"What are we doing, Shane?"

"I thought that was obvious."

"I mean, what are we doing together? I want to believe you're just trying to seduce me so I'll sell the Crown. But..." She hesitated, realizing that admitting the truth would be giving up something of value. "I'm not sure I actually believe it."

He met her gaze, frowning. "It's not like that, I mean, I'm ashamed to admit it, but at first I thought that was what I'd do." He scrubbed his jaw. Miriam felt a sting to her pride, but didn't interrupt him. "But I really do like you. Everything I've done up to this point... I wanted to get close to you to understand why you'd hang on to a decrepit old building. I think I'm starting to get it now. There's...for lack of a better word...magic here. I don't know how else to describe it. It's the same way I feel about this town. I can't fault you for wanting to hold on to that."

She smiled a little sadly. Just because he understood didn't mean she'd swayed him to her thinking. "So where does that leave us?"

Dear Reader,

Have you ever slept over in a museum or spent the night in an aquarium? I've always wanted to stay someplace that could be my personal playground, alone after all the doors are shut and the public is gone. Knowing all the little secrets of a special place somehow adds to the magic, especially at night.

Unfortunately, these days I value sleep too much to go on such an adventure. As of the writing of this letter, my baby girl is just over six months old. It's been quite an adventure. Writing *Matinees with Miriam* was one part wish fulfillment, one part *Castaway* in an old movie theater. How would you live in an historic abandoned building like the Crown? What would you do for fun? How would you shower?

Committing to that lifestyle takes a special kind of person. Miriam Bateman became my pragmatic dreamer, practical in every aspect of her life except for the fact that she lives in her own fantasyland. She's fearless when it comes to protecting the things that matter to her, but she's also scared of the world that has only ever hurt and disappointed her. Exploring a character who was so contradictory in her nature was a lot of fun and a lot of hard work.

My little town of Everville is seeing lots of changes, which is what life is all about. I owe this story to my husband, who is a city-planning nerd and helped me understand a lot about why municipal policy and bylaws are so important. So much of daily life is taken for granted until you threaten the status quo—something else I'm learning as a new mother.

Enjoy your latest visit to Everville, "The Town that Endures!"

Vicki

VICKI ESSEX

Matinees with Miriam

ISBN-13: 978-0-373-61012-9

Matinees with Miriam

This edition published by arrangement with Harlequin Books S.A.

For questions and comments about the quality of this book, please contact us at CustomerService@Harlequin.com.

Printed in U.S.A.

Vicki Essex loves movies, but requires regular "movie forcenings" to get through the canon of quintessential nineties films and blockbusters, Hollywood golden-age classics and best picture nominees. She doesn't live in a theater, but eats popcorn as though she does. She lives in Toronto, Canada, with a man, a baby, a cat and The King of Centipedes as a tenant.

Books by Vicki Essex

HARLEQUIN SUPERROMANCE

Red Carpet Arrangement
A Recipe for Reunion
In Her Corner
Back to the Good Fortune Diner
Her Son's Hero

Other titles by this author available in ebook format.

Thanks to my editor, Karen Reid, and the rest of the Harlequin Superromance team for being awesome guides in my romance writing journey.

Thanks to my agent, Courtney Miller-Callihan of Handspun Literary, for all her support.

To my mom and dad, my sisters, my in-laws and the whole village of relatives and friends who came out to make my journey into motherhood less terrifying and more joyful: thank you.

To my little Mara: “When you smile, you knock me out, I fall apart/And I thought I was so smart.”

And to my husband, John, without whom none of this would be possible: there aren’t enough words to say thank you for your love and staunch support. Best of fathers, best of husbands.

CHAPTER ONE

SHANE WAS PRETTY sure the Keep Out sign was clear. Then again, teenagers carrying six-packs of beer and what looked like a bolt cutter weren't the kind of people who obeyed signs.

The three boys clipped the edges of the chain-link fence and pulled up the corner. With surreptitious looks around, they ducked beneath it, then hurried around the back of the building. Shane clenched his jaw. After the three-hour drive from Brooklyn, he'd wanted to go straight to the bed-and-breakfast, but he hadn't been able to resist driving by the properties before calling it a night. *Good thing*, he thought as he got out of his car. While the block of buildings would eventually be knocked down, he still didn't like trespassers on his property.

Well, it wasn't *all* his yet. But it would be soon.

As he slipped through the gap in the fence, his blazer caught on a wire and tore. Great. It occurred to him that he should've called the police instead of going after the punks, but he could take care of himself.

The abandoned buildings on either side of the

old Crown Theater were boarded up tight, but the rear fire door of the theater was ajar. He hesitated. The Keep Out sign aside, the owner had made it clear she wouldn't welcome his presence.

But those punks were in there. It was his civic duty to stop them.

He slipped into the darkened building, quietly pulling the door shut behind him. The sound of breaking glass followed by a snide laugh reached his ears. He'd never understood bored teens and their need to get into trouble, especially in picturesque Everville. This town was straight out of a Norman Rockwell painting—watering holes, beaches, ice-cream parlors and a whole slew of awesome hangouts. And yet, they were in *this* building, messing around. His blood pumped hard. He didn't get mad easily, but he took the intrusion personally.

His eyes adjusted to the eerie red glow of exit signs. It'd been over a decade since he'd visited the theater, and coming in from the back, he didn't recognize where he was immediately. He climbed the short flight of stairs leading to the main lobby, a vaulted space that reminded him of the rib cage of some huge, starving beast. An empty vending machine hummed in one corner, its cold inner light flickering. He listened hard, but heard no further sign of the teens.

He wasn't sure how he'd confront them—maybe just tell them to buzz off, or threaten them with calling the cops. He hadn't been able to tell how old or big the intruders were in the half dark. Now that he thought about it, three against one weren't great odds.

Something fluttered in the dark to his right. He whipped his head around—nothing. Just more tomb-like silence and a slightly dank smell. Sweat broke out on his upper lip. He stifled the urge to call out. What if those kids were armed? He was starting to regret not calling the cops.

A faint scuffle and some low murmurs reached his ears. With all the stealth he could manage in a suit and dress shoes, he crept along the wall and wedged himself against the corner by a pillar. A whiff of freshly made buttery popcorn tickled his nose. The Crown had been out of commission for nearly ten years—who'd be making popcorn now?

"C'mon, man, hold that light still," a raspy voice said. Not that old, then—maybe sixteen or so.

"You're so full of bullshit, Jacob. You don't know how to pick a lock," another voice, a touch lower, drawled.

"Shut up. I totally do, but it's kinda hard with you shaking that light everywhere."

"That's cuz he's freakin' scared, man," the third voice sneered. "You don't believe those ghost stories about old man Bateman, do you?"

"Woo-oo!" The first guy cackled. "I heard that old guy hung himself off the balcony."

"I heard he blew his brains out in the projector room."

"I heard he was murdered by someone in his family."

Shane's skin prickled. He hadn't heard any of these grisly tales. If *any* proved to be true, he'd have to disclose it to the development board. It could affect sales of the units.

The darkness stirred again, like shadows moving through smoke. He searched for the source but saw nothing. Maybe it was a rat…

The PA system suddenly crackled to life. A funereal carnival dirge played on a tinny piano warbled through the lobby, making the hairs on his neck stand up.

"What the hell?" one of the boys whispered.

The raspy voice quavered. "Someone else is here."

More scuffling. Shane pressed against the wall, heart hammering. The boys were headed his way.

Suddenly, all the lights went out. He hadn't noticed the ambient hum of electronics, but the air was dead silent now. Only the piano continued its forlorn melody. His veins filled with ice. Ghost stories that his *chachi* Priya had told him rose from the depths of his memory. He suddenly felt very exposed.

"Holy—"

"Go, go, go!"

Something metal clanged. A crash, and one of the boys yelped.

In the pitch black, Shane sensed movement. A pair of doors leading to the auditorium banged open, and a blast of cold air hit him.

The red exit signs flickered. A dark *something* glided soundlessly across the lobby, and Shane's chest seized. He caught sight of the boys, the three of them heaped in a pile on the floor, staring wide-eyed at the approaching figure in black.

And then it spoke.

"Get. Out."

The lights went out again. From beneath billowing black robes, the outline of a skeleton glowed neon green.

The boys screamed. Shane squinted against the strobe light flickering from within the empty vending machine, catching the stop-motion-like progress of the teens as they tripped over each other sprinting toward the front door.

One of them paused to look back, the way an emboldened and inexperienced lion cub might when facing an angry badger.

The shadowy figure stopped. It raised its arms. A series of soft cracking noises punctuated the piano melody. The boy yelped as bright green globs exploded on his chest and arms.

Was that ghost using a paintball gun?

The doors burst open as the three trespassers stumbled out. The wraith stood there a moment longer, then drifted toward the exit. It set the bolts on the top of the door, then locked a large dead bolt.

Shane was still plastered to the corner when the figure turned around. It pulled out a smart phone and hit a few buttons. The strobe light stopped, and blinding emergency floodlights turned on, washing the lobby in dirty brown light. A second later, the piano music ceased. The figure in black wasn't quite so menacing now. It stood barely five-three, draped head to toe in filmy, artfully ragged cloth. Not an inch of skin showed, not even the small, delicate hands. An indigo-hued black light hung from a chain around its neck, which explained how the skeletal figure could be seen in the dark.

This was no ghost.

Relief and amusement swamped him. He stepped out from the corner and cleared his throat. "Miriam Bateman, I presume?"

He thought catching her off guard would shock her into revealing herself. He was wrong.

With lightning reflexes, the figure raised the paintball gun and pulled the trigger.

MIRA HAD NO tolerance for trespassers. Why anyone thought they could simply waltz into her theater to hang out, drink beer and piss against the walls like a bunch of animals...

The little bastards were lucky she didn't own a real gun.

The paintball gun huffed a fierce volley of Day-Glo green pellets at the remaining intruder. Not only would he be cleaning the stuff out of his clothes for days, but he'd probably have some nice bruises, too. The sheriff wouldn't have a hard time finding him or his friends.

As the first volley hit him square in the chest, he twisted away, hands shielding his head, exposing his ribs and thigh to the assault instead. He reeled back as she stepped forward. The closer she got, the worse the impact would hurt.

She let go of the trigger briefly. "Get out," she gritted, though it didn't have the menace the voice-changing app on her phone gave her. "You're trespassing. The sheriff is on his way. Get out or I'll put one through your eye."

"I followed those boys in here. I thought they were causing trouble—"

"I'll cause *you* trouble. Get out!" She pulled the trigger again. Three paintballs hit him square in the crotch. His face contorted, his mouth opened in a silent scream and, eyes crossed, he collapsed.

Mira lowered the gun. He wasn't getting up. And she was pretty sure he wasn't faking his agony. Crap. That wasn't good. She put the gun aside and dialed the sheriff, filling him in on her situation.

"I'm driving as fast as I can, Mira," Ralph

McKinnon told her gruffly, "but I'm still about ten minutes out. I called Arty. He'll probably get there before me."

"There was a fourth one, Ralph. Older guy. I shot him in the nuts with my paintball gun. He's down." She kept her gun pointed at him and leaned in far enough to ascertain if the man was still breathing. He had his hands cupped around his crotch and his eyes squeezed shut.

Only a little remorse broke through her self-righteous fury. He was wearing a fairly nice gray suit and a pink tie, all of it now splattered with neon green paint. Clearly he hadn't been with those punks. Not that it excused him from breaking into the Crown.

The sheriff sighed. "I should never have given you those shooting lessons."

"Hey, you were the one who was all about standing your ground."

"Does he need an ambulance?"

"Hey, you," she said to the stranger. "Do you need an ambulance?"

The man gurgled something that sounded like a no.

"Nah," Mira told Ralph. "But get over here quick. If he tries to get up, I might have to unload on him again."

"Please don't." The man rolled over and looked up at her with wide eyes. "I just wanted to drive those kids off."

"I'll see you soon, Sheriff." Mira slipped her phone back into her pocket, muzzle still trained on the man. He was dark skinned with jet-black hair and large, dark eyes. No rings on his fingers, so he wasn't married—no wife to come after her in case she'd accidentally neutered him.

She hefted the paintball gun menacingly. "So you're, what, a good Samaritan?"

"I'm Shane Patel from Sagmar Corp.," he said hoarsely, easing himself up. Worried he might try to disarm her, she brandished the paintball gun. He raised his hands. "Are you Miriam Bateman?"

Mira realized she still wore the head-to-toe wraith costume. He wouldn't have recognized her anyhow—she didn't have much in the way of a social media profile and preferred to stay anonymous online. All the same, she kept the cowl and veil on.

"Why are you here, Mr. Patel?" She recognized his name, of course. All those letters from the property developer had gotten on every last one of her nerves.

"I wanted to speak with you personally." He sat up, his knees pinched together protectively. Contrition inched onto his face. "I wanted—"

"I already told you, the Crown's not for sale. Sheriff McKinnon will be here shortly to escort you off my property."

He straightened, ready to argue. "My associates—" She gestured with the muzzle of her weapon, and he got the hint, cutting off his sales pitch sharply. "It was rude of me to call on you so late," he amended hastily. "I'm sorry for barging in on you like this. Seriously, I meant no harm. I was only driving by when I saw those kids."

Doubt stirred inside her. He hadn't tried to hurt her or damage the Crown as far as she could tell. Nor did he seem to be trying to burn down the place to expedite the sale of the property—she'd heard stories of developers doing just that. His nice suit was ruined, and he'd probably be covered in bruises tomorrow. She'd be lucky if he didn't press charges against *her.*

She lowered the gun. "Sorry about your suit," she said reluctantly. "You can send me a bill for the dry cleaning."

"Not to worry. It was in need of a little color anyhow." He got to his feet. "I'll wait for the sheriff. I can give him a description of those guys who broke in."

"That's not necessary." She didn't want him there any longer than he had to be. "You can go."

He looked around, lingering, as if waiting for an invitation to sit and have a coffee.

"You're here rather late," he remarked.

She stiffened. "I'm often here late."

"The back door was open." The almost-fatherly condescension in his tone irritated her. "Do you normally leave it unlocked?"

"It's a tricky lock. Been like that forever."

He frowned. "Maybe you should board the door up."

Mira glared. She didn't like to be told how to run her life. She held up the gun. "I think I have security covered."

"Mira?" Arty's gruff voice echoed from the back lobby. "Where are you?"

"I'm here. Everything's fine."

A moment later, Arty Bolton strode in, his sweater inside out, his graying hair flying in all directions. She could see him putting it all together in his mind as he took in the scene, and he sagged in relief. "Christsakes, Mira, that costume could scare the black off a zebra. What the hell is going on?" His gaze narrowed on the man from Sagmar. "Who's this?"

"Shane Patel." He wore his smile as readily as his ruined tailored suit. "We've had a misunderstanding. I was trying to rescue Ms. Bateman from some teens who broke into the building—"

Rescue? What a lying piece of—

"Mira, what have I said about barring and locking all the doors?" Arty glowered at her.

She glared right back, then realized he couldn't see her face. She pulled away the cowl and unhooked the veil. "You know how that back door is."

"And if it weren't for this brave young man—"

"I wouldn't go that far," Shane said modestly. Mira felt a flicker of appreciation for the correction, but Shane Patel wasn't anywhere near the vicinity of her good graces yet. "She had me dead to rights. As you can see." He gestured at his green-spattered suit.

The lines in the older man's face deepened. He gave a put-upon sigh. "Mira…"

"Why are you mad at me?" she asked, irritated. "He was trespassing."

"I was trying to do my neighborly duty, honestly." He sounded sincere, but all Mira could hear was the slime beneath his words. And yet, he was winning Arty over. The older man's expression eased with sympathy and gratitude.

Mira summoned her outrage. "Arty, *this* is the guy I was telling you about. The one who wants to buy the theater."

"Oh." He regarded him a moment, then held out a hand. "Arty Bolton. I own the Everville Grocery down the way."

"I know." He grinned. "I guess you don't remember me, Mr. Bolton. My family and I used to come to Everville every summer when I was a kid. I came by the grocery store frequently to get bubble gum cards."

"Wait a sec." Arty squinted. Mira looked between the two, flabbergasted this intruder could have any possible connection to the man who'd been watching out for her since her grandfather had died four years ago. The grocer pointed. "I do remember you, I think. You were tiny, and you had huge ears. You were friends with the Latimers. Your parents used to stay at one of the big cottages by Silver Lake, right? I'm trying to remember… Ran… Ranjeet?"

"That's my dad." Shane's face broke out into a brilliant grin.

"Well, hot dog. How is your family?" They got to talking about a past Mira knew nothing about. She was feeling steadily more and more uncomfortable. She hated being out of the loop, hated that strangers had been in her home, hated how she was simultaneously being ignored and made the center of attention. She rubbed her arms and huffed. Her personal space felt violated.

Sheriff McKinnon arrived a few minutes later. One hand rested on his service piece as he assessed Shane and listened to what he had to say. Mira then told her side of the story—she'd been working when the silent perimeter alarm she'd installed alerted her to the intruders. From there, she'd called him, put on her costume and taken up her post, initiating her "haunting protocol" program to play itself out.

The sheriff rubbed his eyes. "I don't see why you can't have a normal security system like everyone else," he said. "Or a guard dog."

"Those kids came in here looking for trouble." She raised her chin. "I just gave them what they wanted."

"Always one for theatrics, just like your grandfather," Arty said with a touch of exasperation. "They could've been more than kids, Mira. It's not safe for a girl on her own. You need to move out of here."

She glared at Arty in warning. Not everyone who knew her knew that she lived in the theater. It wasn't something she openly shared, especially not with the law or strangers like Mr. Patel.

The sheriff glanced around disinterestedly. "Is anything missing? Any property damage?"

"There's a broken beer bottle in one corner—they were drinking. They were trying to pick a lock on that storage closet, too. Nothing in there of value, though." She pointed to one corner. Ralph checked it out and declared it hadn't been damaged.

The sheriff made a note on his pad. "Mr. Patel… I presume you won't be pressing charges?" The question was a half warning.

"Not at all, Sheriff." Again, that too-big smile. It gave Mira goose bumps.

"Mira?"

She shook her head reluctantly. No sense in causing more trouble or giving Shane Patel reason to sue her.

"All right. If either of you remember anything else about what you saw, call me. I'll do a drive around the neighborhood—see if I spot those troublemakers. If I catch them, I might need you both to come down to the office and identify them for me."

"I'm staying at the Sunshine B and B," Shane said. "I'm here on business."

"For how long?"

He slid Mira a lopsided grin. She met his stare head-on, her face fixed with stony dislike. "As long as it takes."

CHAPTER TWO

IT WAS CLOSE to nine by the time Shane left the Crown. That he'd gotten off with only a stink eye from the sheriff was a point in his column. He'd have to be more careful when approaching Miriam Bateman.

And, boy, was he ever going to have to watch himself around her. He'd expected an older woman, someone as hard and obdurate as her refusals had been. He hadn't thought she'd be so young and pretty. Even in that billowing pseudo-Dementor's robe, those big blue eyes had glowed against her round, pale face, framed by that mass of dark brown hair. Girls like that spelled trouble for him, and not just because she'd shot him in the balls.

He winced, still feeling the burning ache. It'd been tough to smile in front of the sheriff.

He parked outside the Sunshine B and B. The house was a fairly ordinary-looking two-story Colonial off Main Street with a screened-in porch, a well-manicured garden and a short driveway. Exactly the kind of place a couple might get away to for a weekend while touring Upstate New York.

In the main foyer, an older woman with dyed blond hair and blue eyeliner greeted him cheerfully. "Nancy Gibbons," she introduced herself. "You must be Shane. You're the only one booked for the week..." Her face fell as she took in his state. "Oh my—what happened to you?"

"Had a run-in with some neighborhood kids and a paintball gun," he explained, which was as close to the truth as he wanted to go. He was sure some version of that story would make its way around the small town eventually.

Nancy scowled. "Their parents must be mortified. I've been saying we need to give these kids more to do around here than cause trouble, but the town doesn't have the money for those kinds of programs." She sighed. "Back in my day, we had jobs to keep us busy. Now it's hard enough to even keep the young folks *in* town."

Shane nodded. This was the story in small towns everywhere. As factories and mines shut down or pulled out and the economy shrank, people lost their jobs and had to move on to find new opportunities. As a result, the towns collapsed.

"Your room is at the end of the hall, top of the stairs," Nancy said, handing him a key. "Get out of that suit and I'll send it to the dry cleaners in the morning. I'll bring you supper."

"And an ice pack, if you please."

Nancy frowned. “Are you hurt?”

“Just my pride,” he said with a grimace.

After a stinging-hot shower, he applied the ice pack where he needed it most and sat down to his laptop, connecting it to the in-room Wi-Fi. In minutes, his inbox flashed nineteen new messages.

Typical. The partners at Sagmar had been hesitant about sending him as the rep because of what they perceived as a “soft heart” toward the town that had hosted him during so many childhood summers. “We need you to go for the jugular,” the senior project manager, Laura Kessler, had told him. “Companies will be swarming this place looking to buy up real estate for development as soon as they realize what a gold mine it is.”

Sure enough, there was an email from Laura, reminding him that the longer he took to convince Miriam Bateman to sell, the higher the price for the Crown would go. Rumors of a new high-speed commuter rail line hadn’t yet leaked to the general public, though, so the town’s property values hadn’t changed. And as long as Miriam Bateman remained in the dark, she couldn’t necessarily demand a higher price.

It wasn’t exactly all aboveboard as deals like this went, but the rail project wasn’t set in stone, which was the only reason Shane didn’t feel completely deceitful. It was a shady enough deal as it was, since the president of Sagmar received the tip off-the-record. Laura had told Shane they wouldn't be prosecuted if the information was leaked, but he wasn't reassured.

The rest of his emails were mostly minutiae from work. There was one from his parents in Brooklyn reminding him of his sister's birthday next week. They knew he was working hard on this deal, but they didn't know *why*: he had his heart set on buying one of the condo units so his parents would have a place to retire. They always talked about coming back to Everville for an extended stay, and Shane wanted them to have that. Besides, a new condo would be the perfect income generator and secondary leisure home.

He was certain he could convince Miriam to sell before Priti's party. He just needed more information about the theater owner. It was why he'd come to Everville—he wanted to face Ms. Bateman and get a sense of who she was. Emails and letters didn't cut it. He was a people person. Once he figured out what motivated Miriam and what kinds of dreams she had, he'd know how to get her to sell.

THE NEXT MORNING, he walked downtown, marveling at how much Everville had changed. Unlike many of the locations he'd scouted in Upstate New York, this town had managed to evolve, avoiding stagnation against all odds. Where there had once been feed stores and midsize department stores, there were now trendy cafés, galleries and boutiques. There were still lots of empty storefronts, though. He remembered how busy and vibrant Everville had been when he was a child, but the town hadn't suffered nearly as badly as other places Sagmar Corp. had considered for the condo.

It was nice to see some things hadn't changed: the local Chinese eatery, the Good Fortune Diner, was still thriving after all these years. It was the only place in the States he'd ever found sweet-and-sour chicken balls—he'd learned it was mainly a pseudo-Chinese staple on Canadian and British menus. He'd go in for a plate later.

He headed for the grocery store. He preferred to fend for himself rather than eat out all the time. He didn't need much—as fancy as his suits were, instant ramen, microwave dinners and peanut butter sandwiches suited him fine. He'd save the fine dining to woo Miriam Bateman, if it came down to it.

As he was waiting at the checkout, Arty Bolton pushed a cart piled with boxes of groceries past. Shane paid and followed the older man to the parking lot, where he was loading a delivery van.

"Good morning, Mr. Bolton," he greeted cheerfully. Arty was as good a source of information on Miriam Bateman as anyone. He was definitely some kind of guardian figure in her life—Shane's research on her hadn't turned up any family connections apart from the Crown's previous owner, Jack Bateman. "Need a hand?"

Arty looked up and grinned. "Mr. Patel, good morning." He stretched his back and winced. "My guy who usually loads the truck is off today. If you don't mind…?"

"Just Shane, please." He placed his own bags on the ground and hefted one of the heavier boxes into the van.

"And just Arty to you, young man." The grocer craned his neck and spine with an audible pop. "Thing about getting older, you feel a lack of sleep a lot more keenly."

The man had unwittingly provided the perfect opening for Shane's queries. "Did Ms. Bateman have any more issues after I left?"

"Mira? Not at all. In fact, the sheriff tracked one of those kids down already. Local boy, barely sixteen. Ralph will probably be calling on you to ID him later."

"How was Ms. Bateman after I left?"

"Mira's tough," Arty reassured him. "Gets it from her grandpa, God rest his soul. Stubborn as a mule. If I haven't said it, thank you for rushing to her rescue."

"It was nothing." After all, he'd been the one who needed rescuing in the end. "I'm glad to hear she hasn't suffered from the incident."

Arty regarded him speculatively. "So you're here 'cause you want to buy the Crown?"

"The company I represent has been pursuing Ms. Bateman the past six months, but so far, she's refused all offers."

"Yeah, she showed me the letters." His tone revealed nothing of his opinion. "What're you doing with the property once you get your hands on it?"

"I think you'll like it. Sagmar has plans for a twelve-story living complex with ground-floor retail space, more than sixty family-sized units—"

"Condos," Arty summarized with a frown.

Shane smiled tightly. For some reason, people reacted negatively to the term. "Well, yes, but—"

The grocer gave a dry chuckle as Shane handed him another box from the shopping cart. "You may have spent summers here, son, but clearly no one told you that you need to get to the point around these parts if you want to try to sell us anything."

"My team has spoken at length with the mayor about redeveloping that vacant block. This project has been in the works for a long time."

The older man shrugged. "I'm not sure people will welcome a condo as readily as you think. We've had a lot of change around here lately—all the water main construction, the wind turbines, the old businesses shutting down…it's been difficult. Putting up condos, though, is another thing."

Shane knew that. No matter where Sagmar built, they always faced opposition from not-in-my-backyarders—or NIMBYs—environmental groups, heritage preservationists, even religious groups. His specialty was answering questions, presenting facts and changing minds. It was why he was the top negotiator at the firm. His record for closing the deal was perfect; he wasn't about to break that streak.

He finished loading Arty's van. The grocer offered him a ride back to the B and B, and Shane accepted.

"I'd like to give Ms. Bateman a gift to apologize for my intrusion last night," Shane ventured as Arty drove. "Would you happen to know what she'd like?"

Arty scratched his chin. "To be honest, I don't know that a gift would get you out of the dog house. I did mention she's stubborn, right?" He sent him a loaded though not unfriendly look. "But you can't go wrong with flowers and chocolates. Women like those. Visit the Main Street Florist. Talk to Janice. She'll take care of you."

Shane suppressed a smirk. If he didn't know better, he'd think the old man was trying his hand at matchmaking. Not that he wasn't above a little flirting to grease the wheels on the deal—a smile and a wink could be just as effective as a firm handshake. "Main Street Florist. Gotcha. Thanks, Arty."

"FLOWERS AND CHOCOLATES?" Janice Heinlein rolled her eyes. "Really, Arty, that's about as subtle as telling him to buy her a diamond ring."

"Don't see what's the big deal. And anyhow, I'm sending business your way. Can't argue with that, can you?" He picked up the bucket of bouquets the florist had put together for his shop. Janice could have sent one of her boys to deliver them to the grocery store directly, but he liked to visit when he could and see her in her natural habitat—a rare orchid among dandelions.

Now that's what you call maudlin claptrap, he scolded himself for his bad poetry. Jack would've laughed him out of the store.

"You know, if he gets here before you're gone, he'll know you're up to something."

"Up to something? Me?" He grinned. "Whatever could you mean?"

"Don't play coy." She gave him a lopsided grin. "You want Mira to find a man."

Arty smirked, not denying her allegation. They'd both worried over Mira since Jack's death. She'd had a rough start to life, and as much as she'd grown and matured, she'd never really come out of her shell entirely and had only seemed to retreat further since her grandfather's death. Finding a man who'd look after her wasn't out of the question, but he wasn't entirely ready to push Mira out of her comfort zone, either. The girl was sensitive.

"If you want my advice, you need to steer the man toward other avenues. Women like men who put a little thought and creativity into their gifts.

Miriam needs more than fresh-cut flowers if you want her to be wooed out of that cave of hers."

Janice shook her head. The sunlight through the flower shop window made her white-blond hair glow as it tumbled around her ears. Arty longed to touch her. He kept his hands stuffed in his pockets instead. "Anyhow, what makes you think this Shane Patel is any good for her? Sounds like he's only after her property, and I doubt he's the kind to stick around."

"A man knows when another man is interested," he said firmly. "He lit up like a lightbulb when he saw her last night."

"Maybe it was just the paint from that paint gun. You should take that thing away from her before someone loses an eye."

"And do what? Give her a real gun? She needs some kind of protection, but hell if I give her anything worse than a BB."

"What she needs is to move out of that place." Janice huffed. "I know Jack would be grateful for how you're looking out for her, but he wouldn't have wanted her alone in that old theater for the rest of her life."

Arty's chest ached, hearing Janice's wistful tone. They all missed Jack Bateman. Miriam's grandfather had been a fixture in Everville, a grinning beanstalk of a man who was as at ease camping with his granddaughter as he was running the projector at the Crown. He and Arty had been friends since childhood. The man would have known better how to handle Mira.

"I think Mira is happy," Arty said gruffly. "Her definition of it, anyhow."

"She didn't pick up her own groceries this week," Janice pointed out.

"She had deadlines to meet. You know how she gets when she's focused on work."

"It's not healthy, Arty. She needs to be around people, too."

He lifted his shoulders. "She talks to people on the internet."

"That's not the same."

"Jan, she's twenty-eight, not twelve. She's an adult. Her life isn't conventional to us, sure, but times have changed. She likes her privacy. She's not starving. She's got a job, a roof over her head…all things considered, she's doing all right." He wasn't sure whether he was trying to convince her or himself.

"'All right' isn't always enough," Janice returned staunchly. "Before you know it, she'll be an old woman living alone in a decrepit theater."

Arty grimaced. He usually deferred to Janice when it came to Mira's well-being, being a woman and all, but they frequently disagreed on how to handle the young woman's introversion. The fact was, he wanted to honor his friend by helping his granddaughter become the woman *she* wanted to be. If it meant arguing with the woman Jack—and Arty—had been sweet on most of their lives, so be it.

His main concern was that Mira was alone—and that would bother him less if he were younger and knew he had many more years to keep an eye on her. But the incident with the trespassers had hammered home how perilous her situation was. Next time, it could be someone far less benign than a bunch of troublemaking kids. Someone who wouldn't be scared off by Halloween costumes and paintball guns.

Shane Patel wasn't exactly forever material: he didn't see a long-term relationship between him and Mira flourishing. But Arty also knew folks these days didn't need long-term to be happy, and Mira had always been pragmatic. When it came to relationships, anyhow.

If he could get her to simply open up to the idea of dating, he'd consider his job done. The problem was that the men in town were less than appealing to Mira. Too many knew about the Batemans, and Mira in particular.

"You think we should convince her to sell the Crown?" he asked casually. He couldn't picture Mira giving up the theater—Jack had loved that place.

The florist shook her head. "That's something she has to decide for herself. What I'm suggesting is she get a taste of what else is out there. She can't live her life in front of a screen."

Arty raised an eyebrow. It was uncharacteristic of Janice to talk about casual flings. She'd always been much more serious when it came to relationships. She'd been married for twenty-four years before her husband, Bill, had passed, and after that, she'd refused to remarry. Even when Jack, a widower himself, had come a-calling, she still hadn't budged, and Jack had been no slouch when it came to charming the ladies. Hesitantly, he said, "A taste…of this Shane Patel, maybe?"

She shrugged. "He's convenient—I don't deny that. Temporary, which isn't necessarily bad. Mira needs her life shaken up a bit. He'd get her beyond the theater's walls, too."

"He's not bad-looking, either," Arty said, almost giddy that he and Janice were on the same page for once. "And he's got money."

At Janice's disapproving look, he added, "What? Money never hurt anyone's chances."

"If we're going to play matchmaker, there's a lot you need to learn about the female psyche," she said wryly. "If money were something she cared about, she'd have sold the theater a long time ago. Right now, all Mira sees in that man is an enemy. He wants to buy the Crown from her, and you and I both know she'll cling to it tooth and nail."

"So how do we get her to even look at him?"

Janice tapped a finger against her lips. "I may know the way to her heart."

MIRA TOSSED THE scrub brush into the bucket and stood, stretching. Getting the neon-green paintball stains out of the old carpet had been tough, but all traces of it were gone now. She'd have to go easy on the trigger next time.

"Sorry, Grandpa," she said out loud. "Won't be doing that again."

She was met with silence, though she liked to imagine the rush of air seeping through the auditorium doors was her grandfather's put-upon sigh. To her, the Crown housed Jack Bateman's spirit, which was why being alone there had never bothered her. Not even when her silent alarm had been tripped. Arty and various others had warned her time and again it wasn't safe to sleep in that huge, abandoned building, but if she hadn't been there, those boys could have done a lot more damage, defiling the Crown and her grandfather's memory. No, as long as she was alive, she'd never let anything happen to Grandpa's pride and joy.

Besides, this was the only place she felt truly safe.

Her cell phone blipped as the front door proximity alarm was triggered. The problem with having an old theater for a home was that there were no doorbells, and it was impossible to hear anyone knocking. So instead, she'd installed a special silent security system around the building. It was amazing what one could buy on the internet.

Who could it be? Arty had already delivered

her groceries—had he forgotten something? She checked the phone feed to the web cameras outside the theater.

It was Shane Patel. He stood staring up at the Crown's old marquee, wearing a fresh suit that fit him as well as the one she'd painted with neon-green polka dots. He pressed his face to the cracked glass of the old ticket booth, then tried each of the locked doors. He pounded out a knock. How had he known she'd be in the theater now? Then again, she'd ignored his calls and emails, and the only address he had for her was the theater. She supposed knocking was his only recourse. Maybe if she waited, he'd go away…

Or maybe he'd break in again to do God knew what.

She'd checked his online profile after last night's debacle. He was definitely who he said he was, but she hadn't expected the Sagmar real estate developer to be quite so…well, *heroic* was too strong a word, but it was the only one she could think of for some damned reason.

Then again, she supposed he could've hired those punks to break into the theater so he could look like a hero.

Don't be paranoid, Mira. Life isn't a movie. He isn't some nefarious villain planning complicated ruses to get his hands on your property. He didn't even know you lived here.

She considered meeting Mr. Patel at the door

with her paint gun, but decided sharp words would be sufficient to warn him off. She was an adult, not some child hiding from the boogeyman.

She unbolted the front fire door and swung open the exterior door. The facade had been boarded up on both the outside and inside to preserve the glass.

Shane Patel looked up, startled. In the light of day, she could see he was tall and quite handsome, square jawed with thick, expressive eyebrows as dark as his jet-black hair. Something about his neatly tailored suit and the lavender shirt, no tie, put her in mind of a luxury car salesman. Maybe that was her bias, though.

"What do you want?" she asked bluntly.

He smiled wide, a perfect set of pearly whites gleaming against his equally brilliant and clear complexion. "I thought I'd bring this by." He held out a box of chocolate nut clusters. "A peace offering to apologize for my intrusion last night."

She regarded him and the box flatly. "I don't like chocolate."

That was a lie, but it was worth it to see his face fall, his confidence shaken. This was a guy used to having his charms work on members of the opposite sex—she added that brick of insight into the wall she was building around herself against him. "I suppose I should ask how you're feeling." A show of sympathy could go a long way toward keeping a lawsuit at bay, after all.

"I'm a little sore, but nothing I can't handle." He rubbed his arm, where she remembered he'd been hit. She studiously kept her eyes above his belt and her mind away from any kind of speculation. "I've done paintball before. Do you play a lot?"

He was trying to engage her in conversation. Maybe he was simply a friendly guy, but she was certain these were just tactics for making her linger and talk. There was only one thing he was here for. "No. Now, if that's all, I have work to do." She started to close the door.

"The sheriff caught one of the young men who broke in last night," he said quickly, and that made her pause. "I ID'd him earlier. I think he'll tell on the others, too. Will you press charges?"

She thought about it briefly. "No. They're just a bunch of bored kids. Sheriff'll scare 'em straight."

"You should reconsider. They'll come back. Might try to look for revenge."

"Or they might figure out that they should leave me alone unless they want a crotchful of paintballs." Unlike some people who couldn't take a hint. She gave him her most unimpressed look. "You and your nut clusters should go now, Mr. Patel. You have nothing I want, and I have a lot of work to do."

"What is it you do, exactly?" he asked, sliding his words in as effectively as a foot in the door.

"Work." Some guys didn't know how to take

no for an answer. "And it's not getting done. Now please, get off my property. I have absolutely no intention of selling to you or anyone else. The Crown is my grandfather's legacy. No dollar amount could make me give it up."

"Ms. Bateman—"

She closed the door firmly and bolted it tight, the booming sound punctuating the end of their interaction. It echoed through the building, shuddering through the cavernous halls until it was swallowed up by darkness and silence.

She waited one minute more for her cell phone to chime, indicating that Shane Patel had left the premises. It beeped once. Gone.

She let out a breath. Well. If that wasn't a clear enough message, she wasn't sure what would be.

CHAPTER THREE

SHANE STUDIED THE mostly blank profile he'd composed of Miriam Bateman as if it would provide some clue about the mysterious theater owner. He'd never met anyone so obstinately unfriendly—especially in Everville. Everyone was nice, or at least, that's how he remembered them. The kids at the beach on Silver Lake and in town had all been cool with him and his sister, and he'd gotten along with everyone he met. Of course, he'd been gifted with the ability to charm people—something his mother had warned him about. But Miriam was a conundrum.

Arty Bolton had suggested chocolates, but clearly, the old man didn't know what she liked. He supposed a gift basket might be more appropriate than flowers. He reserved fancy bouquets for hospitalizations, funerals and first dates. He didn't want Ms. Bateman getting the wrong idea.

Yet.

The problem was, she was hard to read. She had an almost-impenetrable stare, narrow and glassy at the same time, as if she were studying a festering lump underneath a microscope and trying to decide if it was fascinating or disgusting. She used that look liberally on him. It was a little disconcerting. He could usually pick up when a woman was attracted to him and then leverage that attraction for professional gain. *Amma* disapproved, mainly because her son wouldn't settle down.

At the very least, Miriam hadn't completely dismissed him. She'd been intrigued enough to speak to him, even if it was crisply and briefly. She could've called the sheriff if she'd really wanted him gone. But she'd answered his innocuous questions. That was a start. A crack in her facade. Now all he had to do was figure out how to chip away the rest of her defenses.

He scanned the profile, adding notes as he went.

Miriam Bateman, mid to late twenties.
Brown hair, blue eyes.
Proprietor of the defunct Crown Theater in Everville, NY.
Friends/Allies: Arty Bolton, grocery store owner?

He added the question mark because while the old man had come to her aid when she was in trouble, he was a lot older, making him more of a father figure who'd protect her rather than dish out any good intel. Shane had been hoping to find someone who was closer to Miriam's age, maybe a girlfriend, a confidante, someone he could charm.

Did she even have friends? He shook his head. He wasn't going to take her prickly attitude personally. She had every right not to like or trust him. He'd just have to figure out what made her tick and get her to open up. With that in mind, he headed out to explore the town, maybe have a beer. He'd talk to locals and see what they could tell him about the Crown's elusive owner. It would take as long as it took. Persistence was the key—what had always made him a winner.

He'd convince her to sell him the Crown one way or another. Personal pride depended on it.

"IT'S FROM WHO?" Mira studied the potted orchid suspiciously. As pretty as it was, and as much as she was thrilled to receive it, she couldn't imagine anyone in town wanting to buy her such a gift.

"A secret admirer, according to the tag." Janice Heinlein grinned. "He came in while I was out, made the order with Pete. Even if I knew who it was, which I don't, I'm not allowed to say more than that. Customer right to privacy and all that, you know." She winked.

Mira sighed. It had to be from Shane Patel. He'd come by twice more over the past week bearing gifts, which she'd reluctantly accepted, though she'd reiterated both times that she wasn't selling the Crown. He hadn't seemed fazed by her rebuttals—in fact, he'd looked as though he was simply happy to bring her presents. The first had been a basket of assorted baked goods from Georgette's Books and Bakery, along with two pounds of fresh ground coffee beans from the Grindery, a café on Main. There was simply no way to turn that down—Saul, the café owner, would be insulted. And no one could resist cookies from Georgette's.

The second gift had been just as nonrefundable: a deli tray from Everville Grocery. Apparently, Mr. Patel was bent on feeding her *and* ingratiating himself with the local businesses. Since the platter had come from Arty's, she couldn't say no.

Mira had no doubt that the real estate developer was buttering her up for negotiations. She imagined he'd come by to show her his plans for whatever he was going to build, tell her how it would benefit the community, do some song and dance while avoiding any actual discussion of sales or price tags. The initial offer for the building had been reasonable, she supposed, for what most people thought was an abandoned building. But it wasn't nearly enough in Mira's estimation. Of course, she wouldn't sell the place for anything, unless Shane could magically bring her grandfather back from the dead. Maybe not even then. Grandpa had loved the Crown with all his heart.

She turned the potted orchid in her hand, admiring the deep fuchsia blooming from the center of the blossom and lightening to a blush at the tips of the petals. How had the man known she loved orchids?

"How are the tomatoes doing?" Janice asked, rocking up onto her toes eagerly.

Mira smirked. Janice was usually too busy to make deliveries herself. She'd come to see the garden. "Come."

The florist grinned and clapped her hands. She quickly followed Mira up to the balcony fire exit. Mira unwound the chains from around the push bar and unlocked the padlock. People had tried breaking through that door before. She'd also had to put a bike lock on the fire escape ladder to keep trespassers from climbing to the roof where her precious garden was. It wasn't technically legal or safe, but no one was using the theater except her.

With the orchid in a backpack, they climbed the ladder. Mira stayed beneath Janice in case the older woman made a misstep. Mira was used to heights—the Crown was her home, her playground, and she could walk this place in the dark. The florist went up slowly, and eventually, they clambered over the edge of the roof and onto Mira's gravel-topped oasis.

She never got tired of the view up here. With careful attention to where and how things were planted, the garden thrived with little interference, and in mid-May, the place was like Eden.

Thick, healthy vines and climbing plants twined around the freestanding trellises, providing cool shade for the more delicate plants. Marigolds and citronella protected many of the produce plants from bugs. A few sparkly rainbow-colored pinwheels and flapping pennants warned birds away. A wind chime she'd made as a child for Grandpa out of shells, beads and tiny jingle bells clattered and tinkled in the breeze from one decorative arch.

Janice headed straight for the bean and tomato boxes. She fingered the leaves and gently turned the tiny yellow blossoms. "Looking good. The extra shade's a good idea up here, too." She nodded at the faded patio umbrellas arranged around the boxes of produce that couldn't handle full sun. She stuck her fingers in the soil. "Good drainage. Nice and moist. I think you'll get a bumper crop."

"I hope so." Mira picked some stray weeds out of a planter full of squash and filled a watering can from one of the many rain barrels placed around the roof.

"Your grandfather would be proud of what you've done with his garden."

Mira smiled sadly. Grandpa had had a crush on the florist and had often wistfully joked about marrying Janice so Mira could have a grandmother. And he'd been a hell of a flirt. When Mira had gotten a little older, she'd wondered if the two had ever had some kind of relationship. But as far as she could tell, they'd only ever been friends.

They placed the new orchid in the small plastic greenhouse with her other tropical plants and chatted about the various health issues some of her specimens were having. Mira had worked this garden alongside her grandpa since her early teens. Jack Bateman had loved growing things. When they'd lived together, his bungalow hadn't had much in the way of a front or backyard, which was why the rooftop garden had been his pride. Keeping it alive was just as important to Mira as keeping the Crown in her possession.

After half an hour of puttering, Janice and Mira climbed back down the ladder and headed into the theater. "Be honest, Janice. Was it Shane Patel who bought me that orchid?" Unwanted warmth wormed through her with the mere mention of his name.

"I really couldn't say." The older woman's shrug and secretive smile suggested otherwise.

Mira rolled her eyes as she relocked the balcony door. "Well, at least he didn't bring it himself. He's been bugging me all week. I don't have time for him. I have a lot of work to do."

"Oh?"

"Life of a freelance writer," she said, with no resentment. She enjoyed her work—it was just a lot of juggling projects.

"I didn't mean 'Oh' about your work. I meant

'Oh' as in, I didn't realize Mr. Patel was courting you."

Mira's cheeks burned. "He's not *courting*," she corrected prudishly. "He's looking for a way to buy the Crown from me. Honestly, I've no idea why he won't take a hint. I've been pretty clear."

Janice scratched her nose. "Maybe you should talk to him, see what his plans are."

Mira shook her head. Handsome, charming men like Shane could not be trusted. He wanted her property. That was it. She couldn't trust a single compliment, kind word or platitude from him.

"If there's nothing he can say to convince you," Janice went on reasonably, "then it wouldn't hurt to listen, would it?"

"I have more important things to do than sit through a sales pitch."

"Well, if you won't talk to him directly, come to the open house he's having down at B. H. Everett. I heard from Cheyenne he's giving a presentation about his project and what it'll mean for the town."

That gave Mira pause. Mayor Cheyenne Welks had pushed important infrastructure projects through and secured funding to do the much-needed upgrades to the water mains and sewer lines. She'd been a real boon for the town, a progressive liberal thinker who'd swayed some of the conservative cronies on town council to invest in the future.

That Shane Patel had the new mayor's ear was significant. Cheyenne's agenda had been one of growth and change, and her vision had done much to improve life in Everville. If she thought the Sagmar project was a good thing, Mira would have a battle on her hands.

What would Grandpa do? He'd always said keeping Everville alive was all about growing and changing.

But not the Crown, Mira insisted. Some things had to stay the same—everyone needed an anchor in a storm. The theater had once been the cultural heart of the town, and it would be again—as soon as she could figure out how to reopen.

Maybe the first step was to make her intentions public.

SHANE WENT THROUGH his mental checklist as he scanned the pamphlets, Sagmar-branded swag and hors d'oeuvres being laid out. This informal presentation of the condo project was meant to keep things transparent with the locals. He'd dealt with NIMBYs before, and had convinced the company that spending the time and resources to assuage their fears was paramount to their success. A small investment early could save them huge headaches later.

And so, it was with a big smile and a huge spread of locally purchased treats from the various small businesses in town that Shane opened the doors to the B. H. Everett High School's gymnasium. All week, he'd put up flyers around Everville inviting folks to find out more about the new downtown development.

He'd hoped for a good-sized turnout. He hadn't imagined the place would be packed by eight o'clock.

"If you feed them, they will come," Arty Bolton said with a chuckle. The grocer had provided numerous catered trays of deli meats, similar to the one Shane had ordered for Miriam last week. She'd accepted it grimly, so he considered that progress.

"I'm glad for all the interest," Shane said, though he kept an eye on the wrinkled brows and scowls circulating around the professionally done display boards. A couple of strong, dissenting voices could turn a crowd against the project. "Do you know if Ms. Bateman is coming?"

"Mira? I doubt it. She doesn't get out much. Always working, that one." Arty cleared his throat. "Course, this does all concern her, so it'd make sense if she did show up. Then again, if she's not selling to you, then none of this matters, does it?"

"I hope to change her mind," Shane said confidently.

"Been talkin' to some folks," Arty ventured, scratching his nose. "Seems your people have been working on this deal awhile."

"It began almost four years ago, just as I was

joining the firm," Shane confirmed, wanting to ensure Arty understood Sagmar had nothing to hide. "But I didn't take over this project until about two years ago when Mayor Welks was elected. Soon as I heard they were considering Everville for the location, I fought to have it placed here and took the project on."

"Means something to you, then?"

"A lot. I loved this town when I was a kid. We only came for the summer, but I looked forward to it every year. I want to see it thrive. I'm willing to put money on it, too," he admitted. "I have my eye on one of these units so my parents have a place they can escape to during the summers. Maybe I'll retire here myself one day."

"You'll have to build it first." Arty studied him. "You wouldn't consider moving it to another location in town?"

Shane glanced away, keeping his cards close to his vest. He didn't want to reveal *too* much. Sagmar already owned the properties on either side of the Crown; Miriam's theater was the lone holdout. While the project could technically be moved to another location, it would mean months if not years before he could proceed, and even then, there was no guarantee the same situation wouldn't arise with any other property. No, this development would be built where the Crown stood. He just had to make Miriam Bateman see its benefits. "If there were better venues, we would've taken the project there."

He excused himself as people waved him down. He spent the next hour or so fielding concerns from the locals—most of them perfectly sensible questions about the environmental impact, the property values, how the new build would affect traffic and so forth. He could see, though, that despite his answers, people weren't altogether convinced.

"I just don't think this project is suited for Everville," one man said boldly. "It doesn't fit with the rest of the town."

Shane turned toward the bombastic voice. "I assure you, Mister…?"

"Bob Fordingham, former mayor." The beefy, balding man with a ruddy complexion and prominent paunch put out a meaty hand. Shane shook it, clenching his teeth as the man squeezed unnecessarily hard.

"Mr. Fordingham, yes, of course, my Sagmar colleagues mentioned your involvement in the initial stages of planning." He kept his tone light, reminding himself that the current mayor, Cheyenne Welks, had trounced the man in the last election. "I thought you supported this project wholeheartedly."

"Things have changed." He pointed a fat finger at the display boards. "Now I'm not so sure this is what we need, what with all the money we've already spent on the water mains and such."

Shane was pretty sure the man's objections were more about ego than the development. "I'd think it was in the interests of any town to provide affordable quality housing to draw in new residents, and Sagmar can do that. As for commercial space, I've always believed in small businesses being the heart of any town. Let me show you the floor plans and I think you'll agree the space can more than adequately accommodate any business type..."

He spent some time chatting with the former mayor, but could tell the frowning man wasn't listening. Bob Fordingham had made up his mind, and whatever his agenda, he was going to fight Shane and Sagmar. Eventually, the ruddy man left, muttering just loud enough to be heard. A few of the townsfolk went to chat with Bob and shake his hand. Shane would have to watch out for that group.

Out of the blue, his skin lifted with goose bumps. He wasn't sure how he knew it, but his eyes were drawn toward the lone woman hovering by the side door. She must have slipped in from a different entrance, unnoticed by anyone else. In black jeans and a dark blue hoodie drawn up around her face, Miriam Bateman skulked around the perimeter of the gymnasium away from the bulk of the crowd gathered at the food tables. Thick-framed glasses rested on her face—they would've almost seemed comical, the way she kept pushing them up her nose, as if they were part of a disguise. She was trying very hard not to be detected.

He excused himself and made his way through the crowd. "Ms. Bateman," he called.

Her head whipped around, eyes wide as he approached. She flinched away from his extended hand. "I'm glad you could make it."

She looked from his hand to his face, her lips a thin line. Conflict flickered in her cobalt-blue eyes. She cleared her throat. "Yes. Well. I thought I'd come to at least say thank you for the orchid."

Shane continued smiling, but he had no idea what she was talking about. "You're welcome." It wasn't in his nature to take credit for other people's work, but this was the first tiny smile he'd seen from the Crown's owner. Small, tentative, a minor puckering of rosebud lips, but a smile nonetheless. If only he could coax a laugh out of her. "Please, come enjoy some food. I'd love to give you a personal tour of the project—"

"That's not necessary." She glanced around nervously. "I thought it'd only be polite to tell you in person that as much as I appreciate your efforts, you shouldn't waste any more of your time or money here."

"I hardly think supporting local businesses is a waste of money," he said smoothly.

She flushed, her gaze darting to her toes. "Of course not. But when it comes to the Crown, I've made myself clear. One day, I'll reopen the theater. I made that promise to myself and to my grandfather. I intend to keep it."

Shane regarded her thoughtfully. The conviction in her eyes was clear, but he wondered if she understood the magnitude of what she was proposing. It wasn't just a matter of taking all those boards off the doors and flipping some switches. New building codes and safety standards would have to be adhered to. The investment needed for capital costs alone would be astronomical. As a business, a small second-run theater simply wasn't sustainable. Even if she did reopen, how long would that last? Would she hold up progress in Everville just to satisfy her own ego? "I understand your position," he said cautiously, "but I'm hoping to change your mind."

She stared at him uncomprehendingly. "You won't. I've made myself as clear as I possibly can. Why can't you accept that?" She was growing more agitated by the second, her voice rising. "I'll never sell the Crown, not to you, not to *anyone*." People started to turn and stare. "The theater is my grandfather's legacy, and I won't see it torn down for a bunch of yuppie condos!"

"Ms. Bateman—"

"No, don't talk. Don't interrupt me. You're not listening to me. Why aren't you listening to me?"

He thought she might start flapping like a panicked goose. This was a woman who'd faced four trespassers armed with only a paintball gun. Now she was trembling, almost shaking with rage. The tears gathering in the corners of her eyes made his stomach clench.

"Mira." Arty hurried over, whispering harshly. "You're making a scene."

"I won't sell the Crown. I won't sell the Crown," she repeated in a quavering mantra. Arty said something to her that Shane couldn't hear. It was then she seemed to notice all the eyes on her.

With startling speed, she spun and hurried out, knocking one of the foam-core-mounted posters of the condo off its easel. The whole setup clattered loudly across the floor as Miriam Bateman tripped on one of the easel legs and scrambled for the exit like a frightened deer skidding across an icy pond.

Shane stood there, gut churning. What on earth had just happened?

CHAPTER FOUR

"MIRA? HONEY, ARE you okay?"

"I'm busy."

Arty stared around the empty theater, the aisle lights and dingy stage floods the only illumination. "Where are you, girl?"

"I can't talk right now, Arty, I'm concentrating." The echo of her voice gave him some inkling of where she was. He sighed, cursing his old bones as he climbed the ladder into the fly loft above the stage. Sure enough, he found Mira hanging from one of the cables, strapped into a well-used nylon harness, tinkering with the sliding mechanisms. He gripped the railing. "I wish you'd stop playing on this old thing. It's not safe."

"It's fine. I made modifications so I don't need anyone else to help me use it," she said as she took a grease gun from her tool belt and applied a glob to the track.

"I'm not worried about you needing help to use it. I'm worried about you getting hurt."

"This was a state-of-the-art rig in its day, Arty. I can't let such an investment go to waste."

"'Its day' was over twenty-five years ago. It's

almost as old as you. It's never going to get used again, Mira."

She glared at him defiantly. "No? Then what do you call this?"

With a heart-lurching lunge, she flung her whole weight to one side. Arty yelped as she dived toward the ground headfirst, but at the last minute, she flipped around and lightly touched the floor with her toe before ascending once more. Her path around the stage stopped abruptly, however, as the rig juddered. She gave a little *oof*, then laughed as she took up the slack from a connecting rope and dragged herself back to the platform Arty clung to.

"Are you crazy?" he screamed. "Do you have a death wish?" His heart pounded. "Get down from there this instant!"

"Relax, Arty. I've been playing on this thing nearly my whole life. Grandpa taught me how it all works and I've made it so it's perfectly safe."

"So it'll be your grandpa's fault when you fall and crack your skull open. I'll be sure to thank him when I die of a heart attack."

She pouted. "I didn't mean to scare you."

"You scare me all the time, Mira. I worry about you." He wiped a hand over his brow. "What happened tonight? You haven't had a panic attack like that in years."

She climbed down the ladder ahead of him

so he couldn't read her expression. "That school brings out the worst in me."

"Mira…"

"It wasn't a panic attack. I'm too old for those now."

Arty sighed. She acted tough, but he knew she was fragile inside. Jack had always indulged her because of it. "You got pretty upset."

"I'm upset because Shane Patel won't get the hint." She started taking the harness off. "I can't sell the Crown. This place is my home. It's all I have left of Grandpa."

"That's all well and good, honey, but it doesn't explain what happened to you out there."

Her shoulders sagged. "It was nothing. You know I don't like it when people pressure me. Or stare."

Yeah, he knew. Miriam's parents had been a couple of deadbeats from the start, and when they did pay attention to her between drunken binges, they either berated her ruthlessly or expected her to perform like some kind of circus monkey. Jack had pulled her out of that hellhole away from his no-good son when he'd discovered they'd been leaving her alone for days at a time. That rough beginning had made her an easy target for gossip and bullying in school, too.

"I didn't think you'd show," Arty said.

"I didn't, either. But I had to make myself clear to Mr. Patel."

Arty studied the flush in her cheeks when she said his name. He knew Janice had brought that orchid to her from a nonexistent secret admirer. It seemed Mira had fallen for the ruse. "He's not a bad guy. Used to spend his summers in Everville. He's practically one of us."

"He isn't." She said it so sharply, Arty wondered at her hostility. He decided to push the matter.

"I don't know. He's easygoing, knows the terrain, the people. For a kid who only spent two months a year here, he's got a better memory for folks' names and occupations than most."

She made a dismissive "Pfft" sound, but didn't say anything to contradict his claim.

"Y'know, I don't think he's going to stop trying to convince you to sell."

She paused. "I know."

"So…what? You gonna call Sheriff McKinnon to kick him off your property every time he comes around?"

"Ralph has better things to do." She turned, a shrewd look in her eye. "No, I've got better ways to stop him in his tracks."

"They don't involve more weapons, do they?"

"Give me some credit. There's more than one way to crack a nut."

"MS. WELKS." SHANE greeted Everville's mayor. She looked up from her paperwork, smile lines radiating around her face. Her dark red hair was the color of a banked ember. He was put in mind of a lioness watching her cubs from a hot, flat rock.

"Mr. Patel, thank you for coming." She gestured at the visitor's chair across from her cluttered desk. "Can I offer you some tea? Coffee?"

"Nothing for me, thank you." He wasn't sure the tiny "mayor's office" even had room for an electric kettle. There wasn't much in the way of a town hall in Everville. The main administrative building housed a bevy of municipal functions, but Ms. Welks's office was barely the size of his living room in his Brooklyn condo. Filing cabinets stacked with bulging folders and yellowing binders surrounded the perimeter. An overgrown mother-of-millions plant by the window spilled out of its cracked pot, its progeny scattered over the water-stained credenza and linoleum floor.

"Sorry about the mess," she said, noticing his silent assessment. "Life of a municipal bureaucrat."

"I've seen worse," he said, though the paperwork was usually spread over offices ten times this size in other cities he'd worked in. And there were usually assistants to help with this kind of thing. The mayor of Everville didn't even have a secretary. "You wanted to talk?"

She nodded. "I heard you made quite an impression with your condo presentation at the high school."

"I sure hope so. The people who attended certainly made a good impression on the food tables." He studied her surreptitiously, trying to gauge her feelings. Certainly there were some who'd voiced their concerns to her over the past two days.

Mayor Welks chuckled. "Sorry I couldn't make it myself, but I have to appear somewhat impartial. I've been hearing talk around town. You've got people buzzing, which is always good. Well, usually."

"You heard about Bob Fordingham?"

She rolled her eyes. "He's a man of his own convictions, even when he's contradicting himself." She sniffed. "I won't be coy about it. He hates me for winning the election. He'll do anything to undermine my administration."

"I've dealt with guys like that before. He's just one man, though. It's really a matter of who he'll sway to his way of thinking."

"He has the ear of some more conservative thinkers. Older folks who haven't appreciated the way the town's changed over the past few years."

"I've dealt with folks like that, too."

"I'm glad to hear that, Mr. Patel."

"Shane is fine."

She nodded. "Unfortunately, Bob Fordingham isn't the only one I wanted to talk to you about."

She slid a folder toward him. “Miriam Bateman’s lodged a formal protest to Everville’s town council against the rezoning of her property.”

The pit of his stomach swooped at the mention of Miriam. “But the zoning board hasn’t even voted on this yet.”

“Seems she’s getting a jump on it. She’s really not keen on selling the theater.”

“Do you have any insight into her reason?”

“I don’t know her personally, and I never knew Jack Bateman. From what I hear, he was a good man.”

He hesitated. “Do you know how he died?”

“You’re referring to the suicide rumors.” She shook her head. “I don’t know if they’re true. Stories get conflated around here. All I do know is that he left everything to his only grandchild, Miriam.”

He added that to his mental file on Miriam. He’d ask Arty or someone else about Jack Bateman. Getting to the root of Miriam’s attachment to the Crown was key to taking it off her hands.

“You understand that you’ll probably have to defend your project at the next town meeting. Miriam’s protest will likely be followed by others.”

“You’ve had success changing people’s minds before,” he noted.

“I don’t change minds, Mr. Patel. I support projects that will ensure Everville endures and grows." She dropped her pen on the notepad in front of her. "It's not my job to convince people what's good for them. All these infrastructure projects I've supported are about shoring up the foundations of this town, prepping it for growth. Your condo is one of the first major private investment opportunities the town has seen in years. But no matter how good it looks on paper, I serve my constituents."

"And does the project still look good to you?" he asked carefully. He'd heard from Laura that former mayor Fordingham hadn't been coy about seeking a bribe from Sagmar in exchange for his support. The company had already offered other cosmetic and peripheral infrastructure incentives—a splash pad and playground, a new park, all kinds of beautification—but Big Bob had wanted his fat palms greased.

"I think affordable modern housing is what this town needs. The jobs and new blood it'll bring in will benefit the whole community. Nothing is worse for the economy than stagnation. Nonetheless, my job is to serve the people." She paused, gazing out the window. "The zoning meeting is about a month away. I'll listen to any and all concerns the townspeople have, as will the other members of the board. You'll understand if I tell you now that we should limit our private meetings until the zoning board vote is over."

"Of course." After all, optics were important.

Everyone in town would know by the end of the day that he'd been by to see the mayor. She rightfully wouldn't want anyone thinking those visits had affected her decision.

"I'll ask that you conduct yourself professionally while you're in town. It's hard not to trip over elected officials here."

"I understand." Plenty of council members had businesses in town—he'd have to be careful about who to patronize. He didn't want to be seen as favoring a few shops or services over others.

"Good. Nothing's more important to me than the relationship between people and community, and I believe in good, democratic governance. The foundation for that is trust, transparency and truthfulness. That is something I will not jeopardize."

"I hear you loud and clear."

They parted ways soon after that. Shane headed back for the B and B, chewing over the mayor's words.

She was a woman of strict morals—honest, dutiful and clearly intelligent. It was no less than he'd expected, considering the thoughtful, articulate emails and phone calls they'd exchanged. There'd be no bribing her or the other council members. Not that Shane would resort to that—not ostentatiously, at any rate. Miriam Bateman was a different story, though.

A month. He hadn't thought he'd have to wait

quite that long, though he supposed he could head back to New York in that time and return for the zoning board meeting.

Then again, he hadn't yet secured the Crown, and from what he could tell, he would have to work hard to pry it from Miriam Bateman's claws.

There were worse things than hanging out in Everville during the summer. Reacquainting himself with the town that had been like a second home to him wouldn't be a trial.

MIRA FINISHED HER last blog post for the day and hit Publish. It'd been a grueling week with her deadlines. While she appreciated how much her editors liked her work, writing ten or more pieces daily was exhausting. The money was too good to turn away, though, and she needed every penny to pay the property taxes.

She frowned at the time—almost eight. She'd thought she'd be able to water her garden, but she preferred not to climb up to the roof in the dark. She thought again about the never-ending list of repairs and improvements and where "install rooftop patio lights" fell. Too far down, unfortunately. Working locks, busted plumbing and wonky electrical were top priority. While she could do a lot herself—the internet was great at teaching her all the DIY she needed to maintain the theater—she wasn't stupid enough to think she could take on a job that required a certified professional.

"Don't worry, Grandpa, I'll get it all done, starting with the wiring," she promised to the empty room as she got up to heat a can of soup in the little pot on the hot plate. "Or do you think the leaking urinals in the men's room are more important?"

A hollow whistle broke the silence as changing air pressure creaked through the cavernous building. The wind outside was picking up—she knew the sound of every groan and thump like the beat of her own heart. She sighed. "I know, I don't need to use them, but I'm worried about the pipes cracking in the walls, leaking all over the place. You know what water damage does." Water was the most patient and most destructive of the threats to the Crown.

Well, except maybe for Shane Patel.

The man was insufferable. She hadn't seen him since that presentation at the school gymnasium. Filing that formal complaint to the mayor must have finally put him off. Thank God. She wasn't sure she could deal with his big, stupid smile, as if he was friends with everyone in Everville…

If the movies had taught her anything, it was to never trust handsome charmers.

She screwed up her face. "He's not handsome, he's just…new and different."

The theater's old ventilation shafts shuddered softly, as if with laughter, and she glared up at them. Tightening the bolts on the shaft brackets moved up the to-do list. Shane Patel was nothing more than a novelty, and an unwelcome one at that. He was like Harold Hill in *The Music Man*, a huckster after every red cent he could get, or in Mr. Patel's case, her building. He would get what he wanted and be out of there as soon as the deal was done.

Well, that deal was never going to be done. She'd make sure of it.

Her perimeter alarm chimed. She checked her phone, wary about who was on her property at this time of night. She grabbed her paintball gun as the shadow moved across the security camera's view, but then paused. She recognized that broad-shouldered silhouette and wide-stepped saunter. The figure banged on the front door.

With a disgusted grunt, she put the gun down, hastened toward the entrance and opened it. "What do you want?"

Shane's eyes twinkled. Was he laughing at her? "Sorry for coming by so late. I wanted to talk to you before I left town."

She blinked. "You're...leaving Everville?" She didn't know why her stomach dipped, or why disappointment pricked her so keenly.

"Just for the weekend. I'm heading back to New York for a family gathering, but I should return Monday. Tuesday at the latest."

"Oh." It came out stupidly. She wished she had some witty, cutting remark.

"I spoke with the mayor the other day. I understand you've filed a formal complaint against the development of the condo."

She straightened, unsure why she felt a surge of guilt. "I have. And I won't be the only one."

"I didn't think you would be. I've encountered plenty of resistance to other Sagmar projects, but we've always managed to address community concerns." He held out a thick file. "I wanted to give you this. It's a portfolio containing the specifics of the Sagmar condo we're proposing for the site—almost identical to the one I filed with city planning."

She glanced between him and the file warily. "I don't need that. I already got all your emails. This won't change anything."

"Maybe not, but you might find the information helpful for your deputation."

"Deputation?"

"At the next town meeting. You submitted a formal complaint, so you'll get to give a five-minute presentation to the council about why you don't want a condo here."

She stared at him, feeling as though a trap were closing around her. She didn't need to speak publicly about why she didn't want the condo there. The Crown was her home. Not that anyone openly acknowledged it. Then again, Shane Patel probably didn't know she *lived* there.

"But...why would you give me this?" She nodded at the folder. In her experience, opponents didn't try to help each other.

Shane gave a light chuckle. The sound brushed against her senses with a featherlight caress, and her skin prickled. She liked that sound too much. "I don't want to hide anything from you. I'm giving you this information so you can do your research properly. No one at Sagmar will hold any nonprivate information back from you, either. The company firmly believes in working with the community so that we can make sure we have the best fit, the best use of space, the best mix of business and residence. We don't just drop concrete boxes into towns so people can spend years complaining about how they look or how terrible they are. We build homes." He held the file out to her. "I want to work with you, Miriam."

Awareness shimmied through her. He sounded sincere, but she didn't always trust the way things sounded. She couldn't let him past her defenses. Not for a second.

"I'm sorry—" his nose lifted as he looked past her "—but is something burning?"

CHAPTER FIVE

AT FIRST MIRA thought he was pulling some kind of ruse. Then she smelled it, too.

"My soup!" She bolted inside, tripping across the worn carpets through the semi-darkness to the rear office. Thick steam and gray fumes billowed from the tiny pot on the hot plate and filled the room in two distinct layers like a miasma parfait. She reached for the pot, but snatched her hand back from the handle. The soup had boiled dry and the pot itself was red-hot. Bits of what had once been chicken and vegetables popped and flared briefly into tiny flames before becoming greasy black smoke.

"Here." Suddenly, Shane was there with his suit jacket wrapped around his hand. He picked up the pot and looked around. "Sink?"

"Bathroom." She pointed down the hall.

He hurried out of the office, smoke blowing into his face. She yelled, "To the right!" when he hesitated, and he paused at the door to the ladies' room. She pulled the door open for him, turned on the faucet and shouted at him to put the pot into the sink.

A cloud of steam wafted up as the cold water hit the red-hot metal. Shane hissed and spun away from the superheated vapor.

"Are you okay?" She looked between him and the mess in the sink.

"Burned my hand on the steam," he said, shaking his fingers. "My jacket isn't as good as an oven mitt."

Crap. Visions of lawsuits danced in her head as she ran for the first aid kit in the smoke-filled office. The Crown's building insurance had ceased coverage after Grandpa died and the theater closed. She'd have no way to pay for a lawyer or anything if Shane Patel—

Mira froze, the blood turning to ice in her veins. For a moment, the hazy shape in the doorway looked just like Grandpa, rangy and powerful. He flapped his jacket as if it was a bullfighter's cape, trying to clear the smoke, and the ghostly image disappeared.

"The hot plate's still plugged in." Shane Patel's voice cut through her momentary lapse. She dazedly went to unplug the machine. It was a lucky thing nothing else in her makeshift kitchen had caught on fire. "Leave the door open, let that air clear," he said, using his jacket to waft the steam out.

"I should look at your hand," she said, agitated. "Run it under some cold water."

"It's fine. It's minor. Do you have ventilation fans? AC? Anything like that?"

She bit her lip. "Grandpa had a bunch of fans to keep the lobby cool during the summer."

"Then let's open the doors and get the air moving."

It took a few minutes to unlock and unbolt all of the front and rear doors—the first time they'd all been opened since Grandpa had died. Shane helped her lug out the heavy commercial turbo fans. Eventually, they got a strong cross draft blowing through the theater, and by the time they'd finished setting up the fans, the worst of the smoke and charred smell had dissipated.

"How's your hand?" she asked apprehensively.

The real estate developer flexed his palm grimly. "It'll pass."

She grabbed his wrist and turned it over. A blister the size of a dime had formed on the top of his right index finger. "Oh, my God. You need to get that under cold water right now."

"It's fine." He winced as she pulled him back toward the bathroom.

"It's not fine. You want it to get infected?" Was he trying to make it worse? Maybe he was hoping it'd get so bad it'd leave a lawsuit-worthy scar.

Her first aid kit was the most complete one she could afford. She'd patched herself up several times when she'd cut herself on the stage rigs or hurt herself in the garden. It saved her from leaving the theater to go to the doctor's office.

"You seem to know what you're doing," Shane said as she applied the burn ointment.

"It's not rocket science. This is a small second-degree burn. You can go to the doctor if you think you need to, though," she added hastily. "I don't want you blaming me for any injuries you got trying to help. I would've been fine on my own. You didn't need to come to my rescue."

"You're welcome."

She let out a long breath, chastened. "Sorry, I don't mean to sound ungrateful."

"It was my fault. I should've used something other than my jacket." He flapped it out and checked it over, then sighed as he held up the singed sleeve cuff. "Must've touched the element when I picked up the pot."

"I'll pay for that." Great. Now she'd ruined two of his suits. "This place is a curse on your wardrobe."

He chuckled again, and his laughter buzzed along her spine. They were standing close, and she was still rubbing ointment on his hand in soothing little circles…

She let go abruptly. "Let that sit and breathe. I don't want to bandage it just yet. You need to let the heat out."

They left the ladies' room. The fans were now bringing fresh, cool night air into the theater.

The Crown seemed to breathe deeply for the first time in years. Mira had a sudden flashback of double feature Thursdays during the summers when people would come to watch back-to-back classics and eat popcorn. They'd always kept the doors open then so the place didn't get too hot. Grandpa would talk with his lips pressed against the fan's grille and pretend he was a spaceman speaking to her from a spaceship far, far away. She'd reply in kind from another fan, shouting across the lobby. He'd made her believe for a long time that the fans actually made sound waves go faster.

"Really, this was my fault," Shane said, bringing her back to the present. "I distracted you from your cooking."

"I shouldn't have left that thing on. I'm usually more careful." But then she didn't usually have men badgering her on her doorstep, though she wasn't about to provoke him. They'd reached an uneasy truce for now. "I guess you spoiled me with all that meat and stuff. I didn't have to cook for days."

"I'm glad you liked it. Is there anything I can bring you back from New York? Pizza? Pastrami and bagels from Katz's Deli? A hot dog from Yankee Stadium?"

"I don't need anything."

"It's not about need. I like bringing you things."

His grin sent another wave of unwanted pleasure through her, and she stuffed down the urge to return his smile. She wouldn't be won over, dammit, not even after he'd supposedly "saved" her. "There must be something you want. Something you can't get here in Everville."

She set her jaw, grasping for the coolness she'd first met him with. It was harder now, though, after everything she'd put him through and his incessant need to be kind to her. There was only one thing he wanted, she reminded herself. She took a deep breath.

"All I want is to be left alone, Mr. Patel."

His smile flickered briefly. She could see the first tiny spark of doubt, the barest hint of defeat edging into his confidence. She almost felt bad snuffing out his hopes, but it had to be done.

"Well, if you change your mind—" he took out a business card and scribbled on the back "—that's my personal cell phone number. Call me. Anytime. I'll answer."

A rebellious part of her wanted to toss the card back in his face. She didn't, though. That card felt like a talisman, somehow, and even if he were being nice just to get his hands on her property, she had the strangest sense he didn't often write his personal phone number on his cards.

No. She would not let him manipulate her. She frowned and said, "There's very little I want from *you*." Then she walked away, leaving him alone in the lobby.

And she kind of hated herself for needing to do that.

"WHAT'S WITH THE angry eyebrows, Shekhar?" Shane's mother, Nisha, chided him. "Your sister will worry you're mad at her on her birthday."

Shane hadn't realized he'd been scowling. He was still thinking about Miriam Bateman and how stubbornly unfriendly she'd been, even after he'd helped save the Crown from burning to the ground. He could've done nothing and had all his problems solved for him. Two days later and it was still bothering him. "Just thinking about work, *Amma*."

"Well, stop. You work too hard. Never have time for your family and your poor old *amma*." She patted his cheek. "Now go be social. Your sister doesn't turn thirty every day."

The banquet hall they'd rented for his sister's birthday was packed with friends and family and his parents' business associates. There were probably a hundred people there—a fairly small gathering. His cousin Poonam's wedding had hosted close to five hundred guests. His sister, Priti, hadn't wanted a big affair, but his parents loved parties—they'd make an event out of anything. Shane had a feeling that they were hoping their terminally single children would finally meet someone at one of these shindigs and get married so they could throw a "real" party.

He spotted Priti surrounded by a group of her old high school friends, sipping machine-made margaritas and dancing. She looked happy, maybe a little drunk. She waved him over.

"You guys," she addressed her friends loudly, "you remember my brother, Shekhar, right?"

"Shane," he corrected automatically.

"You changed your name?" One of the women peered at him speculatively, eyes gliding up and down his body. Her name was Chloe, he remembered—the sporty one who'd been Priti's friend since forever.

"He changed it in college. He's a bad Indian son. No pride in his family-given name." Priti batted her lashes and laughed.

He shrugged. Anglicizing his name had simply been easier for everyone. It was awkward having to repeat his name several times to people as he shook hands with them. That, and he'd hated the nicknames people came up with.

"So what do you do, Shane?" another of his sister's friends asked politely.

"Real estate development. I work at a company called Sagmar."

"My apartment's a Sagmar building!" Chloe exclaimed. "What do you do there?"

He explained his role in the company, how he negotiated and acquired property and scouted out sites. He loved his job and was happy to chat about it. Soon, he was talking about the condo project in Everville and all the problems he'd been having acquiring the Crown Theater. Some of the girls' eyes glazed over, and a few of Priti's friends drifted away or excused themselves to get a drink. But his sister remained rapt. She had fond memories of Everville, too.

She tapped a finger to her lips. "So…this woman won't sell her building because…?"

"Honestly, I'm not sure. I mean, it has sentimental value to her, but from what I've seen, the place is falling apart. I don't know how she even affords the taxes on the place. It seems like she can barely keep the lights on. It's actually a bit depressing."

"Just because she doesn't have an apartment in Brooklyn and earn six figures doesn't mean she's not happy."

"I think she might be a bit of a shut-in."

"Why? Is she some kind of crone, wearing tissue box shoes and collecting her urine?"

"She's only twenty-eight." He swirled the ice cubes around his glass. "It's just that she's *always* at the theater. God knows what she's doing there. And the one public event I saw her at didn't go well—she kinda freaked out. Like some kind of panic attack."

"You can't just assume she's a shut-in. You hardly know her."

"That's the problem. I can't find out anything about her. She isn't on Facebook or Twitter or anything. Not under her real name, anyhow. Her best friend in town is the old man who runs the grocery store, and he couldn't even tell me what she was into."

Priti regarded him, chin tilted, then smiled slowly. "You like her."

"What?"

"You *like* her," she teased. "And you're frustrated you can't do your usual wine and dine to get her to like you back."

"That's ridiculous. She shot me in the nuts with a paintball gun. She barely said thank you for all the gifts I brought—"

"See, that's your problem right there. You think a woman owes you something just because you pay attention to her."

He was taken aback. He wasn't that entitled—was he? Then again, Miriam Bateman was probably the first woman he couldn't coax a real smile out of. And it did annoy him.

He suddenly felt a little sick about himself.

"Even if she were interested, you still want to take away something that obviously means a lot to her," Priti added. "Of course she's suspicious of your motives."

"I'm just trying to be nice."

"So that she'll sell you her property. C'mon, Shekky, don't act like the injured party here." His sister swigged her drink. "I've never seen you go after anyone seriously enough to believe it would last. You like the chase, and you like to win. This woman can smell a predator a mile away. I'd have shot you in the nuts, too, if I saw you coming."

"*I* wouldn't have." Chloe beamed at him, flicking him a flirty look.

Any other day he might have offered to get her a drink, but he was too preoccupied with the conundrum of Miriam Bateman.

His father waved him over. He was standing with his cousin Sanjay, who worked at the electronics store Shane's father ran. A year older than Shane, Sanjay had always been the dutiful one, the one Shane assumed would take over the family business if and when his father retired. Shane had helped out at the shop when he was younger, but while he was a good salesman, he wasn't as savvy with electronics as Sanjay.

"We were just talking about you," Sanjay said by way of greeting. "Ranjeet was thinking of expanding the business, maybe opening a smaller branch just for repairs."

It always weirded him out how his cousin addressed his father by his first name rather than Uncle like all his other cousins did. "Where would you open it?"

"Ideally, not far from the shop, but the rents are pretty high. Don't suppose you know any good real estate agents?"

"I'll get you some names." He nodded to his father. "Things going okay, *Baap*? How's your knee?"

"It's fine." Ranjeet waved him off. "Nothing I can't handle."

"I try to make him sit at the front, but he won't." Sanjay gave a put-upon sigh.

His father didn't like to be reminded that he was closing in on seventy. Shane had meant the query to subtly clue him in on the advance of his years, and that maybe expanding the business at this stage was questionable, but his father knew his son's tactics too well and dodged. "How's Everville these days?"

"It's great. A lot has changed since our last vacation there."

"I miss that place," his father said wistfully. "The fishing on Silver Lake is still the best."

Sanjay and Shane both chuckled. If Ran wasn't talking about the business or the latest cricket match, he was talking about fishing.

"Well, maybe you should take some time off and visit for a weekend. I'll be staying there for a few weeks."

"A vacation? That's unlike you, Shekhar."

"Not exactly." He told them about the Crown and Miriam Bateman, and the town meeting scheduled in June. "It's my personal time, but it's an unofficial working vacation."

"Ah. Apples don't fall far from the tree. Just

like you, Ran, he doesn't know how to relax." Sanjay toasted him with his drink.

Ranjeet ignored him. "I remember that old theater. I took you kids to see all the Indiana Jones movies there. Shame it closed."

"There's a new big theater in Welksville."

"Yes, but these old independent movie houses are an endangered species, you know. A whole industry has collapsed because of digital projection."

"For someone whose business revolves around selling the latest and greatest in technology, I wouldn't think you'd defend the obsolete for nostalgia's sake."

"You can't put a price on nostalgia. Theaters like the Crown remind me of the ones I went to in Mumbai as a teen..." He lapsed into Hindi as he described the classic Bollywood films he'd seen when they were still new then, and how he'd met his wife, who'd been a movie set manager back in the day. Shane's connection with his Indian roots had always been tentative at best—he'd been born and raised in New York and had lived all his life in the Tri-State area. While he appreciated his father's point of view, Shane was a man of the here, now and future.

"Well, the Crown's defunct. It'll be condemned before it ever opens again," Shane said. Strangely, the thought made him feel a bit guilty.

His father shrugged. "Too bad. But you know

what they say. 'Change is the law of life. And those who look only to the past or the present are certain to miss the future.'"

Shane narrowed his eyes in thought. "Gandhi?"

Ranjeet frowned. "No, JFK. Read a book now and again, son." He went to refill his drink, limping slightly.

His cousin chuckled. "Gotta give your dad credit. His health's not the best, but his mind is sharp as ever."

Shane thought about the condo in Everville, about how nice it would be for his parents to have a place to retire to. He prompted his cousin. "Sanjay, I was wondering if you'd help me with something. How are your hacking skills these days?"

"Depends," he said slowly.

"Nothing illegal, promise. I'm just trying to learn more about Miriam Bateman. I can't find anything about her on the internet. She's like a ghost."

"You mean she's smart." Sanjay smirked. "It's not safe out there with all the weirdo real estate developers stalking you."

"I'm not *stalking* her. I just want to find out what she likes, what her interests are. I need to connect with her. Can you help?"

"Sorry, that's beyond my skill, though I do have an old buddy from MIT who might help. He's a private investigator who specializes in digital identities."

"Yes. Perfect. That'd be great."

Sanjay sent him an odd look. "You sure you're not stalking her?"

"Yes, I'm sure." He suppressed the exasperation climbing through him. Why did his family think he was such a creep? He was only doing his job. "All I'm interested in is the building, and she's pretty much the last hurdle. The rest is up to town council, but at this stage I doubt they'll turn the project down."

"You mean turn *you* down." Sanjay grinned.

He toasted his cousin. "Tell me more about this PI."

CHAPTER SIX

SHANE DIDN'T GET back to Everville until the middle of the following week. He'd had paperwork to do at the Sagmar offices, and then he'd had to arrange for a more permanent place to stay for his "vacation" and pack. The B and B was nice, but he needed a better Wi-Fi connection if he was going to work. He wouldn't waste this vacation relaxing.

He found a sublet near Silver Lake—a little house just down the road from the beach, much like the place his family used to vacation in. It took him an additional day to settle in. He bought groceries, set up the internet connection and then made some phone calls. The PI Sanjay had recommended worked fast—he'd already emailed a preliminary report on Miriam Bateman. Shane sat down to read it.

Miriam Bateman
Born: December 1, 1986,
Hudson Falls, NY
Parents: Jeannie Ansen (mother)—deceased (overdose)

Richard Bateman (father)—incarcerated at Rochester Penitentiary, serving twenty years for drug possession, drug trafficking, possession of a firearm, perjury in the first degree, contempt of court, assault on a police officer…

The list went on. Shane grimaced. He kept reading.

Education: BA in Film Studies, CUNY
Currently employed: Freelance writer for various publications under the pseudonym M. J. Baille.

A list of writing credits was included, with hyperlinks to her articles. She wrote on a number of subjects, mainly about pop culture, with copious movie and book reviews. Shane read through a few of the shorter ones. Her tone and style were whip-smart and a little snarky. And these weren't just typical plot summaries with thumbs up or down: they delved into deeper issues, criticizing Hollywood for its lack of diversity and strong roles for women. She went on at length about several films that had missed major storyline opportunities. She dissected the themes and significance of several works.

He found more articles by M. J. Baille on the decline of independent second-run theaters. She waxed on about the lost nostalgia of the smaller theater. She complained about how difficult it was to fill seats in expensive megaplexes with good independent films when people could download movies illegally. It seemed she knew everything there was to know about the movie industry, and had even interviewed some of Hollywood's biggest names.

Shane sat back after nearly three hours of intense reading. It was fascinating stuff, and he agreed, or at least sympathized, with some of her views. No wonder she was so invested in the Crown. It wasn't just a representation of her grandfather's legacy—it was the last stronghold in her ongoing war against change and progress.

Prying the property from her hands would be a lot more difficult than he first thought. But every battle had a turning point, every defense a weakness. He just had to find hers.

MIRA CLOSED HER laptop after a long, hard day of writing. Her neck cracked as she rolled her shoulders. She really needed to get away from her desk more often, but freelancing meant longer hours and more work by necessity. People often smarmily remarked on how nice it must be to work from home in her pajamas, but they had no idea how hard she worked for so little pay and zero benefits or job security. Frankly, she'd probably be better off if she served coffee at the local café. Human interaction and food service were not her calling, however. The lingering smell of burned soup was proof of that.

Her thoughts strayed to Shane. He had said he'd be back Monday, but he hadn't phoned, emailed or come by, and it was now Thursday. Not that she was expecting him to—in fact, it was a good thing he hadn't. Maybe he'd finally given up.

That was only wishful thinking on her part, though. Since Grandpa's passing, she'd felt as though she'd been waiting for the other shoe to drop. That shoe was the demise of the Crown. If she didn't get the theater open and generating income again, the city could condemn the building.

Mira rubbed her eyes. Worrying about it wouldn't solve anything, and she didn't need another sleepless night. She needed to relax.

She rummaged through her collection and pulled out *Casablanca*. It'd been her and Grandpa's favorite movie. She'd cut her teeth on film storytelling listening to him talk about all the ways it'd become the timeless classic that it was. She'd made it the subject of numerous projects and essays in film school.

She popped the DVD into the player connected to the older model digital projector she'd bought secondhand online. It wasn't a theater-quality piece of equipment—it was mostly used for office presentations and not much good for projecting on anything bigger than Mira herself, plus the replacement bulbs were hard to find—but it was better than her laptop screen. She'd always believed in watching movies the way they were meant to be watched.

As the on-disc commercials and advertisements played, she put a bag of popcorn into the microwave, then on a whim, decided to hook herself into the harness to have another go at that busted rig coupling. She didn't need to sit through the film to enjoy it—she knew all the lines by heart, though she did love that moment when Ilsa meets Rick again for the first time in the film.

In short order, she was hooked into the rig and was pulling herself along the track, checking every inch as she went. The broken coupling that joined one part of the track to the next was bent just enough that she couldn't get the wheels of the stock to jump the gap. Replacing it would be best, but the more she looked at it, the more she wondered if shifting it a few millimeters over would solve the problem. She studied the bolts in the ceiling—she wasn't sure she had the equipment to take them out, or the strength, but she had to try.

Stretching, she pulled herself up and grabbed the wrench from her tool belt. She could barely get a grip on the bolt. Her arms were about two inches too short to get any real purchase, but she twisted anyway, torquing her whole body in the hopes that something would give.

Something gave, all right. Her biceps protested sharply, and pain shot through her wrist. The wrench clattered onto the stage below. The sudden release of tension made her tip downward, almost headfirst, and the sudden shift in weight made her spin in place. She flailed, trying to right herself like a wildly tilting helicopter blade. Tools slipped from her belt and rained down onto the stage below before she managed to grab hold of the track to stop her wild midair pirouette. She caught her breath and waited for the world to stop spinning.

That had never happened before. She looked up and groaned: part of the ceiling where the track was bolted had come loose. A steady drip of dirty brown water leaked from the gaping hole.

No need to panic. The track was still connected, so all she had to do was pull herself back to the catwalk. She reached for the tether rope, then swore when a tug didn't return her to safety. The rope had tangled up around the rig.

She spent ten minutes trying to use the slack to get it unlooped from the tangle, but it was hopeless. She gave a frustrated whimper as the music in *Casablanca* swelled. She had no choice—she'd have to call Arty or Janice to help get her down.

And get yelled at, most likely. She could just imagine the smug satisfaction with which Arty would tell her he'd been right about the rig. Or the utter disappointment and worry on Janice's aged face as the older woman gently told her for the billionth time that everything she did was risky and dangerous. She set her teeth as she pulled out her cell phone. At least that hadn't fallen in her wild spin.

The perimeter alarm chimed. The feed brought up an image of a tall man in jeans and a T-shirt with something in his arms.

It was Shane Patel.

Relief and elation flooded her, overriding the dread that came with confronting the man after her public breakdown. In spite of her humiliation, she'd never been so glad to see the real estate developer.

She dialed his number. She'd programmed it into her contacts list after he'd given her his card only because she wanted to make sure she could screen his calls, not because she'd ever intended to call him.

"Shane Patel."

"Mr. Patel, it's Mira—Miriam Bateman." She was a little chagrined by how breathless she sounded. "I can see you're standing outside the Crown."

He paused. She imagined he was searching for a camera.

"The back door is open. Listen, I'm in the auditorium. I… I need your help."

"Is everything all right?"

"I just need you to hurry in, please." She didn't

want to be beholden to him, but she'd prefer he help her down rather than Arty or worse, the fire department.

"Okay, hang on. I'm keeping the line open. Are you hurt? What's the problem?"

Mira hesitated. "It's kind of hard to explain."

"Not another fire, I hope?"

"No."

"Are you sure you're not hurt? Do you need an ambulance?"

"I'm fine. Just get in here," she said impatiently.

She heard the outer back door groan open. His footsteps were muffled by the carpeting, and then the doors to the auditorium opened. "Miriam?"

The music to the film chose that precise moment to swell. Ilsa and Rick, meeting again after years apart. Her face flushed as Shane approached the stage, his head swiveling as he scanned the rows of worn velvet-covered seats. "Ms. Bateman?" he called again. "Where are you?"

"Up here."

He squinted and shaded his eyes against the floodlights above her. "How…?"

"It's a fly rig," she explained. "It was installed years ago for a production of *Peter Pan*. I was doing some maintenance, but the track broke loose and I'm stuck."

"Holy—" Shane leaped onto the stage and stared up into the fly gallery from beneath her.

Thank God she wasn't wearing a skirt. "I'll call the fire department."

"Please, don't. I'm fine. The rig will hold." She hoped. "I just need to get down."

"How?"

"My lead line is tangled." She gave the rope a wave to demonstrate. "If you can find a long stick or something to get it off the rig, I can pull myself back."

He disappeared behind the heavy, faded curtain. She could hear him rummaging around. "I don't see anything here. Is there a broom or something in your office?"

"No. A rope will do, if you can throw it to me."

He reappeared a minute later, rope in hand. "How's this?"

"Great! Now, the ladder to the catwalk above the stage is to your right." She pointed. "Climb up and throw me one end."

He looked up, frowning. "Maybe I should just call the fire department."

"No need for that." She couldn't bear it if they saw her like this. And who knew what the fire marshal might say if he discovered she was living here. "A lot of them are volunteers from around the county. They'll probably be getting ready for bed. Or they might have a real emergency."

She could see Shane's brow furrow even from up there, and she got a feeling he was holding something back. "What's wrong?"

"Is the ladder safe?"

"I've never fallen from it."

"And the catwalk?"

She huffed. "What's the matter?"

He wiped a hand across his mouth. "I should call the fire department."

"No! Please, Shane—" she gripped the rope and spun herself around "—I'm begging you. I don't want them here." She couldn't handle a bunch of townspeople shaking their heads at her. Whispering about her. *Stupid girl, getting herself tangled up there...*

He didn't look convinced. Desperate, she made a bargain. "Look, if you help me down, I'll listen to anything you have to say, sit in on all your presentations, whatever. Just don't call anyone else."

He hesitated. "All right. Hang on."

It took a really long time for him to climb the ladder. The rungs rang with each step. The higher he got, the longer the pauses between clangs. Eventually, he reached the catwalk. He gripped both rails, the rope he'd found slung over his shoulder. His jaw worked as he focused on her. He'd gone quite pale.

"Are you all right?"

"I...have a thing...about heights."

"It's not that high up," she assured him hastily, though Grandpa had told her a stagehand had once fallen and broken both legs decades ago. "Just don't look down."

"Wasn't my plan." His voice was thin, coming out on a shaky breath.

"Can you throw me the rope from there?"

He slowly uncoiled the rope from around his shoulder. Carefully, one hand still white-knuckled on the railing, he tossed her the end.

He missed, and she saw immediately why. It wasn't a rope at all. It was a yellow extension cord—the ten-foot one she kept by the stage, most likely.

"That's too short," she told him. "Climb down. I'll think of something else."

He edged his way quickly off and then down the ladder. Frankly, she was relieved he was back on solid ground—if he fell, she'd have to call the sheriff, the fire department, an ambulance *and* a lawyer.

The harness bit into her thighs as she thought hard. "There are a set of counterweights that keep me up here. If you untie them, I might be able to swing myself far enough over the track to reach the floor."

She directed him to the pulley and rope system and instructed him on how to safely get her down. "You sure this is a good idea?" he asked.

"No." She judged the distance along the track, praying the rig didn't drop her like a deadweight.

"I can still call the fire department," Shane said.

I'd rather fall and break my neck. "I'll be fine."

She felt the line slacken. The cables gave a slight *zi-ip* sound as the counterweights were released. She took hold of the tether rope and threw her weight forward, pulling as hard as she could. The harness snapped against her stomach and winded her. She had just enough presence of mind to release the tether before it could leave rope burns on her hands as she plummeted straight toward a wide-eyed Shane.

"Look out!"

They crashed in a tangle of limbs, and Shane went "Oof!" as she thudded against his solid chest. She dug her fingers into his muscled back as the counterweights yanked her back upward. Her claws sank in, and he let out a strangled cry.

"Don't let go!" she rasped. "I need to get this harness off—if I go back up, I'll be stuck worse than ever."

"You couldn't have said something about that earlier?" He threaded his arms under hers and locked her to him, chest to chest. The counterweights, however, were still lifting her a couple of inches off the ground, so she couldn't quite touch the floor.

They hung there, locked in a full-body stranglehold. Sweat pooled in her armpits. Shane was overwarm, too, the lingering funk of fear mixing with his spicy cologne—he seemed to be getting hotter under his T-shirt by the second. "Okay," she panted. "This is awkward."

"I would've taken you to dinner first, you know." Shane pulled back from her slightly to look into her face. He smirked. "No need to throw yourself at me."

She scowled, but didn't smack him in case he let go. "Can you reach the D ring above me?"

"I think so." He reached up, and she had to cling tighter, practically climbing down his body to make sure he had enough slack to unhook her.

"Don't let it go once you get me out."

"Easier said than done," he grunted. "Hang on. I need to use both hands."

She clung to his waist, her nose now firmly planted against his sternum. He was fit, not too lean, and even had a few softer spots. Perfectly average, she told herself, though she didn't have much to reference. Her entire romantic experience had been limited to the one guy she'd dated in college.

Not that she was entertaining romantic notions with Shane Patel.

The upward pull on her suddenly slackened. "Got it."

She unlatched herself from around his waist and scrambled to her feet. "Hang on to that for a little longer." She ran and retied the counterweights backstage, then shouted, "Okay, let go!"

When she came back onstage, Shane was shaking his hands out and stretching. The line dangled in front of him. "Are you all right?"

"Yeah. I'm good." A sudden sheepishness overtook her. "Thank you," she mumbled as a fresh wave of heat shot into her face. She busied herself unstrapping the harness. "If you wouldn't mind, I'd like to keep this from Arty. And the rest of the world."

"My lips are sealed." He mimed zipping his upturned lips and locking them. Awareness flushed through Mira, a rush of not unpleasant tingles skittering across her skin. She fumbled with the numerous clips and buckles to hide her reaction.

"Need help with that?"

"No," she said sharply. The last thing she wanted was for him to be that close to her again, his hands on her in places she really didn't want to be thinking about. She quickly unsnapped the buckles around her thighs and freed herself from the apparatus.

"How'd you end up there, anyhow?" Shane looked up at the ceiling.

"I'm up there all the time." She didn't know why she was being so defensive. She struggled to rein in her hostility—he'd just saved her from yet another humiliating situation. What was it about this guy that brought out the worst in her, apart from the fact that he was trying to take her home from her? "I like to be up there. It feels…safe."

"Safe." He grimaced at the water trickling down. It'd slowed to a drip, so it wasn't likely a burst pipe. Probably water that had pooled on the roof. "Maybe you should stay off of it for now."

She rolled her eyes inwardly. Why did everyone treat her as if she didn't know any better? But she kept her mouth shut—goodwill and keeping secrets came at a price.

"Let me help clean up," he offered.

"Oh, no, that's not—"

He was already jogging up the aisle. "I saw a mop and bucket in your office. I'll grab them. You can check all your ropes and things, make sure everything's out of the way and that nothing will fall on our heads."

MINUTES LATER, HE was sopping up puddles onstage. Mira silently monitored him while she secured the rigging and checked the ropes and cables for damage. She sighed—she wouldn't be up there again for a while. One more thing to add to her to-do list. One more bit of solace taken from her.

"As Time Goes By" crooned on in the background as Ilsa and Rick argued. If she'd called Arty, he would've been griping about his aches and pains and berating her for her recklessness. She loved her grandfather's dear old friend, but he could be a real crank. Shane, however, worked quickly, quietly and without complaint or criticism. She might have resented his presence in her life, but right now, she was grateful for it.

Which meant she needed to get him and his confusing presence away as quickly as possible.

"Did you come by for something?" she prompted.

He grinned and went to one of the rows of seats. "I got back in town yesterday but didn't have time to stop by. I wanted to bring you this." He picked up a potted orchid. "It's from a specialty florist in Manhattan. I thought you might like it."

She suppressed a delighted "Oh!" It was pure white with delicate tendrils spread like wings—a wild white egret orchid. "It's gorgeous…but…why?"

"You like flowers. I thought I'd bring you one."

Of course, it was all part of his scheme to win her approval *and* the Crown. She opened her mouth to point that out to him, but hesitated. "Thank you," she said instead. "You didn't need to bring me anything, though."

"Is it just orchids, or do you like other flowers?"

Strange question to ask—she'd assumed he'd known about her garden to give her such a specific plant. "I keep a bunch of different tropical hothouse plants in the greenhouse, but I grow other things, too."

He looked confused. "You have a greenhouse?"

"In my garden. On the roof."

"Oh." He glanced up again, almost nervously. "Maybe that's where this leak is coming from?"

“We haven’t had a lot of rain. And I’m pretty sure none of the plumbing runs up this high.” She grimaced at the gap in the ceiling.

The swell of music reminded her the DVD was still playing. She went to stop it.

“Funny, I’ve never watched *Casablanca* all the way through,” Shane mused.

Every thought inside her ground to a halt, and she whipped around to face him. “Are you serious?”

He flinched. “It’s not a crime.”

Yes, it was. “How can you never have— It’s a classic! It’s *the* classic. The defining film of cinema history!”

“I’m more of an action film kind of guy.”

“Oh, my God.” She threw her hands up in the air. “Okay, that’s it. Until you watch it, I can’t talk to you.”

“Is that an invitation?”

She supposed it was. She hadn’t exactly meant it to be, but confronting someone who’d never seen *Casablanca* was anathema to her. It was like telling her they hadn’t been vaccinated against the plague. “Sit down. I’ll make more popcorn.”

She supposed she owed him for saving her life, after all.

CHAPTER SEVEN

SHANE COULDN'T BELIEVE his luck—if anyone could call it that. He'd expected a brief visit, maybe a door slammed in his face. But now he was sitting comfortably next to Miriam, eating microwave popcorn and watching her favorite movie.

It was true he'd never seen the whole film beginning to end, though he was certainly familiar with the classic lines. But watching Humphrey Bogart on-screen wasn't half as interesting as watching Miriam out of the corner of his eye.

She was rapt. She must have watched the film hundreds of times—she lip-synched the lines, and yet still laughed at all the jokes. She had an odd laugh, a guffaw that came out in little chuffs, as if she were trying to suppress the real mirth bubbling up from beneath that dour facade.

When the film got sappy, her eyes grew dewy. She chewed her nails as the Nazis invaded Paris, and Bogart and Ilsa had to part ways. He hadn't thought Miriam the romantic type, but she actually sighed and put a hand over her heart. He didn't know people really did that, but maybe that was the cynical New Yorker in him.

As the film ended, with Bogart and the French police chief strolling off into the unknown, Miriam turned to him. "Well?"

"Fantastic. Loved it." It was a genuine sentiment. "Makes me wonder why Hollywood hasn't done a remake."

"Sacrilege!" Her eyes burned. "You could never remake this movie. No one has Bogart's gravitas or cool. And you can't imitate the feeling of helplessness that 1942 inspired, with everyone steeped in World War II."

"What about a modern remake? Change Casablanca out for… I don't know, Kabul…"

Miriam shook her head and launched into even more reasons why it wouldn't work. Shane was baiting her, of course. He knew she'd defend her position and the sanctity of *Casablanca* with her dying breath. He'd read enough of her essays to know she would. She'd probably break out singing "La Marseillaise" in a few minutes.

She wasn't sanctimonious about it, though—he bandied possibilities for modern-day dream casts, and she considered each one thoroughly, citing roles that were similar or pointing out why his chosen actors weren't worthy of the vaunted roles.

"You just don't mess with the classics," she said definitively, then paused thoughtfully. "Although, a remake might work if it were an international story. I'd like to see a version of *Casablanca* set in North Korea. Wouldn't that be cool?" She grinned.

"You really know your movies," he said.

She lifted a shoulder casually. "It's what I do for a living. I write reviews and critical pieces for a bunch of blogs."

He knew that, too, but getting her to open up about her life was a huge accomplishment. "I would think you'd have to live closer to New York to attend all the advance media screenings."

"I'll go for the big movies if my gas and accommodations get covered. I've even been invited to some Hollywood premieres. I went to the *Infinite Destinies* premiere last year in LA, and that was insane. But I mostly get copies of indie and international films couriered to me. Quiet, short-run films that have critical praise, but no marketing budget."

"Where do you watch the more popular stuff?"

"Here." She nodded at her projector. "But *everyone* does reviews for those, so I don't have to stay too current. I've got a niche in indie film and film history."

He'd gathered as much from her portfolio of work. But even if he was pretending, he found himself drawn into her world. "Have you met any celebrities?"

She laughed. "No one likes to meet their critics. Although, I did meet Riley Lee Jackson briefly at his premiere."

His head popped up. "Really?" The *Infinite*

Destinies star was a household name these days. “What was he like?”

“Meh.” That ambiguous shrug said a lot more about Miriam than it did the A-list actor. “I didn’t talk to him much. He’s just a guy. Has a kid, a girlfriend. I know what you’re going to say,” she said with an admonishing look. *“‘I thought all women threw themselves at his feet?’”* She rolled her eyes. “He’s not really my type.”

And what is your type? It was on the tip of Shane’s tongue to ask, but that was a line he might’ve used on a woman at a bar. Miriam wouldn’t appreciate it, and this rapport had been hard-won. He wouldn’t risk ruining it. “I really liked *Infinite Destinies*.”

“You and about $1.8 billion worth of worldwide viewers.” She smirked. “I mean, it was all right, but if you really want to talk superhero films…”

He let her continue, studying her animated hands, the way her blue eyes glowed as she spoke. Movies were her passion. It was hard to reconcile this Miriam with the black-clad wraith who’d warned him off with a fierce glower and a loaded paint gun, or the small, panicked animal who’d scampered out of the high school gym. It wasn’t just her articulation and critical knowledge that captivated him; her enthusiasm was infectious. He didn’t have a whole lot to add, but he wanted to engage her in more verbal sparring—which might have been why he provoked her into defending her positions on several classic films, which she claimed all others were derived from.

They talked for a long time. He glanced at his watch and was shocked to find it was close to midnight.

"Holy cow, it's late." He gave her an apologetic look, though he didn't feel all that sorry. "I didn't mean to keep you up."

She ran a hand through her shoulder-length bob, brushing it away from her slender neck. "Don't worry. I'm a night owl." Her heavy-lidded eyes cast downward. "And a bit of an insomniac."

He studied the angle of her chin, the way her lips were slightly parted. Damn. If this were anyone else, he'd be brushing a fingertip along that plump lower lip and proposing they spend the rest of the night together working on her sleeping problem. She was primed for seduction—at least, that was what her body language told him. But Miriam Bateman was not a conquest. He wouldn't put the moves on her as if she were some casual fling.

"Would you join me for dinner tomorrow?" he asked.

She blinked. "Dinner?"

"You do eat, don't you? Something other than popcorn and burned soup, I mean."

She shriveled like a wilting flower in a time-lapse video. Her expression went from open and bright to closed and cold. "I don't really eat out much."

He'd said something wrong. Maybe she couldn't afford to eat out. "My treat. Nothing fancy—you like Chinese? I've been jonesing for some sweet-and-sour chicken balls from the Good Fortune Diner."

"It's not that," she said, turning slightly away.

"What, are you a shut-in or something?" He chuckled.

The daggered look she sent him stopped his laughter as effectively as another paintball in the nuts.

"I'm not a shut-in," she snapped. "I'm just busy. And I have to keep an eye on things here. You saw how easy those kids got in."

So she felt as though she had to guard the place like a dog? "Guess you haven't replaced that lock on the back door yet."

"You know I haven't." Bitterness rose in her voice, the lines in her face growing more pronounced the more he irritated her.

"All right, then. No problem." He backed off reluctantly. "I'll bring dinner to you. In fact, I'll swing by the hardware store tomorrow and see what we can do about getting that fixed." He nodded at the rig.

She blinked at him. "You don't have to do that."

"Sure I do," he said, though he had no idea how he was going to get up there. It didn't look that high from the ground, but nothing ever did. He'd hated that Miriam had seen his one real weakness, but he also realized he'd won points by exposing his vulnerability to her. It wasn't intentional—his only concern at the time had been to help her. "I can't just leave your stuff dangling and broken like that."

"Well, if anything needs fixing, it's the roof. I have to find out where that water is coming from before it rains again."

The roof. Great. "I'll get a bucket of tar and some supplies," he said through a tight smile.

"You know how to patch roofing?"

"I know the basics. It's not that hard. That's what YouTube's for, right?"

Miriam's lips pursed. She looked ready to argue but then nodded. "All right. But bring me the receipt for anything you buy. This is my building, after all."

Shane quirked his lips. He was well aware of that.

"YOU WOULDN'T BELIEVE who I just ran into."

Janice looked up as Arty burst into the florist's shop. He was already breathless from hurrying over to see her, but now his heart stopped. She was never prettier than when she was at work among her flowers. For a moment, he forgot what he was going to say. She prompted, "Well?"

He cleared his throat. "Shane Patel's back in town. He's staying by the lake for a few weeks. Bumped into him at the hardware store. He was getting supplies to—get this—help Mira fix the roof."

"The roof of the Crown?"

He nodded, giddy. "Was all smiles, that one—more so than usual. He was obviously happy to be helping her. I got the impression they've been spending quality time together."

Worry lines appeared around Janice's delicate mouth. "You think he knows what he's doing?"

"Judging by what he was getting and what he was asking for? Not a foggy clue. Don't worry," he reassured her. "Herman straightened him out. He and Mira will do fine between the two of them, I'm sure."

The concern didn't disappear from her face, though. "What's wrong, Jan?"

"I'm not sure I feel right about this. It all sounded fine in my head when we were just talking about her having sex—" Arty squirmed. He'd never heard Jan say S-E-X before, and it made him feel self-conscious "—but you know Mira's a softy at heart. I don't want her to get hurt."

"If anyone does any hurting, it'll be her." Mira could be anxious and cranky, but she was resilient. Arty believed she'd bounce back from anything. "Besides, our part in this was tiny. We just gave things a little nudge."

"I hope our nudge doesn't make either of them fall on their face," Janice murmured.

"Mira'll be fine," he said again, and reached out to grip Jan's hand. His arm tingled as her fingers curled around his. "They'll both be fine."

Slowly, she nodded. "You're right," she conceded. "They're adults. Perfectly capable of taking care of themselves."

A golden slice of sunlight peeked through the thin cloud cover, making the whole shop glow. Nothing was as radiant as Janice, though.

THIS WAS SUCH a bad idea.

Why had he volunteered to help Mira fix the leaky roof? Hadn't the word *roof* told him everything he needed to know about what he'd face? He'd humiliated himself last night on the catwalk above the stage—why had he thought this would be any better?

Because you're a manly man and you're too stubbornly male to acknowledge your weaknesses. Years of being teased for his fear of heights might have played a part in his show of heroics. He was a winner, after all, and hated that gravity and distance could reduce him to a quivering mess.

Shane had had a hard enough time looking down from the theater balcony as he'd carried the supplies to the fire escape. Now, as he stared up the ladder to the roof, he thought he might throw up. There was nothing to keep a person from slipping and falling to their death.

How old was the fire escape, anyhow? He scanned the black wrought iron for a clue. The theater itself had been built in 1900, but the fire escapes had to be slightly newer than that, right? Orange rust spotted a few joints and bolt heads, and he noticed a touch of corrosion on the bottom rung. Miriam stood on the landing without any concern as she rearranged the supplies.

"I'm not sure I can carry this bucket of tar up the ladder," Shane said.

"Not to worry. I have something for exactly this purpose." She scaled the ladder quick as a squirrel. Shane watched her nervously, then made the mistake of glancing down through the slats of the wrought-iron landing.

He clutched the door frame and breathed deep, eyes closed as he fought vertigo. It was a long way to fall.

"Heads up," Miriam called a minute later. Shane pried himself away from the door and cautiously leaned out. A shallow square wood box measuring about four by four feet was rapidly descending on a series of ropes and cables, which were threaded through a pulley hanging from an arm over the edge of the roof. He caught the box as it reached eye level and gently guided it down.

"Homemade elevator?"

"For the stuff I can't carry up," she replied. "Not for you, though." She notched her chin at him. "Load the platform, but try to balance everything so it sits straight. Use the bungee cords inside to strap things down if necessary."

Shane braced himself as he stepped onto the fire escape landing. The ground below seemed to loom up through the thin metal strips of the lattice, threatening to smash into him. He shut his eyes and muttered, "It's just carpet," before focusing on loading the platform.

He didn't know when or how his fear of heights had developed—he'd simply never enjoyed being high up. He remembered a particularly aggravating family trip to a country fair when he was thirteen—his sister and cousins went on all the roller coasters and high-flying spinning rides, and had made fun of him when he'd absolutely refused to go with them. They'd called him a chicken, but Shane had reasonably told them he didn't trust any ride that could be dismantled and reassembled in less than two hours.

Shane had preferred to play the midway games, both feet firmly planted on the ground. He'd gotten particularly good at Whack-A-Mole, though it had cost his father quite a bit of cash.

"Shekhar, it's perfectly safe, I promise," his father had cajoled, hoping his son would join the others. "A little risk is okay in life. You think I built my business and life here without risk?"

"What's the point of all that, though?" Shane had argued, upset that his father was trying, yet again, to force him into something he didn't want to do. He'd pointed at the roller coaster his family was lined up for. "Half hour lineup for a two-minute ride that costs five bucks each? I call that a rip-off."

"Meanwhile, you've spent twenty dollars to win a plush elephant."

"At least it's a *thing* I can take home. All I have to do is win." And he did. He just had to figure out the trick, the angle, the right combination. Every game could be won, and in the end, he'd had enough prizes to hand out to his nauseated cousins and sister to shut them up.

His father hadn't had the same point of view. "Son, there are some things that are worth experiencing, even if they end badly. Life isn't all about the payoff. Sometimes, you just have to *live*."

Shane finished loading the box, thinking about that long ago lesson. He still didn't do roller coasters, though he had learned to take more risks. Not that many, though—he preferred sure bets. He liked to win. That was why he was one of Sagmar's top agents. Risk meant a greater opportunity for loss, and Shane hated to lose. Still, he knew his father was right—and maybe this rooftop experience, however it turned out, would also lead to a practical, tangible reward.

"All set," he called up.

"You need to come up here," Miriam called back. "I can't pull that full box up on my own."

Up. Right. Gripping the railing hand over hand, he made his way to the ladder. His head spun as he looked up to where she peered over the edge of the roof. It was only about eight or ten feet up, but it felt farther. He focused on the look of concern on Miriam's face.

"You all right?" she asked.

"Good," he grumbled back.

"Ladder's perfectly safe, I promise." And yet, she hovered as if he were a child taking his first steps, ready to catch him if he fell.

That image irritated him. He was a grown man, for God's sake. He couldn't let her see how much he was shaking.

He set his foot on the first rung. The ladder creaked ominously.

"C'mon," Miriam said, her tone neither impatient nor encouraging. "I can't do this without you."

On the ladder last night, the stage had been dark, the ground below much harder to discern, the interior of the theater like a cocoon that ensured some modicum of safety. But out in the open, it was different. The ground four stories below was lethally horizontal. The afternoon sun beat down on his neck, and sweat beaded on his forehead and dampened his palms. As he grabbed the next rung above him, he snapped his hand back with a hiss.

"Oh, the ladder might be a bit hot," Miriam said. It was then that he noticed she wore fingerless work gloves.

Great. A hot metal ladder high up in the air and he was climbing it with bare, sweaty palms.

"Hang on, I'll throw you some gloves." Mira disappeared. A moment later, a pair of flowery pink gardening gloves with bright pink rubber nibs all over the palms fluttered down. He grimaced—was she making fun of him?

"Sorry, they're the only pair I could find that might fit," she said, grinning.

Wordlessly, he pulled them on and went for the ladder again. Frilly and pink as the gloves were, they did help with his grip. Now all he had to worry about was that rickety ladder collapsing under his weight.

Just keep moving, he told himself firmly, keeping his focus glued to the next rung. *She got up here fine; you will, too.*

Finally, he was peeking over the top of the roof. Miriam stood back, arms akimbo, an expectant look on her face. She'd donned a pair of clip-on sunglasses which hid her eyes. The corner of her lips twitched. "You did it."

He gritted his teeth and pulled himself over

the edge, tiny rocks biting into his palms and knees as he crawled over the gravel-covered surface of the roof. He didn't care. This was solider ground than the ladder, and he thanked the gods he'd made it.

Conscious of Miriam watching him, he pushed to his feet and took three big steps away from the gap where the ladder was. He was grateful for the three-foot-high wall surrounding the roof; it made him feel contained, safe, and hid the vertigo-inducing view of the street below.

He turned, and it took him a moment to absorb what he was looking at.

"Whoa." Green. Everywhere, plants in bloom, large gardening boxes overflowing with hearty plants of all kinds. Shoulder-high fronds of some kind of decorative grass bowed and sighed gently in the breeze. Faded patio umbrellas of different hues sprang up like weird giant flowers. A sweet, earthy scent filled the air. In a few corners, small Plexiglas greenhouses provided shelter for even more plants, reminding him of roadside shrines. It was the complete opposite of the dark, empty theater beneath their feet—a green crown for the Crown.

"Help me with the rope, will you?" Miriam prompted.

He studied the swinging arm bolted to the roof. It was a simple contraption, and not very old. Maybe Miriam or her grandfather had built it.

He took one end of the rope, and they hauled up the platform until she could swing the arm back over the roof wall.

Shane helped her unload the roofing supplies. "So your grandfather put all this together?" He nodded at the garden.

"Some of it. I added most of those flower boxes there." She pointed. "Grandpa loved growing things. He owned a farm once, but sold it to buy the Crown. Said he wanted to keep the magic of theater alive."

"Seems like a risky business venture."

"Not at the time it wasn't. Back then, the Crown still did live theater, and eventually Grandpa saved enough to get a good projector and turn the place into a movie house." She scanned the rooftop, seeming to take in the whole theater with that soft blue gaze. "This place has a lot of history."

And it was crumbling to bits. Not that he wanted to think about anything falling apart while he was up there. His next step could send him crashing through the ceiling of the auditorium. He turned his thoughts back to the task at hand. "Any idea where the leak is?" The whole roof was almost entirely covered in gravel.

"I have a few suspicions. But if the actual hole is under one of the soil boxes, we're gonna be here awhile."

Shane wiped his brow and grimaced as he squinted up at the blistering sun. In for a penny…

CHAPTER EIGHT

MIRA LED SHANE around the rooftop garden, answering his questions about the plants and vegetables she was growing. She was impressed he'd scaled that ladder, despite his fear of heights. Hell, that ladder scared *her* sometimes. But he'd done it. And he definitely wasn't faking his phobia. She could still detect the sour stench of fear on him. It made her feel a little guilty.

Then again, he'd been the one who'd insisted on helping. She hadn't asked him to. He was doing this for his own reasons, and probably ones that involved impressing her enough to soften her stance against selling the Crown.

She wasn't *that* impressed. But she did appreciate that it was Shane and not Arty or Janice who was helping her with the roof. She didn't want her elderly friends out in the heat up here.

She focused on the task at hand and shifted one of the half-full rain barrels. She checked the ground around it. No signs of cracks in the barrel, no leaks in the hoses that redirected the overflow to the eaves and downspouts. They checked the rest of the barrels. When they found a crack in the last barrel, Mira groaned.

"I knew I should've replaced this old thing." She gave the thick plastic shell a kick. "Okay. We need to clear the gravel around this area and see how far the damage extends."

They used push brooms to move the gravel and expose the black tar paper beneath. The spongy surface made Mira frown. If the spot was rotted through, she wasn't sure she could fix it.

"We should peel up everything here, see what we're looking at," Shane said, picking up a crowbar.

"Do we have to? I get the feeling this is one of those scab-picking projects—the more we pick at it, the worse it'll get."

He wrinkled his nose. "You've certainly got a way with words, Miriam."

"Mira," she said almost automatically. He cocked his head. "Miriam is what my parents called me. I prefer Mira."

"Mira." He tried the name out. She held back a smile—maybe she was just imagining it, but he said it almost reverently, with a hint of wonder. "If we only fix the top layer without looking under the surface, we'll never know what's really wrong. You could spring another leak, or miss the real issues."

She sighed and planted her hands on her hips.

"I guess you're right. I just don't want to end up replacing the whole roof."

"If that happens," Shane said with a bright grin, "I'm here to help."

He used the crowbar to pry up the soft, rotted sheets of tar paper and bits of particle board that made up the base of the roof. Pulling back that skin exposed another layer of wood that, fortunately, wasn't as spongy as the top layer.

As they tore away the rotting outer layer, she wondered why Shane was fixing a building he had every intention of tearing down. Not that she was about to stop him. What he did with his time was his business. For now, she supposed she should simply be thankful he was there.

THEY WORKED FOR nearly five hours, taking short breaks beneath the shade of the patio umbrellas. As long as he didn't look over the edge and remind himself he was four stories in the air, Shane could fool himself into believing he was in a beautiful garden with a pretty woman working beside him.

Red-faced and sweating beneath the sun, Mira—he liked that name—was a picture of good health, despite the color-sapping black she wore. She'd put on a sun hat and found him a worn trucker cap in the small toolshed. It was a blazing hot day, though the greenery did a lot to relieve the glare. Despite the leak in the roof, the garden was probably doing a lot to keep even more water from getting into the theater while providing an insulating layer against the oppressive heat. He'd read about the benefits of green roofs. Maybe he'd recommend that the builders for the new condo consider adding one on to the project. Environmental incentives often went a long way to fostering goodwill in communities.

They'd only managed to tear up the worst of the water-damaged boards by the time they were both ready to call it quits. Shane should've known it wouldn't be a quick two-hour patch job, but he didn't mind. Hard as the work was, he enjoyed Mira's quiet company, sporadically punctuated by talk about movies and TV shows they both liked. That seemed to be the topic she was most comfortable with so he stuck to it.

They decided to leave the roof exposed overnight to dry out—the forecast wasn't calling for rain for the next few days—and they'd work on it tomorrow.

"Getting supplies up here to replace what we took out is going to be hell." Shane nodded at the makeshift lift.

"It could be worse." Her eyes narrowed against the sun. For a moment she looked like a pirate captain scanning the horizon from the prow of her ship—if her ship were the *Titanic*, he supposed. She nodded at the garden. "That dirt didn't crawl up the sides of the building on its own."

He glanced around, doing a quick estimate of the stress all those tons of dirt might be adding to the rooftop. He shifted his weight nervously as heat gathered around his collar. “You don’t think all that added weight is messing with the roof’s support, do you?”

“Nah. They don’t make buildings like this anymore.” She stomped her heel, making Shane jump. “You could park twenty cars up here and still be fine.”

Even so, Shane’s sense of security was rapidly deteriorating. “How’d you like to get dinner now?” he prompted with forced cheer. He needed to get off that rooftop. “I’ve worked up a hell of an appetite.”

“If anything, I owe *you* dinner.”

He shoved his hands in his pockets. “I wouldn’t be a gentleman if I didn’t fight you for the check. But if you did pay, I would have to take you out again to even things up.”

“Something tells me your idea of even will never work out in my favor.” She chuckled, and inside, Shane danced.

They headed for the ladder. His chest seized as Mira swung over the edge and rapidly disappeared. The moment he glanced past the lip of the roof, his head started spinning.

He backed away rapidly and gulped in shallow breaths.

“Shane?”

"Just a minute. I think I left something behind." Like his dignity. Going up was always easier than going down. He had to look below to know where he was putting his foot next—and, perversely, to see how far he still had left to fall.

Mira's head popped up above the edge of the roof. "You okay?"

He smiled weakly. "Yeah. I'm…all right."

"I don't hold your fear of heights against you, you know," she said. "I mean, *no one* likes scaling that ladder." She paused. "I was really impressed you did it, especially after last night."

It seemed like an effort for her to admit she was impressed. It wasn't exactly the way he'd hoped to impress her.

"Tell you what," she said. "I'll make you a harness."

"What?"

"I've got some rope in the shed. We thread it around your waist under your arms, tie it off. If you slip, it'll catch you and you won't fall off."

He gave her a skeptical look. She spread her hands. "Trust me. I do it for Arty all the time."

He didn't exactly want his fortitude compared to the old grocer's, but the longer he hesitated, the stupider he felt. "All right." Better to take decisive action than dither.

In short order, Mira had a rope expertly tied to the sturdy swinging arm and was looping it over his shoulders. For a moment, it almost felt like she was coming in for a hug.

"Um…shouldn't you tie it to me?" She'd only slung it loosely around his waist.

"If I tie it, there's more chance of you getting tangled if you fell. It might catch you, but it could snap your spine in half, or maybe snag around your throat and break your neck."

Shane suddenly felt woozy.

"Don't worry." Mira chuckled drily. "I'll catch you if you fall. And the way you're hanging on to me right now, I don't think that'll happen, anyway."

Only then did he notice he was gripping her upper arms. It took a concerted effort to loosen his fingers, but he couldn't completely let go. She felt like the most stable, solid thing up there. His cheeks burned.

"It's okay," she said soothingly, but the heat only spread across his face. "I'll be right here watching you all the way down." She gently extricated herself from his hold.

With small, shaking steps, he approached the ladder, studiously not looking down. He put his feet on the first rung and turned to face Mira, who had the rope threaded through a second pulley she'd hooked to the arm. She wrapped the rope around her waist and gave it a tug, tautening it against his back under his arms. "Feel that? That's me and a whole lot of lifting power right behind you. I'll keep this snug against you all the way down. It's only twelve steps, and then you're on the fire escape landing, safe and sound." She smiled. "You made your way up—you can make your way down."

"Right." Never mind that Mira's claim to "a whole lot of lifting power" consisted of a hardware store pulley attached to a homemade rig attached to a hundred-year-old building with a spongy, leaky roof, and only Mira's wiry hundred-and-twenty-pounds-soaking-wet frame.

And never mind that she could be rid of him if she simply let go.

He couldn't think like that. Nothing about her indicated a murderous streak—except her aim with that paintball gun.

"C'mon," Mira cajoled. "Those chicken balls you want so bad are getting cold."

Shane slid his grip down the railing and traced the inner edge of the ladder with his foot until it hit the next rung. He kept his eyes forward as he lifted the other foot and let it sink through open space. It hit the rung. One step down.

"Good! Keep going. Only eleven more steps."

It took an agonizing five minutes to climb down that ladder. It got harder when he lost sight of the roof and was about halfway down, his gaze having nothing but the crumbling old brick to focus on. Every crack before him looked monstrously huge, as if they were widening and would drop the ladder and him at any moment. Only the rope around his back and the woman holding it made him feel remotely secure.

Finally, his feet hit the landing with a clang. He reached shakily for the wall and crept along it to the open doorway, stumbling into the cool theater and taking deep, gulping breaths. He reeked of sweat, and his limbs felt weak. He scrubbed his palms over his face. He'd gotten through the day and he was alive.

A moment later, Mira popped in. He felt as if she'd seen him with his pants down. "Hey." She studied him curiously. "You all right?"

He nodded stiffly. "I think I should go home for a shower."

She tilted her chin up. "Don't get fancy on my account. It's just the diner."

He rubbed the back of his neck. He supposed that was true, but it wasn't just about food. He needed to pull himself together. He was in no state of mind to seduce this woman.

Seduce? No, that wasn't the right word. He was trying to befriend her. Make her trust him. That'd been the whole point of this day, hadn't it? To ingratiate himself with her? To inveigle himself into her life so he'd have reasons to talk to her?

"I'd like to wash up anyhow." He was feeling better now that he was back on solid ground. "How about I meet you at the Good Fortune in two hours?"

This is not a date.

Mira stared at herself in the steamed-over mirror, dark dripping hair hanging limply around her pale face. Makeup would take some of that washed-out look from her features, but makeup would also signify she was trying to impress someone, and she didn't need to impress Shane Patel.

She settled on the bare minimum—a few dabs of moisturizer, a quick blow-dry and a touch of mousse to tame the flyaways, and a bit of tinted lip gloss. No one could fault her for wanting unchapped lips.

All the better to kiss him with. The thought sang through her head in myriad different voices, ranging from admonishing to teasing in tone. They were the voices of the people who judged her, who liked to point out everything she did wrong in her life, who laughed at her…

She grimaced. Just because she hadn't been on a date since college didn't mean she was prettying up for a guy. She'd learned long ago that you couldn't trust anyone with your happiness or well-being. You didn't need to risk more heartbreak or waste any effort on someone who could disappoint you, or whom you could disappoint.

She didn't do anything for anyone else anymore. Never again.

Except you, Grandpa.

She set her teeth as guilt drove a little wedge

deeper into her chest. Shane Patel was the enemy, the man trying to take the Crown from her, and here she was, about to have dinner with him.

She glared into the mirror and wiped the lip gloss off roughly. She should call and cancel. But she'd been the one to offer to buy him dinner after all the work he'd put in on the roof. So how was she supposed to sit across from him and share a meal, knowing all he wanted was the theater?

She was readying to make the call when her cell phone blared.

"Hi, Arty," she answered. "What's up?"

"I called to check on you. Heard you were working on some repairs today."

She bit the inside of her cheek. "Heard from whom?"

"Herman," he said after a short pause. "At the hardware store."

Considering Shane had been the one to pick up the supplies, all she could think was that Arty had either jumped to conclusions or Shane had blabbed about helping her. Not that she expected him to not talk about what he was doing with all those supplies—she just hated it when people talked about her business.

"It was the roof." She explained the progress she and Shane had made.

"So you and Shane are working *together* now?"

"He offered to help. I don't know why, honestly." She hesitated. "I told him he didn't have to, but he insisted."

"Some people are just decent folk," Arty said.

"Or he's buttering me up. *Or* he's trying to sabotage the building to force me to sell."

"That's paranoia talking."

She paced. "It just doesn't seem… I dunno." She waved her hand in the air helplessly. "I'm supposed to have dinner with him at the Good Fortune Diner—" She bit out a curse. She hadn't meant to mention it.

"Oh! Well, don't let me keep you—"

"Actually," she broke in, "I was about to call to cancel."

"What? Why?"

She wrinkled her nose. "It's not right, Arty. Grandpa wouldn't approve."

"Why not? Shane's a nice young man."

"He's only nice because he wants something."

"No one will think any more or less of you for wanting to have a meal out with a friend. You should get out more."

She frowned. "What's *that* supposed to mean?" She knew, of course. She'd had enough people say it to her. *You should get out more. Stop hiding in that drafty old theater. Why don't you have any friends? Are you a hermit? What is wrong with you?*

"All I meant was—"

"Never mind. I have to go." She hung up. Arty

meant well. But he had a knack for sticking his nose where she didn't need it.

She had to call Shane and cancel. She didn't need the Everville rumor mill grinding out news about their local shut-in dating the real estate developer who wanted her building.

She dialed his number.

"I'm right outside," he said without any preamble. "Ready to go?"

She tripped over her words as she checked the time. Dear lord, had she spent that much time getting ready? "I… I'll be right out."

Crap. That wasn't what she'd meant to say. In a panic, she hung up. Double crap. There was no way out now. She searched for her keys and purse and… What else would she need? A jacket? She hadn't been out after dark in so long she couldn't remember what summer nights were like.

She threw her phone, wallet and keys into a purse and headed for the door.

She paused, then grabbed the tube of lip gloss. What the hell.

CHAPTER NINE

As casual as Shane tried to be, dinner was a stilted affair. Mira ate with singular focus, digging into her fried rice and chow mein without saying much. She answered his ice-breaking banter with short, clipped words. Maybe the long day had made them both tired and hungry.

He let her pay, but only because she insisted. It wasn't an expensive meal—Shane would take her somewhere nice for a real dinner date—if he ever got to that point. As she polished off her plate, he wondered what he'd done wrong.

"It's still early," he said as they left the Chinese diner. "You wanna go for a drive?"

"Drive?" She said it as though she'd never heard the word before.

"My family and I used to drive around after dinner, look at the trees and greenery. We'd stop at the chip truck for dessert fries." At her confused look, he added, "Just regular fries and gravy. We called them dessert fries because they came after dinner."

She looked as though she was going to refuse. Shane could see the wariness in her eyes.

"I know," he said, snapping his fingers. "Let's watch a movie."

"At the Welksville theater?"

"At *your* theater." He relaxed when her eyes brightened a fraction. "You mentioned a bunch of films I should watch. Now's as good a time as any for a movie forcening."

"Movie forcening?"

"It's—"

"Self-explanatory." They were walking back toward the Crown. The evening was clear and warm with just enough of a breeze to keep them comfy after the day's dry heat. She hunched her shoulders as she stuck her hands in her pockets. "Why are you doing this?"

He blinked at her. "I don't want to go home just yet."

"I mean, why are you being nice to me?"

He understood her suspicions. He rubbed the back of his neck. "I'll be up-front. Clearly you're too smart not to wonder about my motivations. And frankly, you wouldn't be wrong about them. I do want to convince you to sell. The opportunity is too good for both of us not to explore. But apart from that, I find you...interesting. I like spending time with you."

Her cheeks turned tomato red and she glanced around as if searching for the nearest exit. He hadn't exaggerated: even if there were long, awkward silences, he truly enjoyed her quiet company. He was used to filling every second with chatter—his dates often involved a constant thread of inane conversation. But with Mira, he had to work hard to get her to talk. Perhaps the challenge was part of the intrigue.

"I don't understand," she said, discomfited.

She didn't understand the opportunity? Or the kindness? Not wanting to condescend, he picked his words carefully.

"When my father first moved to the States from Mumbai and started his business in the early eighties, he was one of the few Indian businessmen in the neighborhood. He got a lot of support from the landlords. They were this older couple who shared my dad's vision of the future of personal computing and electronics. They let him pay his rent late at the beginning, and helped him invest in stock he wanted for the shop but couldn't afford. He eventually paid them back, but he wanted to give them something to thank them for their trust and kindness. Yet to them, the investment in the community was payment enough. They credit my father's business with helping turn around a rough part of the neighborhood.

"This couple, the Latimers, was originally from Everville. Every summer, they'd invite my family to stay with them at their summer home here by the lake. They were like my surrogate grandparents. After they passed away, my father kept on the tradition of coming here to honor their memory and give back to the generous community they came from."

Mira studied him, the lines between her eyes deepening. "That doesn't explain why you're being nice to me," she said blandly.

He smirked. "Would you rather I not be?"

"I don't know." Her lips pinched as she quietly admitted, "I don't trust easily."

No kidding. He pressed on optimistically. "What I'm doing a terrible job of saying is that the people of Everville, starting with the Latimers, have always been kind to me and my family. I feel it's my personal mission to give back, one person at a time."

"I don't think I was living in Everville when you would've been here."

"That doesn't matter to me. You needed help. I was here."

Her face settled into a mask of cool composure. "Let me say what's on my mind." Her tone was as precise and vaguely threatening as the barrel of a paintball gun. "I appreciate everything you did today. And I know that your phobia of heights made everything that much harder." He started to deny it, but she held up a hand. "Going up and down that ladder wasn't easy, and it means a lot to me that you put yourself through that. What I'm struggling with is why, when you're here to buy the theater. You could've let things be, not put yourself through that. You don't owe me anything."

"And you could've pushed me off the roof and claimed it was an accident."

Her shock and outrage were reassuring. "I know you wouldn't have, Mira. But the bottom line is I couldn't let you deal with this on your own any more than you could've fathomed taking advantage of me at my most vulnerable."

The sun was dipping behind the buildings as they arrived back at the Crown. Shane shivered. It was chilly in the shadow of the theater.

"If it's all right with you, I'd like to skip the movie and turn in for the night," Mira said quietly. "It's been a long day."

He nodded despite his disappointment. "Of course. I'll come by tomorrow morning to help you finish the roof."

"You don't have to. I could call Arty or hire some workmen."

"I'm sure he's capable, but I'm available. Besides," he added, grinning, "I like to finish what I start."

Their eyes locked, and he thought he could see her sifting through his words for deeper meaning or deception. He wondered who or what in her life had made her so cautious and distrustful of people.

She relented with a short huff. "All right. Come around ten. I'll have coffee and croissants."

"Great."

He didn't know why he did it, or even if he really meant to. But he found himself leaning in and planting a quick peck on her cheek. It felt so natural he almost didn't register the buzz of electricity humming through him. The moment he recognized it for what it was, though, it was like a bee sting, the shock of desire spreading through him like fire. His breathing hitched in his throat.

Just as quickly, the sensation evaporated. Mira's head snapped back, her eyes wide. Before he could apologize, though, she whipped away, short hair flying as she disappeared around the corner of the theater.

"Mira—" He barely got her name out before the door slammed shut behind her.

Dammit. He couldn't seem to do anything right with her.

HOW *DARE* HE!

Mira gingerly touched her cheek again. The hot, lingering sensation bristled like fryer oil, as though he'd planted an ember on her skin. Her whole body seemed to fizz.

She'd been kissed before, of course. She'd had a boyfriend in college. But Shane's touch even after she'd scrubbed her cheek and pressed a cool cloth to it stayed with her as she got ready for bed.

How dare he, she thought again, but with less heated indignation. She hated feeling this way—

like she wanted to crawl out of her skin, confused and warm and flustered.

She started up *Singin' In the Rain* on her laptop. She often put on a movie at night so she didn't have to listen to the theater groan and creak. Back when she'd first moved to Everville to live with Grandpa, he'd shown her classics on the VCR in his office, the room she now called her bedroom. Falling asleep curled up on the mustard-colored corduroy couch under a plaid flannel blanket was one of her best memories, and even now it made her feel safe.

The couch had been replaced by a futon, the VCR had long since broken down and the VHS tapes were probably degrading. But the spirit was still the same; this place had always been more of a home to her than any place she'd ever lived. She could still sense Grandpa's presence here.

As she climbed into bed, stiff and sore and still buzzing from Shane's peck on the cheek, she lay quietly and listened to the theater breathe in the night.

"It's not as if he *likes* me," she said aloud, staring at the ceiling. From the soft glow of the laptop, Gene Kelly wooed Debbie Reynolds atop her makeshift soundstage balcony, singing "You Were Meant For Me." The stutter of her fridge sounded too much like a chuckle in her ears. Mira turned her head and closed the laptop.

She punched her pillow and turned over. So

what if he'd kissed her? A guy like him probably kissed every woman he was on a first-name basis with on the cheek. She wouldn't be sucked in by his charm. He was a salesman, bred and trained to manipulate people into thinking they needed something they didn't. She certainly didn't need him.

Romantic notions were best confined to the movies. Real life was too complicated and awkward for big sweep-me-off-my-feet romance. People didn't break into song and dance to express their burgeoning feelings, and life did not end with happy-ever-afters and scrolling marquees.

Unfortunately, her subconscious didn't get the memo. As she drifted off, she dreamed of curtains closing on a kiss with Shane.

CLIMBING THE LADDER to repair the roof the next day went a lot more smoothly. Shane told himself it was because he was focused on getting the two sheets of plywood up to the roof. The truth was, he was distracted by Mira.

And she seemed distracted, too, though she blamed the heat, which soared into the midnineties by noon. He just hoped he hadn't made her feel uncomfortable. Though if she were, he assumed she would've told him to scram—she'd had no problem doing that before. Still, kissing her had been a bad move. He wasn't sure he regretted it, though.

With minimal chitchat, they patched the hole in the roof. The tar product and paper had to set overnight before they could cover it with gravel. Shane watched Mira as she drifted around the raised garden beds, picking out weeds, ignoring him.

"Need help?" he asked. "I can pull weeds."

"Please don't." She shot him a look. "You might rip out the wrong thing."

"So show me what not to pull. This isn't the first time I've played in the dirt. I used to help my aunt in her garden."

Mira's ears perked up. "What did she grow?"

He'd thought she might be interested. "Peppers, mostly, but also onions and tomatoes. They were always going on about how peppers in the States weren't spicy enough, and insisted on growing their own. My mother made me help my aunt, hauling watering cans and fertilizer. Said it would be good for my character to do something other than play video games and study."

"She was right." With only the slightest hesitation, she beckoned and pointed. "See these spiky leaves? They're dandelions, and I don't want them spreading. Get them out by the root, otherwise they'll grow back. You can leave the tiny plants—anything smaller than half your thumb."

Shane dutifully obeyed while Mira went to work on another bed of vegetables. He silently thanked *Amma* and *Chachi* Priya for the long hours in the garden that today gave him an excuse to stick around and stay in Mira's good graces.

CHAPTER TEN

AT THE END of the day, Mira was dirty, sweaty and sore, but in a good way. Her discomfort meant she'd accomplished something. Seeing Shane in an equally dirty, sweaty state, and then watching him gingerly make his way down the ladder once more, she knew she owed him big-time for all he'd done. Even if she wasn't sure of his motives, she was still grateful for his help.

He'd heartily accepted her offer to share a frozen pizza and watch *The Maltese Falcon* on her projector. Feeding him was the least she could do—the movie was simply a way to avoid awkward conversations. About midway through the film, though, the picture turned yellowy green and the sound fizzled out.

"Dammit." Mira bumped the projector with the heel of her palm and huffed. "It's been doing this a lot lately."

"Maybe it needs a new bulb," Shane said.

"This model projector is pretty old, so finding parts for it is hard and expensive." Besides which, she was supposed to be prioritizing the theater's projector, not her personal one. She whacked the side of the machine again. The picture blacked out. Her heart sank. “Crap.”

“We could finish the movie on your laptop.”

She grimaced. “It’s not the same.”

“Well…there’s a big-screen TV and DVD player back at my place.”

Heat flushed through her. It wasn’t that she was afraid of what might happen—she knew without a doubt she was safe with him. No, she couldn’t accept his offer because the temptation was too great. Sharing a meal and watching movies on her home turf was one thing. Going back to Shane’s place by Silver Lake opened her up to all kinds of possibilities. What if he started inviting her to do other activities, tried getting chummy with her? She knew it was irrational to avoid forging a relationship with him when it was a remote possibility at best. But she didn’t trust him—or herself.

She shook her head. “I’d better not. But I’ll lend you the DVD and you can finish it on your own.” It almost hurt to say the words, though she didn’t understand why. “Anyhow, it’s late,” she added, the words meant to solidify her resolve.

Shane shoved his hands in his pockets. “I was kinda hoping you’d come over, too. I don’t like watching movies on my own.”

“I have to keep an eye on things here.”

“Well, I won’t push.” Shane eased up out of the seat. She hadn’t realized how tall he was, or how good he looked when he stretched, his

T-shirt pulled against his firm torso, his jeans taut against his butt…

Stop ogling the man. She jumped up to eject the disk, but Shane stopped her.

"Hang on to the DVD—I don't want to watch the rest unless you're there."

"But you're so close to the end. It's just as good without another person in the room, you know."

"That may be, but I like your commentary. It makes the slower parts more interesting."

She sucked in her lip. She'd been accused of ruining movies with running annotations. "Sorry. I didn't mean to talk through them like some kind of tour guide."

"Not at all. I like hearing what you have to say."

Man, the guy was a piece of work. He knew exactly what to say to flatter her—and it worked. "I cut my teeth on these films," she said self-consciously. "Sharing them with someone who's never watched is like breaking in a virgin."

Oh, God, had she just said that? "I mean—I…"

"Consider my cherry popped." He winked. A warm, light sensation fluttered across her skin like a feather on fire, leaving cinders in all kinds of secret places she'd become a lot more aware of since Shane Patel entered her life. Damn him.

As he strolled to his car, she called her thanks to him repeatedly until she felt stupid for sounding so obsequiously grateful. Worse, she was almost sad to see him go.

She'd started the day by swearing she wouldn't get caught up by his kindness, his charm, his masculine magnetism. But she couldn't help that she *liked* him. Even if it was in a totally superficial way.

SHE DIDN'T SEE Shane the following day. She didn't know why she expected to now that the roof was fixed. She'd just covered the now-dry patch with gravel when a brief but intense summer shower swallowed the sky and drenched everything. Hours later, there was no sign of a leak.

She was about to call Shane to let him know, but stopped herself. She didn't want to sound needy or overeager. Instead, she threw herself into her writing. By eight in the evening, though, even after banging out a record number of articles and blog posts, she found herself pacing restlessly, and went looking for something to occupy herself. After twenty minutes of furiously polishing the brass railings in the lobby, she realized her thoughts still circled the previous days' events—around Shane, that kiss, their...*relationship*, for lack of a better word, and everything that stood between them. Namely, the Crown. Her home.

Then she thought about the deputation she'd be giving at the next town council meeting and her stomach flipped. She had no idea how she was going to convince the zoning board to save the Crown—there were too many caveats attached to the arguments. The theater *could* be up and running again *if* she came up with the cash to fix everything. It *could* be reopened to the public *if* everyone promised to see a movie there every night for the next five years…

Don't think so negatively. Grandpa had kept the place going for decades on less. She would do whatever it took to open the place again. Make him proud.

She just had to convince town council she could.

"Priorities," she said out loud. "I just need to focus on what needs to get done first."

She made a list of all the things that had to get done before the theater reopened again. Plumbing in the men's room. Parts for the projector. Clean and fix the broken seats. Fix the fire door locks. Clean the popcorn machine and soda fountain… The list went on and on. The top two to-dos were enough to make her head pound—it was why she hadn't addressed them in over four years.

Her cell phone rang. Shane's name popped up on the call display, and her heart jumped into her throat.

Play it cool. She clutched the phone and exhaled. "Hi, Shane. What's up?"

"I have something for you. I was going to wait, but I can't. Can I swing by?"

Another gift? Her first instinct was to say no, to tell him he'd given her too much already in addition to helping her with the roof repairs, but instead she found herself saying, "I'll leave the back door unlocked."

Twenty minutes later, the perimeter alarm alerted her of his arrival. When she greeted him, he was propping the back door open with a concrete block. "Did the roof leak? I caught the tail end of that storm driving in."

"Dry as a bone. I think we got it."

"Awesome. Way to go, team!" He held up a hand for a high five. Mira stared, eyebrow rising. "Don't leave me hanging."

She rolled her eyes and slapped his hand awkwardly. He gripped it for a moment, shaking it high in the air as if she were the new reigning champion after three rounds with him. The way their fingers entwined made everything inside her squirm pleasantly. She pulled away quickly. "What did you come by for?"

"I drove back to New York this morning," he said. "I remembered something my dad had in his shop that he could never sell. Got a great deal off him for a bunch of other gear, too, and booted it back here." He disappeared through the doorway and wheeled a dolly in. Several large boxes rested on it. Mira's jaw slackened as she registered what they were.

"Before you say no, I'm going to tell you that

A, this really did come as a fantastic deal and that we're doing my father a favor by getting it out of his stockroom. B, it's not top-of-the-line but I think it'll work way better than your existing projector. And C, if you don't like it, we can return it."

She stared at the enormous digital projector. It wasn't quite cinema quality, but it would throw a huge picture up on the canvas. "Are you insane?" Tears of exasperation gathered in her eyes. Projectors like this, even if they were older, retailed in the tens of thousands.

"Hey, you left me hanging with *The Maltese Falcon*. I need to watch the rest of it, and you're right. A DVD played on a laptop won't cut it."

"Shane..."

"I got some better sound equipment, too." He patted the boxed speakers. "No offense, but the speakers you've got won't do other movies justice, and I'm thinking we should have an Indiana Jones marathon. It's been years since I've seen those films on the big screen and I had a sudden nostalgic craving since I came back to Everville."

"Shane..."

He clasped his hands in front of him. "Don't refuse this, please. I drove three hours to Brooklyn and three hours back." He widened his dark eyes in a puppy-dog plea. "We've got to at least watch the rest of *Maltese Falcon*. Please?"

Mira tapped her fists against her hips restlessly. It would look pretty cool blown up on the screen. “Well… I suppose as long as it can be returned…”

He grinned. “So can I set this up now? I mean, unless you’re going to bed…”

She couldn’t help the laughter that bubbled up. “All right,” she relented. The chance to see that monster projector in action was too good to pass up.

Shane wheeled the dolly into the auditorium while she grabbed rolls of stereo wire and extension cords. The setup was fairly simple. They placed the projector on a caddy nearer the back of the auditorium so that the picture filled the entire screen, then hooked up the speakers to the DVD and Blu-ray player Shane had also brought.

Mira mentally tallied the net worth of A/V equipment. There was no way she could afford any of it, much less the gas money for Shane’s trip to Brooklyn and back. Surely he knew that. So why had he gone through the effort? Giving her an expensive projector wasn’t likely to push her to sell. If anything, it would make her want to keep the place even more. And if in the end the Crown was sold and torn down, the equipment would go back to Brooklyn.

Maybe that was the whole point. If it was from

his father's shop, he had nothing to lose. He'd return it with zero issues.

"Mira?" Shane's voice brought her out of her thoughts.

She blinked at him. "Sorry, I was woolgathering."

"Well, soon as we get the sound system set up, I guarantee you won't be able to hear yourself think." His gleeful smile did a lot to erode her cynicism. He looked like a ten-year-old on Christmas day setting up that massive projector and sound system.

In short order, Shane popped *The Maltese Falcon* into the DVD player. The marquee scrolled huge against the screen, blurry at first, but they set the auto focus, fidgeted with the color settings and…

"Oh, my God." Mira stared up at the screen, rapt. "It's huge."

"That's what she said." Shane snickered. "Just one more thing…" He handed her a large paper bag. "Caramel popcorn. Thought it'd be a nice change from the microwave stuff."

Mira's mouth watered. "You've doomed me to a night of heartburn, you realize."

He gestured at the seats. "Shall we?"

They sat in the empty auditorium with the bag of popcorn between them, as well as root beers from Mira's fridge. After *The Maltese Falcon*,

Mira put in *Raiders of the Lost Ark*, ostensibly to "test the sound system." They watched it all the way through.

"We need one more test," Shane said as they rummaged through her movie collection. He pulled out *Casablanca*. "For the true silver screen experience."

"It's past midnight. You sure you're up for it?"

"I'm hopped up on sugar and all the caffeine I had on the drive from Brooklyn. I'm going to be awake awhile."

She couldn't remember the last time she'd seen Bogart's face so huge on the screen. She knew the gauzy quality of the old film couldn't be sharpened by the most expensive of projectors, nor could the state-of-the-art sound system hide all the crackles and pops of a weathered soundtrack. Instead, all the flaws of the golden age of cinema were magnified.

It didn't matter to Mira. She let herself be carried away by the heartache and unfairness of a world steeped in war, the struggle between two old lovers whose tie was still strong despite their disparate beliefs and the lengths they were willing to go to protect them.

The movie wound down to the final goodbye on the airstrip, with Rick ushering Ilsa on her way to a new life, the next fight. No matter how many times she saw it, Mira always teared up at this scene. There was something true, not noble, about how Rick let go of Ilsa in the end. The problems of three little people really didn't amount to a hill of beans in this crazy world. Mira felt as if she'd always understood that, but Bogart's dry delivery hammered the sentiment home.

"But what about us?" she whispered along with the soundtrack. She felt the tug on her heart as keenly as if she were the one being torn apart by her love for Rick and her love for Victor and his cause.

"We'll always have Paris."

The words were spoken close to her ear in a deep, meditative baritone. She turned to find Shane watching her with heavy-lidded eyes. Her heart slugged in her chest, in her ears.

The music swelled as his lips pulled into a wide, sensuous smile.

"Here's looking at you, kid."

Mira couldn't name the impulse that swept through her—maybe some mixture of gratitude, romantic sentiment and loneliness—but she let it guide her as she curved one hand around his rough jaw and pressed her lips to his.

CHAPTER ELEVEN

SHANE'S LIPS WERE soft and tasted of caramel popcorn and root beer. He inhaled sharply at first, and Mira pulled away a little, afraid she'd shocked him. She'd surprised herself—she'd never initiated intimacy with her ex-boyfriend, Tom. She'd certainly never pictured this was where she and Shane Patel would end up, either. She started to pull away, mortified, but then he tugged her closer, angling his mouth to deepen the kiss.

Oh. *Oh.*

He glided his fingertips along her neck and into her hairline, cupping her chin briefly, and then cradling the back of her head as if he were holding something precious. She breathed deep, wondering if at any moment he'd push her away in disgust, contempt, shock or fear. It didn't happen. Part of her knew she should stop, but she couldn't. His lips were soft, drugging, firm, sure. She hated that she was so weak.

When his tongue tentatively touched hers, heat surged through her blood. Her fingers curled into his soft T-shirt, brushing against the fine hairs along his muscular arms. Goose bumps pebbled his skin.

Finally, he broke away with a gasp. Mira's swollen lips buzzed.

"I think I found my new favorite film." His chuckle reverberated through her core. He dipped his head and gave her the briefest of pecks on the lips, as if he were reminding himself of how she tasted. "Is it wrong that I've wanted to do that since I first met you?"

She stuttered out a laugh. "Considering I shot you in the nuts, yes."

"Maybe I'm a masochist." He traced her face with light fingertips.

She sighed, unable to ignore her doubts. "What are we doing, Shane?"

"I thought that was obvious."

"I mean, what are we doing together? I want to believe you're just trying to seduce me so I'll sell the Crown. But…" She hesitated, realizing that admitting the truth would be giving up something of value. "I'm not sure I actually believe it."

He met her eyes, frowning. "It's not like that. I mean, at first I thought that was what I'd do." He scrubbed his jaw. Mira felt a sting to her pride, but didn't interrupt him. "I'm ashamed to admit that. But… I really do like you. Everything I've done up to this point… I wanted to get close to you to understand why you'd hang on to a decrepit old building. But I think I'm starting to get it now. There's…for lack of a better word, *magic* here. I don't know how else to describe it. It's the same way I feel about this town."

She smiled a little sadly. Just because he understood didn't mean she'd swayed him to her thinking. "Where does that leave us?"

"I'm not sure." His eyes slid to the screen as if he might find answers scrolling with the end credits. "This kind of complicates things, doesn't it?"

"No kidding." And yet, all she wanted to do was kiss him again. He traced the lines on her palms, studying the calluses like a map to her soul. The longer he did it, the more lost she felt. "I don't suppose you can put your condo elsewhere."

"It's not that simple. We already own the buildings on either side of the Crown. And we can't build *around* the theater."

"So we're back to square one." She drew away, but her hands stayed couched in his. "I can't give up this place, Shane. It's all I have left of my grandfather."

"Your grandfather sounds like he was a great guy. But for what you'd get for the building, I don't think he would've disapproved." He massaged her palms, smiling. "You could even buy one of the new condo units and still be close to him. I could get you a good deal."

Disappointment lanced through her sharply.

"Seriously?" She yanked her hands from his. For a moment she'd believed he'd meant what he'd said about the Crown being *magic*...and then he'd gone straight back to a corporate salesman. She pushed to her feet, disgusted she'd let herself be fooled. "It's late. You should go."

Shane's jaw worked. "I said the wrong thing, didn't I?"

"Gee, ya think?"

"Mira—"

"Forget about it. We just got...carried away." She bit her lip and glanced at the A/V equipment. Taking it all apart and sending it away with Shane would be excruciating.

"Hang on to that stuff for now," he said as if he'd read her thoughts. "Give it a proper test. I can pick it up if you decide you don't want it."

Once he'd left, Mira slouched off to bed. Life wasn't a movie, she reminded herself sternly as she lay wide-awake on the futon. Though she supposed *Casablanca* was a more apt analogy for *her* life since Rick and Ilsa had ended up apart in the end. Their love had been unsustainable—they each had their own convictions and priorities, and a relationship would've meant giving up everything else.

Mira could never abandon the Crown. Not even for a chance at happy-ever-after.

With that thought firmly in place, she focused on preparing for her deputation.

ARTY BURST THROUGH the door of Janice's flower shop, sweat dripping from his brow, his heart in his throat. Janice had called him that morning saying she had urgent news she had to share with him in person.

He couldn't imagine what had her so panicked. Was she sick? Had another one of their friends passed? Ever since Jack had died, it'd felt as if all the people they knew had been disappearing, like grains of sand in an hourglass.

The thought of Jan not being in his life squeezed the air from his lungs.

"Jan?" he called out when he didn't immediately spot her. What if she were ill and couldn't respond? "Janice?" Fear made his voice rise an octave.

"I'm right here, Arty, no need to shout." She bustled in, arms loaded with blooms, a grin on her face. "Sorry I didn't hear you right away. I was in the cooler."

He put his hand to his heart. "You're going to scare me into an early grave." He glanced away, feeling foolish for having worried. "What did you want to talk about?"

Her eyes danced as she held up a slip of paper. "You know I don't give away client information, right?"

"Wouldn't be ethical," he agreed.

"Yes, so I'm just going to put this order slip down right here for a second while I get this bouquet together. Got it first thing this morning and it needs to go out by noon." She placed the receipt on the counter and hummed as she walked away. Arty peered at it and blinked.

"An order from Shane Patel to Mira," he said.

"Read the message."

"'Thank you for a lovely night.'" He looked up in surprise. "You think he spent the night with her?"

"That's the part I'm not sure about. Mira came in here after apparently spending the early part of the morning wandering around town."

That was odd. Mira rarely left the Crown without a purpose. "Was she all right?"

"I'm not sure. She kept sighing, smiling and then frowning, as if she couldn't settle on a mood. I've never seen her like this."

Arty scratched his chin. "What did you two talk about?"

"Said she wanted to get some hints on how to give her deputation to the zoning board next week, but she asked some odd questions. Odd for Mira, anyhow. Wanted to know about how Jack would've handled Shane. Whether she was doing the right thing by not selling."

Arty set his teeth. It definitely wasn't like Mira to doubt her convictions. He glanced again at the order form. "Any clues about what happened with Shane?"

"No more than what you see in front of you.

But I'm convinced something's changed between them." Her grin lit up the room. "If I didn't know better, I'd say she was a little smitten."

"Ha! We did it!" He whooped and grabbed Janice. Before he realized it, he was planting a kiss on her lips.

He snapped back hastily. What was he doing? He let go of her arms and took a big step back. Janice's cheeks were two hot flags of color. "I—I'm sorry, Jan. I got caught up there..."

"Arty—"

"I'd better get back to the store." He hurried out, cursing his boldness, his impulsiveness, his sheer stupidity.

THE FOLLOWING THURSDAY, Shane slipped into the high school auditorium for the town meeting, aware of the eyes on him. He couldn't *not* attend this meeting, no matter how uncomfortable it might make him or the deputants—he had to see who still needed convincing.

He took a seat near the back. Tonight's deputations were meant to guide the zoning board's decision on whether to rezone the block where the Crown stood from commercial to mixed residential. Shane didn't think there'd be too much resistance, despite the turnout at the meeting. Small towns like Everville needed the investment and growth—even the most stubborn resident understood that. It would've helped his cause if everyone knew about the plans for the high-speed rail line. Unfortunately, that information was still classified. If any investors learned of it, there'd be a lot of complications and probably investigations into insider trading. Sagmar's knowledge of the project didn't count—the decision to build in Everville had been made without assurances of the real estate values rising. The rail line had simply been a rumor as far as they were concerned.

He scanned the room for Mira. She'd seemed less than enthusiastic about speaking in public when he mentioned the deputations, but he'd spotted her name on the list of tonight's speakers. He was kind of sad that she was afraid to talk about her passion. She was such a different person when she opened up. It seemed wrong somehow that the world be denied an opportunity to hear what she had to say.

He hadn't seen her since that night in the theater. He'd sent flowers—sending gifts was the only way he knew how to apologize—but none of his calls, texts or emails had been answered with more than one- or two-word responses. He'd asked about the roof leaking, about how the A/V equipment he'd brought was working out. It'd put a tiny dent in his bank account, but seeing the wide-eyed look of sheer delight on her face had been worth every cent.

And that kiss... Boy howdy. The moment their lips had touched, it was magic, cliché as that sounded. His sister had accused him of liking Mira—well, he supposed she was right. Had it been that obvious, or had he simply been too stubborn to admit it?

"Mr. Patel?"

He glanced up into the bright, pointed face of an Asian woman wielding a notebook. "Tiffany Cheung. I'm with the *County Courier*."

"The local paper, right?" He shook her hand. "Not to make any assumptions, but I think I recognize you."

"My family runs the Good Fortune Diner," she confirmed with a nod. "I think I recognize you, too, from a long time ago. You played baseball with my brother. I mean, there weren't a lot of Indian kids in Everville." She gave a sheepish shrug, one he understood well. It was an acknowledgment of their shared differences, growing up as a person of color in a small town. "Would you mind if I asked you some questions? I'm covering the meeting for the paper."

"Sure thing." He gestured at the chair next to him, and she fired away, asking about his hopes for the outcome of the meeting and so forth.

"You have critics." She nodded toward a knot of people near the front of the gym. Shane spotted Bob Fordingham among them, an insincere smile spread across his mottled complexion.

"There's always resistance to change," he said. "But I believe in this project one hundred percent. So did the former mayor, from what I understand. This project started long before Mayor Welks was elected."

"Big Bob's nothing if not inconsistent," she deadpanned, and Shane chuckled. "Fordingham's always been a bit of a blowhard. He needs his daily dose of indignity so he has a reason to shout." She rolled her eyes. "But I'm supposed to be impartial about it."

"I'm sure the former mayor is only interested in the welfare and well-being of the town," Shane said diplomatically.

Just then, Mira crept into the gym from a side door. She wore all black as usual, with a crop-sleeved blazer over her T-shirt that gave her a more professional-looking air. She scanned the room like a soldier checking for snipers, then scurried to a corner seat. When their eyes met, she quickly looked down at her cell phone and stayed glued to it.

"Have you had relations with Miriam Bateman?"

Shane startled. "Excuse me?"

"I mean, have you spoken with her? Negotiated the terms of the Crown Theater's sale? I understand Sagmar hasn't actually purchased the property yet."

Shane cleared his throat. "We're working out the details still." He didn't need news of Mira's stubbornness getting back to the project's investors.

Tiffany eyed Mira speculatively. "Off the record, my dad served you two dinner a while back." She arched an eyebrow, leaving the question unasked.

Ah, small-town rumor mills. "When I can, I like to negotiate on a stomach full of the best North American-style Chinese cuisine in the state." He decided to turn the conversation around. "How's your brother? Daniel, right?"

Thankfully, she went along with his diversion. She told him about how Daniel was living in New Jersey while trying to make things work with his girlfriend. Shane learned Tiffany had gone to NYU and had lived in Manhattan for years before returning to Everville, which got them talking about the big city they both loved and the small town they'd both come back to. Then Tiffany's boyfriend, Chris Jamieson, strode in and wrapped a possessive, muscled arm around her. The guy looked like Farmer Thor.

"Nice to meet you." He bared his teeth and firmly shook Shane's hand. "I wanted to ask you about the LEED certifications on some of the other Sagmar buildings."

"Chris is a bit of a tree hugger," Tiffany said, elbowing him in the ribs. "Watch out for him. He won't give you an easy time when it comes to environmental issues."

"To be clear, I'm for anything that revitalizes the core of the town," Chris said. "And I believe in sustainable communities. Those old buildings have been eyesores long enough. I'm mainly concerned about the most efficient use of resources and what can be done to reduce the carbon footprint of the building and any residents who move in."

"I have a lot of information about the builder's plans," Shane said, glad he'd come prepared. "I'd be happy to forward you a file if you give me your email address. And I'll answer any questions you have."

"The meeting's going to start soon," Tiffany said. "I'll see if I can get a quote out of Miriam Bateman." She gave Chris a peck on the cheek. "Behave," she warned as she slipped out of her seat.

"She can be a pain, but that's why I love her." The light in Chris's eyes as he looked after her made Shane smile.

"Been together long?"

"Nearly two years. I want us to get married, have kids—my son's leaving for college soon, and I'm not sure I can deal with an empty nest at my age. But Tiff's been working on her various careers—reporting, writing, freelance editing and painting… I don't know where she finds the energy." He sighed. "Good things are worth waiting for, though."

Shane wasn't sure he agreed with the man—

if things were good with Tiffany, he should lock that down.

Then again, what did he know about commitment and marriage, or serious relationships for that matter? He realized he was staring at the back of Mira's head as he mulled it over.

The din in the room settled as someone banged a gavel. At the front of the room, three women and two men arranged themselves at tables flanking the podium. Mayor Cheyenne Welks, in a copper-colored flowing two-piece, stood at the microphone, scanning the crowd. "This meeting will now come to order. If you could all settle down, we have quite a few deputations tonight, and I'd like to get started right away so we can all go to bed at a reasonable hour."

The mayor outlined the rules: every deputant had five minutes to speak on the topic of the condo development. Board members would have a chance to question the deputant about his or her case, but in Shane's experience, that rarely happened. These types of meetings were mostly about venting. Board members had likely already made up their minds or else had been directed to vote one way or another by someone of influence. It would take an extraordinary argument to sway their minds.

The first speaker at the microphone set up in the center aisle was a man in his fifties with gray sprinkled through a thinning pate. In a smoker's rasp, he introduced himself as Jonas Randall.

"I, for one, don't think the condo is a good idea," he said, rocking from side to side. "Condos aren't for Everville. We've got enough traffic on the roads as it is. The last thing we need is more people around." He paused, as if expecting applause. "We don't need the wrong element here is what I mean." He seemed to have run out of words. "This is a quiet town for peaceful folks. We should keep it that way." A slight pause. "That's all I have to say."

"Questions from the board?" Mayor Welks asked, her tone as neutral as the color beige. When no one spoke up, she nodded. "Thank you, Mr. Randall."

Faint applause followed him back to his seat. Shane didn't miss the sentiment lurking beneath Mr. Randall's words. "The wrong element" had a lot of different connotations. For reasons he didn't fully understand, a lot of people equated condo dwellers with transients; others simply didn't appreciate the "otherness" element, whether it was ageist, racist, classist or antisuburban. True, many condo owners in larger cities were young people owning their first homes, or people who rented out their properties for income. But most people wouldn't buy a condo in tiny Everville unless they meant to live there themselves. Even if the high-speed rail line went in tomorrow, the town was still pretty out of the way—not exactly a place you'd park your car so you could go clubbing in Manhattan on a Friday night. His intentions for owning a unit were probably the only exception to the rule: he knew what a gem Everville was.

The next four deputants had prepared speeches. He didn't recognize any of the residents from the night he'd hosted the condo presentation, but that wasn't a surprise. People rarely sought out new information if they'd already formed an opinion on something.

Mostly, the concerns were aesthetic: people worried about the shadow a twelve-story building would cast, how the facade would match the rest of the town, or whether the condo would reduce property values. One older woman with dyed orange hair raged about how the condos spelled the death of Everville, spewing some strange theory about gentrification and growth being the scourge of small towns. She went way over her five minutes, and kept talking off her cards about how children in the community would be subjected to more dangerous strangers, then started accusing newcomers of stealing her cats for nefarious purposes. It took the mayor banging on her gavel and shutting off the speaker's microphone to stop her from talking. The congregation looked uncomfortable and people were starting to get restless.

"Mrs. Abbot, while we appreciate your concerns, I'll remind you that every speaker has been allotted five minutes to state their case." Cheyenne's tone was firm, though clearly laced with annoyance. "We kindly ask that to expedite matters and—"

"Well, I didn't vote for you, so you can stick it," the orange-haired Mrs. Abbot spat. "I pay my taxes and I've lived here for forty-three years. The people of Everville have a right to speak up for their community and to defend it from danger. I don't want terrorists as neighbors!"

The crowd looked uneasy, though Shane couldn't help but notice a few nods in the Fordingham camp.

Cheyenne looked on placidly, her cool green gaze settling over the crowd. "We'll take a break before we continue. But first, I'd like to bring up a point of order from my colleague, who has noted that Shane Patel, the representative from Sagmar Corp., is sitting with us in the audience today."

Hundreds of eyes turned toward Shane. Everyone knew who he was, of course—it was hard not to notice the Indian guy in the sea of white faces—but they'd left him alone for the most part. He stood and waved, putting on his most winsome smile.

"Mr. Patel, my colleague has asked whether you'd be willing to address some of the questions or concerns that have been brought up multiple times so far so we don't end up repeating the same points."

He hadn't been prepared to speak, but he already knew he wanted to nip some of the concerns in the bud. "I'm happy to provide information about the project."

The mayor nodded. "As this is a committee, we just need to put this point of order to a vote. All in favor?" All five members of the zoning board raised their hands, and Cheyenne nodded. "Motion carried. We'll recess for ten minutes. Mr. Patel, if you need to prepare anything, now's the time to do so."

The crowd got up and stretched, hurried to the bathroom. Shane stood as Cheyenne approached him.

"Sorry for the short notice. I didn't expect so many deputations tonight." She rubbed her temples. "I don't want to chastise folks for not doing their homework, but I think what you'll have to say will at least cut down on repetition and I'd like to get home before midnight. It's a school night, after all."

"It's no problem." His gaze slid to Mira, perched in her seat, clutching her notecards. She met his eye, then quickly looked away. Something inside him clenched. He didn't want her to treat him as if he were the enemy. They might be on opposite sides in this issue, but that didn't mean he didn't care about her.

It also didn't mean he would go easy on anyone opposing the project. He was here to win, after all.

CHAPTER TWELVE

MIRA SWALLOWED DRILY, trying to suppress the banging of her heart. Sweat gathered on her palms and under her arms. Why was she even here? No one needed to hear from her.

Except that they did. While everyone else was concerned about building shadows, Dumpsters cluttering sidewalks and a lack of parking spaces on Main Street, she had so much more at stake.

She didn't *want* to be here, opening herself up to criticism and ridicule. She wished she could've used instant messaging to give her deputation. She could be articulate and thoughtful on a computer screen. In person, not so much. Still, it wasn't an excuse to not show up. Grandpa would have.

She glanced around, searching for Arty and Janice. She thought for sure they'd be here. She'd really wanted their support—but then, she was more than certain they wouldn't have been too broken up if she was forced out of the Crown. They'd warned her for years about the dangers of living there alone.

The zoning board filed back to their seats, and

Cheyenne took the podium once more. "We've gathered a list of citizens' concerns thus far for Mr. Patel to address. To the deputants, I would highly recommend that before you approach the mic, you listen to what he has to say."

Shane walked up to the front of the room. Mira instantly recognized the foam core boards he'd had at his presentation as he set them up facing the crowd. He moved the mic stand a little farther forward and turned it around so he could face the audience.

"Good evening, everyone," he said with a grin. "I hadn't expected to speak tonight—honestly, I just keep these boards in my car trunk. But I'll jump right into it and keep it short."

He started with the building shadow, pointing out that Main Street ran east-west and that the block slated for the condo was bound on either side by streets, nowhere near any other building that would be greatly affected. He showed pictures of the building facade and how the first four floors were stepped back with terraces covered in green. He reiterated that Sagmar had to adhere to existing code to include parking spaces on the premises for new residents, and that several common green spaces were also being developed.

"This doesn't even begin to cover some of the other benefits Sagmar will provide Everville. We're building a children's splash pad and upgrading the downtown internet connections.

We're even starting a pilot project on this block to provide free high-speed Wi-Fi to residents and small business owners. Some people would call these things frills, but we're building toward the future success of Everville, and communities aren't built on blank concrete alone."

Some of the murmuring turned from suspicious to interested. Mira was intrigued by the prospect of free Wi-Fi, but it wasn't enough to entice her into giving up her grandpa's beloved theater.

"Why don't you tell us the truth, Mr. Patel?" a gruff voice said above the din. Heads whipped around to focus on Bob Fordingham, who stood leering at Shane.

The real estate developer regarded him with a perfectly blank look. "I'm not sure what you mean, sir."

"I mean that you're a salesman, and that all these promises you're making are just that. Promises that can and will be broken."

Some of the people around him muttered their agreement and clapped. The mayor banged her gavel. "Order, please. This time is allotted to Mr. Patel—"

"We know you're in bed with the Sagmar people, Madame Mayor," Fordingham said nastily, voice rising. "Isn't it true you've accepted special benefits in exchange for support for this abomination of a project?"

Mira's eyes narrowed. Surely that wasn't true. Cheyenne homed her basilisk stare on the former mayor. "Mr. Fordingham, I do not appreciate your continued interruptions or your insinuations. You will sit down and listen to the rest of Mr. Patel's presentation. You will also carefully consider the ramifications of your slanderous statements." The implied threat of legal action was as effective as flashing a holstered gun, and the room went silent. Her quelling look blanketed the crowd. "I will not tolerate any more outbursts. This is a civil municipal proceeding. If you have nothing but mud to sling, take it outside."

No one moved except for Bob, who slowly sank back into his chair, a smug look on his face. Mira frowned. The attack hadn't been about the project—it'd been about shaking people's faith in the current mayor, planting a seed of doubt and dissention among her followers. It had also made her sound like a staid schoolmarm wrangling her classroom.

Cheyenne studiously made a note, taking a full five seconds to smooth her ruffled feathers before nodding at Shane to continue.

Shane leveled a look at Fordingham. "To answer your...*concerns*, Mr. Fordingham, Sagmar has always kept its promises when it comes to augmenting communities. Yes, we do offer incentives to municipalities to let us build properties there—we're no different than any other developer in that respect. In fact, it's in the contracts, and it's completely legal. There's nothing underhanded about that."

He angled his chin to one side and bared his teeth in a foxy grin. "I think you'd agree, Mr. Fordingham, that politicians like building things. Nothing is quite as sexy to a town council as a ribbon-cutting ceremony. It makes them look like they're getting things done. Unfortunately, people are less interested in fixing things. You should know. When my predecessor at Sagmar first approached *you* about this project while you were in office, you tried to get us to pay for a multimillion-dollar sports arena instead of accepting the investment we were willing to put up for your water main repairs."

The former mayor's face turned beet red as the audience gasped and turned their collective judgment upon him. Mira remembered how Big Bob had boasted his vision to bring professional football to town, all while insisting they couldn't afford vital upgrades to the aging water and sewage systems. Funding had only been secured after Cheyenne had been voted into office.

Fordingham said loudly, "I believe what I believe. I made that decision in the interests of the taxpayer. The people of Everville—"

"*Thank you*, Mr. Patel," Cheyenne interjected, talking over Fordingham's sputtering. She sounded neither pleased nor dismayed by Shane's criticism of the former mayor. If he'd hoped to win her favor with that stunt, he'd failed. "Let's move on to the next deputant."

Shane gathered his props and marched to the back of the auditorium as if he hadn't just made an enemy out of Big Bob. The mood in the room suggested people were angrier with Fordingham than Shane at the moment, though.

As he passed, he gave Mira an encouraging smile. Her lips tingled, remembering the taste and feel of him, and she looked away. The man was a damned distraction.

The meeting recommenced. A few people did speak in favor of the condo—not surprising since the block in its current state had all the appeal of a haunted ghost town. But those who were against the condo were as vehement about their objections as ever. It didn't seem to matter what Shane said—some people simply didn't want the condo built.

Even with this much opposition to the Sagmar building, Mira didn't feel as if anyone was on her side. They were *against* the condo, not *for* the theater. They didn't care about the history of the place or how hard her grandfather had worked to keep it open for Everville. They didn't care about his sacrifice. They hadn't mentioned him once.

"Miriam Bateman."

She was startled when the clerk called her name. She remembered to breathe and slowly got to her feet. By the time she got to the microphone, she felt every set of eyes on her.

Her hands shook as the moist, crinkled sheets of paper with her speaking notes blurred before her. The mic felt like the barrel of a gun aimed at her forehead. The last few speakers were much taller, so she tried to lower the stand. It tipped over and swung in a wide arc, catching Mrs. Abbot in the shoulder. Her notes scattered all over the ground as she rushed to apologize to the glowering woman.

A snicker in the crowd reached her ears, crumbling what little nerve she'd built up, before someone hurriedly lowered the stand for her and gathered her papers off the ground. Tears burned her eyes.

"Ms. Bateman, I know this is an important issue to you personally," Cheyenne said gently. "I never met Jack Bateman, but I know your grandfather was well respected."

The sound of his name, spoken with respect and reverence, was like a balm, and it bolstered her spirits. She lifted her chin, meeting Cheyenne's smile.

"Please take your time with your arguments. I'll urge the crowd not to interrupt you, as well." Mira heard the warning behind her words to the audience, noted that she was being given special treatment. Because everyone knew she was a nervous wreck? Because she was the town shut-in?

Because she was the poor kid old Jack Bateman had rescued from her druggie parents?

She clenched her jaw and closed her eyes, searching for strength. She was here because of Grandpa. She was doing this for him. She owed him everything. He'd saved her. No matter what anyone thought of her, she had to do this. She had to save the Crown.

"Ladies and gentlemen of the zoning board," she began hoarsely, then cleared her throat. "My fellow neighbors in Everville." She blew out a breath and raised her speaking notes with a trembling hand.

"My name's Miriam Bateman. I'm the owner of the Crown Theater. Some of you may know me. But more of you knew my grandfather, Jack Bateman, who lived in Everville almost his whole life." A lump formed in her throat. She released a breath through her nose and heard it whistle over the speakers. The audience waited.

"When I first came to live with Grandpa Jack, he'd been running the Crown for more than thirty years. One of the first films he ever showed me was *Casablanca*. It was during the town arts festival, an event we've since stopped hosting. He screened a bunch of classics for free. He could've charged for tickets, but he wanted the theater open to everyone coming into town, to give them a place to rest and cool off while he shared his passion for films."

People nodded, seeming to remember that once-great period in Everville's history.

"I was too young to understand everything about the movie that made it great, but I knew I loved it. Sitting in the dark, seeing those faces lit up on the screen, waiting with breathless anticipation for what came next… I know many of you saw that film with me. And I remember all the thank-yous that my grandfather received afterward.

"Many of you watched your first movies at the Crown, as I did. Some of you had your first dates there, met your wives and husbands there, brought your kids to their first movies there. Some of you may even be old enough to remember seeing your first stage production there back when the theatrical society would put on *Peter Pan* or *Romeo and Juliet* or *A Streetcar Named Desire*. The Everville Theater was a stepping stone on the career path for many great stage actors. You can still see their old autographed photos in the town archive. Grandpa donated them because he wanted people to remember the Crown's history after he converted it into a movie theater. He knew it was important to keep arts and culture alive in Everville, especially during tough times."

She paused, took a deep breath. "My grandfather was sorry to close the Crown, but he always knew it would be revived one day. What's old becomes new again eventually, he used to say. And I promised I'd help him achieve his dream."

She kept herself from searching for Shane's face, gauging his reaction. She knew this would drive a wedge between them, but she had to do it for Grandpa.

"All I'm asking for is a chance to show the people of Everville that the Crown can again be the jewel it once was." She set her jaw to keep the tremors from affecting her voice. "Before the month is up, I'll be reopening the theater for an open house. I want to remind everyone what the Crown meant to this town, and what you'll miss if you let Sagmar tear it down." Getting people into the theater was the only way to make them see it was worth keeping. It would be a huge undertaking, but now that she had Shane's projector, she could actually show a movie.

A few folks clapped. It wasn't the rousing applause she'd hoped for—she hadn't exactly given a battle cry–worthy speech to the troops—but it was enough to keep hope afloat. "Thank you for listening," she ended a little lamely. She turned from the mic and sat down hard in an empty seat at the end of the row, willing her lungs to inflate, her heart to slow.

She almost didn't hear Cheyenne.

"I'm certainly looking forward to seeing what you have planned, Ms. Bateman," she said evenly.

"I don't imagine anyone would turn down an opportunity to see the Crown relive its glory days."

It was as direct an endorsement as Mira was likely to get. She managed a smile for Cheyenne and for the first time since the meeting began, felt a sense of relief. She hadn't realized she'd needed someone's approval so desperately.

At the end of the meeting, the mayor declared that the zoning board would take a few weeks to deliberate. Clearly, she expected Mira to make good on her promise to show the town the benefits of keeping the Crown.

Sweat broke out on her brow. What had she been thinking? She couldn't reopen the theater in a month. Sure, she'd dreamed she could, but with her day job and no money to make the repairs she needed…

"Excuse me, Miriam?"

Startled, she looked up into the face of a smiling woman she vaguely recognized. "Maya Hanes," she introduced herself. Her short, spiky hair was dyed royal blue. A pair of red cat-eye glasses hung from a beaded chain around her neck. She wore a vintage style black-and-white polka-dot dress with a high, pinched waist and a wide skirt. "I don't know if you remember me. We went to school together. I own the consignment shop down on Main Street."

"I remember." Maya had been one of the school's top athletes.

Maya sat. "I'm a big fan of the Crown. I was sad when it closed. I used to watch weekend matinees there all the time."

"Oh." Mira didn't know what else to say. She'd never spoken to Maya before.

"I was wondering if we could work together for your open house. I was thinking I could put together some displays for the lobby based on whatever films you're showing. I've got some great props and clothing from a lot of different eras. We could even make it a costume party. It would drive some business to my store, but it'll also make the reopening a big event and not just another night at the movies."

Mira bit her lip. "I was just going to show some royalty-free stock footage I have. I'm not sure I can afford the license to show one full movie, much less more."

Maya tilted her chin thoughtfully. "I have contacts in New York who might be able to help. If they can't, I'll bank your startup costs."

Mira's head whipped up. "What?"

"The Crown's a historic building. It's just like you said—I have a lot of memories attached to the place." She grinned. "Not that I wouldn't be getting something out of it. The exposure for my own business would be phenomenal." She handed her a business card. "Here's my number. Let's meet for coffee to talk. I know tons of people who'd love to help with fund-raising."

Just like that? It couldn't be that simple. A benefactor dropped into her lap was too good to be true—so naturally, it made her wary.

She didn't have any reason to be suspicious of Maya's motives, though. What did she have to lose by accepting her help? She'd been up-front about what she'd get out of helping her. She was more transparent than Shane. She should be glad for Maya's interest. If this was what it'd take to save the Crown, so be it.

Her palms started sweating as she realized she had less than a month to prepare the Crown. She wasn't the only one invested in its success now, and she was on a clock. But setting herself a deadline had lit a fire under her. It seemed it was all she'd needed to get her ass in gear.

She hurried out of the auditorium, her mind racing.

CHAPTER THIRTEEN

A MONTH.

A whole month.

Shane dazedly walked out of the auditorium after his brief conversation with Mayor Welks. He'd hoped there'd be a conclusion to the rezoning issue tonight. He'd thought the board was on his side, especially after being given the chance to speak. He never thought they'd defer judgment for an entire month.

Laura was not going to be happy.

Before he left, Bob Fordingham threw him the stink eye. Shane doubted the ousted former mayor could do much to sway the zoning board, but he'd have to play nice from now on. It wouldn't serve his purpose to poke that bear.

Mira was nowhere to be seen, so he made his way to the theater. He wanted to talk to her. That deputation had taken courage and he wanted to make sure she was okay. He also wanted her to know he had no hard feelings about her renewed fight for the Crown.

He supposed he should have been angry that she'd be using the equipment he'd bought her in order to fight him. She hadn't even offered him money for it. But he wasn't mad. Mostly, he was worried about the optics. If this got back to Laura and the rest of the team…

He shook his head. He wouldn't worry about that right now. He parked his car outside the Crown and dialed Mira's number.

"I just wanted to say you gave a great speech tonight," he said when she picked up. He stared up at the old building. The twilight cast shadows that made the boarded windows and doors look like eyes squeezed tight, as if the theater were flinching from the night. "I know it must have been difficult for you."

She didn't respond. He went on. "Have you picked a date for your open house?"

"Not yet." She let out a breath. "Listen, I'm going to give you some money for the projector—I need to borrow it for the open house. But I can't get a lot together right away. I know you must be upset—"

"I'm not. And I don't want any of your money—" he said it before he could take it back, and it felt right "—think of this as part of the test run. I think an open house is a great idea. Do you know what movies you're going to show?"

"Depends on how much the licenses are. I have a list in mind, but I'm going to talk to some people first…" She trailed off. "Shane… I'm not sure we should see each other again."

His chest tightened. His first thought was to deny they had any such relationship, to make light of their kiss. But he couldn't. He stared at the building as if he could meet her eye through the old brick. "Why?"

"We're on opposite sides of this thing. I need to stay focused, and I don't have a clear head around you."

If she were anyone else, he might have enjoyed the burnish to his ego. But all he felt was a sick sense of loss. "It doesn't have to be that way. Have I done anything to make you believe I didn't want what was best for you?"

"That's the thing. You *don't* know what's best for me. The Crown means everything to me, and you don't seem to get that."

Shane pinched the flesh between his eyebrows, frustration warring with sadness. "Can we talk about this face-to-face?"

A pause. "I can't right now. I have a lot going through my head, and if I see you…" She left the rest unsaid. He knew what she was saying, though, because he felt it as keenly as the ache in the back of his throat.

If I see you, all I'll want to do is kiss you and never let you go.

The thought made his breath catch. At some point, he'd gone from intrigued by her to liking her to something much more potent. It wasn't lust. Not exactly. It was something deeper, though he was confounded by the intensity of the feeling. He shouldn't want to be with Mira. She didn't fit into his life. Besides, his time in Everville was temporary. Anything they might have together would be like his summer stays in town: brief, fun-filled and nonpermanent. Something to look fondly back on. He had a job and a life in Brooklyn.

So why was he thinking forever thoughts with Mira?

He scanned the theater's roof where Mira's Eden lay, wondering if she were hiding up there now, looking down on him like Juliet from her balcony. The warmth of his phone pressed against his cheek, and he closed his eyes. "Mira… I don't want us to fight. I want to be on your side."

"Then move the condo elsewhere," she implored. "Let me keep my home."

He rubbed the back of his neck. He could try. He could go back and tell the board at Sagmar a lie…something to make them turn away from the property in horror. But even if he managed to convince the company to relocate the condo, it didn't mean he would win Mira's hand. In the meantime, Everville would continue to decline, Sagmar would lose its investors and Shane would lose his job.

And yet, the compulsion to do just that tugged on his conscience.

“I should go.” The words snagged in his throat. “That is…if you want me to.”

In the ensuing silence, he thought she’d hung up. But then the front door banged open. Mira stood there, her cell phone clutched in one hand. She looked like a small creature in the maw of the Crown’s doorway about to be swallowed up. And she was inviting him to join her.

Shane walked toward her slowly, slipping his phone into his pocket. As he got closer, he saw the way her chest heaved, the tremble of her fingers, the uncertainty in her eyes. Shane walked right up to her and slipped his arms around her. She shuddered and looked down. He rubbed her back. “What’s wrong?”

“Nothing.” She gently pushed him away and took a deep, shaky breath. “I… I just…” She sucked in her lip.

She didn’t need to say it. The conflict was clear in her face. She wanted him, but couldn’t allow herself to want him.

“C’mon.” He guided her to her office.

The futon couch had been converted into a double bed. He sat her on the edge of the squishy mattress. An electric kettle rested on a table by the hot plate and a basin of dirty dishes. Her “kitchen,” he realized.

And then his gaze hopped to the little fridge, the open armoire he’d thought was simply a storage cabinet but was filled with clothes…

Let me keep my home...

It was only then that he realized Mira *lived* in the Crown. This wasn't just a castle she guarded, a building she haunted. The reason he hadn't been able to find a home address for her was because *this* was her home. She worked, ate and slept here.

A mixture of pity, horror and awe filtered through him as he put the kettle on for a cup of tea. How had he not put two and two together before? He'd only ever found her at the theater, and late at night, to boot. He tried to remember if she'd ever said she lived there; maybe she had and he hadn't processed it. Maybe he thought she meant it metaphorically. He wasn't sure why it'd only struck him now. And he wasn't sure how to feel about it. On the one hand, it was entirely impractical—how did she shower?—but on the other hand, she lived in a movie theater. It was like a childhood dream come true. How often had he wished he'd lived someplace cool? This place wasn't just a monument to her grandfather; it was her playground, her dream palace. Of course she was fighting to keep it.

Which made her conflicted feelings all the more potent. Shane wasn't just flattered; he was honored.

Mira sat quietly on the bed, staring at a spot on the floor. "You want to talk about what's bugging you?" he probed gently. His newfound insight into Mira's world propelled him toward a new goal. He wanted them both to admit their feelings for each other. They could get through the condo debacle as long as they remained on even footing where their feelings were concerned. She already knew too much about how he felt about her—not a strong position to be in sitting down at the bargaining table.

"I just have a hard time with public speaking."

Was that all she had on her mind? "You did really well," he said, trying not to let his disappointment show. She worried her lower lip. "What's wrong?"

She rubbed the heels of her palms over her thighs. "A woman in town, Maya Hanes, wants to help with the open house. She's talking about fund-raising and costume parties and all kinds of stuff. I know I should be grateful, but…" She splayed her hands. "I'm not used to people helping me like that. I don't like being the center of attention…or pity."

"Sounds like she just wants to help."

"Maybe." She sighed, pushing her glasses up. "This is what Grandpa would want. I've just never been good with people. Arty and Janice say I've got anxiety issues, but it's not that. For this, I simply don't know if I can handle all the work."

"I think you're great with people," he said. "And you've got time to get things done."

Inside, the mercenary business part of him

screamed to leverage her fears and doubts to convince her to sell. But instead, he said, "I can help you."

She stared. "I don't get you, Shane. Why would you help me? You can't claim this is about you needing to help people."

"I'm helping 'cause I like it when you smile," he said honestly. "And I like seeing you enthusiastic about something. You want to honor your grandfather by sharing the theater with the world, even though it scares you to bits. That's another reason I like you." He tucked a bit of hair behind her ear.

Her cheeks flushed. Damn, she was adorable. If he didn't get to kiss her again soon, he wasn't sure what he'd do.

"I've got an idea," he said. "Let's go out for dinner tomorrow night. We'll forget about all this and have a night of fun."

"Shane..."

"I'm serious. Just one night. You and me." He studied the conflict on her face, the uncertainty. It wasn't outright suspicion, the way it'd once been, but Mira wasn't convinced. "Please?"

She gave a short laugh. "Why do I get the feeling you rarely beg women to go on dates?"

MIRA CALLED MAYA HANES the following morning, and they met for coffee at the Grindery Café on Main. She ordered a large double shot cappuccino, raising Maya's eyebrows.

"Couldn't sleep," she explained. "Thinking too much about the open house."

That, and her date with Shane scheduled for that evening. She didn't know why she'd agreed to it. Was she that weak-willed and starved for affection that she couldn't say no to him?

She focused on her conversation with Maya, and they worked out a few ideas for the open house. Maya had been busy: she'd spoken with Stephanie Stephens, who'd agreed to organize a fund-raising bake sale. She'd also called the head of the Everville retirement home, who'd said many of the residents were looking for a way to support Mira's campaign to save the Crown.

"That's what we should call it. 'Save the Crown.'" Maya smiled thoughtfully. "Kind of has a nostalgic ring to it, doesn't it?"

Mira nodded a little distractedly. Everything was moving so fast. Maya peered into her face. "Is something wrong?"

"I didn't think people cared enough to do anything for the theater," Mira admitted.

"You wouldn't believe how motivated people suddenly get when they think they're about to lose something they've taken for granted. A paradox, I know. I come across it all the time when I get inventory for the shop. People get attached to things they're used to having around, even if they've never used it." She shrugged. "Change isn't easy for some."

They went to Maya's consignment store, where she showed Mira some outfits she wanted to display at the open house. Each costume was carefully folded within tissue paper inside individual boxes.

"These are amazing." Mira carefully ran gloved hands over the intricate beadwork of a Prohibition-era flapper dress.

"They belonged to my grandmother. She was a costume designer in Los Angeles way back in the day, and had mountains and mountains of period dresses in her collection. I used to go to her house all the time and we'd play dress up, and she'd teach me all about the different kinds of clothes people wore throughout history. She passed down her entire collection to me when she died. You could call this *my* legacy."

Just as Grandpa had entrusted the theater to Mira.

They discussed which outfits could be featured with which films. And before they knew it, they had a whole weekend of films and displays planned.

"If only we could have an entire week," Maya lamented. "There's huge potential for a film festival here."

Mira bit the inside of her cheek. "I have to fix things up, first. The men's washroom is out of order…" She grimaced. "I haven't been able to afford a plumber."

"You know who can help? Chris Jamieson. He's good at fixing plumbing issues. Probably because he's always working on pumps on his farm. He fixed my toilet when it clogged. I'll call him."

"Oh, I don't want to bother him…"

"You won't. He'll help a friend out."

Before Mira could protest, Maya picked up her cell and dialed Chris. A few minutes later, they'd agreed to meet at the theater in an hour.

First Shane, then Maya and now Chris. She didn't know how to feel about allowing more and more people into her sanctuary. It wasn't that she wasn't grateful, but she didn't want people traipsing in and out of her home, poking their noses in her business.

When they arrived at the theater, she let Maya in through the front door hesitantly.

"Oh my," she said quietly, staring around the lobby. "There's a lot more work to be done than I thought."

"The plywood can come off the doors easily. The glass should be intact…" She cringed as she saw what Maya saw—random boxes of old leaflets sitting on the concession stand, cobwebs in darkened corners, detritus littering the carpets despite her best efforts not to track in anything. Between work and her garden and the myriad other make-work projects she'd given herself, she'd neglected the most basic housekeeping. The auditorium was an even bigger mess—she never used more than the front few rows and the stage, and that was still a mess from when the rig and ceiling had collapsed.

Her heart sank into her stomach. Maya must think she was a total slob. How could she possibly have an open house? Who would want to come here? She waited for a tongue-lashing, or some biting remark, preparing for Maya to walk out in a huff and abandon the project altogether.

But Maya simply rubbed her hands together. "Nothing a little elbow grease can't fix up. We just need some help."

"Help?" Mira squeaked.

"I know lots of people who'd be happy to pitch in. I'll email the town business association asking for volunteers to help clean up."

"You don't need to do that," she said quickly.

"Well, you can't do it all yourself. Many hands make light work." She peered at her, and Mira flushed. "What is it?"

Mira pursed her lips. "I've always done things on my own. I'm not used to this... No one except my grandfather ever offered to help me with anything."

"Not even your parents?"

She grimaced. "They weren't really into being parents." She thought everyone in town knew that.

Maya seemed to sense that Mira was uncomfortable talking about her childhood, so she left it alone. “People will want to pitch in. Trust me.”

Mira fidgeted. She couldn’t ask anyone to help her reopen the Crown. That would be wrong, wouldn’t it? This was her project, her problem.

That, at least, had been what she’d believed since childhood. She had to take charge of her own life and deal with her problems by herself. She couldn’t count on anyone to come to her rescue. But then she thought about Shane helping her with the roof, driving all the way to New York to get her a projector, spending time with her. She hadn’t expected anything from him, but he was there, and he had pulled through for her in ways no one else ever had.

She had to admit it’d been really nice to have someone who cared. And though she’d told herself that Shane was only being nice to get her to sell the Crown, she didn’t truly believe it anymore.

CHAPTER FOURTEEN

SHANE CHECKED HIMSELF in the rearview mirror before exiting his car. He hoped Greenfield's was still as good as their five-star reviews claimed. His family would always go to the country club restaurant out by Silver Lake at least once during their summer vacations to enjoy a fancy dinner. Downtown Everville didn't have a whole lot to offer in terms of fine dining, and he wanted Mira to have the best.

He walked up to the theater's front door, knowing Mira would open it before he could knock. He'd finally discovered the sensors that notified her when someone approached the Crown, carefully hidden beneath metal plates attached to the wall. If anyone knew about them, they could be easily disabled, and then Mira would be left defenseless. It compounded his growing worries for her safety—ever since he'd realized her living situation he hadn't been able to stop imagining the worst-case scenarios.

As predicted, she opened the door. "I'm sorry…" She wiped the back of her arm over her forehead. "I lost track of time. I need a quick shower. You mind?"

"No problem. I can wait."

She hurried through the lobby. All the lights were on, casting the place in a gold-hued glow that reminded him of a sepia-toned photo. A garbage bin overflowing with papers and detritus sat in the middle of the room. "What's going on?"

"Cleaning. I've got a lot to do to get the place ready for the open house." She chewed on her lip. "I was so used to the mess I didn't realize how gross the carpets have gotten. I'm going to need to get them shampooed."

"I think Arty has a wet vac for rent at the grocery store. How about I pick it up and bring it by tomorrow?"

"You really don't have to."

"I know." He grinned. "But I want to."

She shook her head. "Something tells me even if I argued, you'd still show up."

She invited him to sit in her office/bedroom while she showered. He wanted to ask her about that shower, maybe even see it. Not because he was some kind of pervert, but because he was curious how she might have cobbled one together in an old theater.

Now that he thought about Mira wet and naked, though…

He clamped down on the notion and looked around. The cabinets and drawers beckoned. Who knew what kinds of secrets about the mysterious Mira they contained? Instead of snooping through every drawer and box in sight, he opened the fridge. It contained a half-empty jug of milk, the end pieces of a loaf of Wonder Bread, a giant jar of peanut butter and quite a few microwave meals as well as several cans of soup. He thought it odd at first that she kept all her food in the fridge, but there wasn't much room elsewhere in the office.

She'd invited him to use her laptop, so he sat at the desk and checked the sports headlines to pass the time. Unable to contain his curiosity, he peeked at Mira's browser history.

Most of the sites were clearly work-related movie blogs and film industry databases. A number of YouTube links directed him to how-to videos that, had he not seen what Mira could accomplish on her own, would've seemed like a random selection of specialized skills for a woman to be interested in. Welding, soldering, replacing corroded pipes…

Of course. She was trying to fix the plumbing in the men's room. She'd mentioned she'd shut the water off there. He did a quick mental calculation, wondering how he could help her out in that department.

Then he stopped himself. He knew he wanted to help her because he liked her, and he wanted her to like him, but he also knew he was doing it because he felt guilty. Because he knew in the end, the Crown would be his. He was there on Sagmar's behalf to do whatever necessary to acquire the property. And he would, regardless of his growing feelings for Mira. He was a closer. He had to do what was best for everyone.

She emerged a few minutes later. She'd changed into black dress pants and a black blouse. It didn't look much different from what she usually wore. She seemed to notice his perusal and she tugged at the top self-consciously. "Sorry, I didn't know how to dress. Where are we going?"

"Greenfield's. There's no dress code." He mentally chastised himself for being so to the point—he was usually much smoother. Quickly, he added, "You look nice," then mentally smacked himself again. *Nice* was too platonic, but *gorgeous* and *beautiful* were a little over-the-top. He had a feeling Mira wouldn't appreciate obsequious flattery.

When had he become so awkward?

The corners of her mouth and eyes tightened. "I'll go put some makeup on." She scurried out before he could tell her she didn't need it.

Five minutes later, she'd brightened her face with a dab of lip gloss and eyeliner. Her hair was still wet but slightly slicked back from her face with gel. She'd also put some cute ballet flats on—somehow those little shoes with the bows on them made her look ten years younger. She clutched a well-worn canvas shoulder bag and picked at the hem of her blouse. "Better?"

"You looked nice before. Now I'm wishing I'd brought you a corsage."

She rolled her eyes and chuckled. It only made him wish he'd brought her a whole bouquet.

The drive to the club was made in silence. It was still bright out, the air infused with summer's hazy gold glow. It was the kind of evening that Shane loved to drive through with the windows down and the radio turned up. Next to him, Mira was a little black cloud of deep thought.

"Are you nervous?" he asked with concern.

"No." She glanced out the window. "What made you pick Greenfield's?"

"They do a great prime rib dinner. And I haven't been there in years." He hoped she wasn't judging him for being too flashy. "Would you rather go somewhere else?"

"No, it's fine. Grandpa used to take me there for special occasions." She fell silent once more, steeped in what he assumed were sad memories. Shane was beginning to regret his choice of restaurants.

Despite her claims that she'd been there before, Mira didn't look particularly comfortable in the country club's dining room. It was Friday, so the place was busy. A raucous party across the room dominated the soundscape, and though Shane couldn't immediately see who it was, he recognized the blustery voice booming above the din.

"Well, if you ask me, I think it's a damn shame," Bob Fordingham's tone rang with false sincerity. The former mayor sat at the head of a table with about nine other people, including a carefully coiffed woman and two children who looked to be under ten. His family, Shane guessed. "Condos are a blight on the town, and they'll attract all the wrong types. This ain't New York. We don't need those people pushing *real* Americans out of Everville."

Shane set his teeth and blocked out the conversation. He was supposed to be on a date with Mira. "Tell me about growing up here. I don't think I ever saw you out at the beach or anywhere around town."

Mira lifted a shoulder. "I wasn't much of a beachgoer." She rubbed her arms absently.

"Where'd you learn about movie critiquing?" He already knew the answers because of the PI, of course.

"CUNY. BA in film studies."

"So you lived in New York for college?"

"Just a year. It was too expensive to stay, so I finished my degree online." Her gaze slid away. "Anyhow, Grandpa needed me here. He was getting older…" The corners of her eyes softened, and she stared at a point in the middle distance. She looked vulnerable, but also accepting.

"How did he die?" He didn't want to bring up bad memories, but Mira seemed open to questions tonight. It was like peeking through a secret door that was locked most of the time and had been left ajar. He wasn't meant to see what was beyond it, but he couldn't help himself.

"Heart attack. He was sitting in the auditorium when I found him. I thought he was just asleep." She stared at her lap.

Shane wanted to take her hand, but she was too far away. "I'm sorry. He sounded like a great man. And he did a great job raising you."

Mira shook her head. "He did what he had to. My parents weren't around much. They drank a lot and did drugs and… Well, Grandpa found out and came and got me. They didn't want me anyhow, except to clean house for them. And for the government checks. I was more trouble than they were willing to put up with. They always said so."

Shane's hands grew clammy as they fisted on the tabletop. He'd figured it was bad, but not that bad. "I'm so sorry."

"It's not your fault." Her gaze flicked away from him. "I was a mistake. I was never supposed to be born." She said it so matter-of-factly, his gut twisted hard.

"You can't believe that."

The corner of her mouth twitched. "When you hear it from your mother and father pretty much every day of your life, you're not inclined to argue." She waved a hand. "Anyhow, they don't matter anymore. Mom OD'd on some bad coke or something. Dad's in jail. He was the one who gave the stuff to her. I try not to think about them."

The blandness of the statement sent a shiver through Shane. It was the kind of story small town communities didn't forget. He couldn't imagine what Mira's childhood had been like in those early years before Jack Bateman had rescued her.

She seemed to read his thoughts because she gave him a flat look. "I don't need your pity."

"I wasn't pitying you," he said honestly. She was a jumble of contradictions—starved for love and affection, but as prickly as a cactus. Clearly, she kept people at arm's length to avoid being hurt by those she trusted, people who would disappoint her the most. What was difficult was figuring out how to get her to see herself as someone deserving of love. "I was just thinking how much I admire you. You overcame all those odds to become the woman you are today."

She looked like she was about to argue—was she that unused to praise?—but then a voice like a bullhorn blared across the room.

"Well, well, isn't this a surprise?"

CHAPTER FIFTEEN

BOB FORDINGHAM SWAGGERED OVER, his face glowing like a heat lamp. He bared his small, evenly spaced teeth in a grin that reminded Shane of a tired old picket fence. “Didn’t expect to see you two being cozy together.”

“Just a friendly dinner.” Shane made to stand to shake the man’s hand. He didn’t want to invite a deeper conversation, but he didn’t like Fordingham looming over him, either. His considerable bulk cast a wide shadow.

“Oh, don’t get up. I just wanted to stop by and say hello. Didn’t think there’d be much on the menu here you’d like. Your people like curries, eh?” He laughed as if it were the funniest thing he’d ever said.

Shane kept his expression neutral. “I’m more of a meat and potatoes guy. That your family over there, Bob?” He nodded toward his table. It was an unsubtle way to remind the man, and himself, to be civil.

“Just the blonde and the two kids. The rest are friends. I have a lot of ’em.” The implied threat wafted from the statement as unsubtly as the alcohol fumes from Bob's mouth.

"How nice for you." Shane knew he'd be better off making this man an ally rather than an enemy, but he'd already burned him in public. And Fordingham didn't strike him as the type to forgive and forget.

The former mayor swung toward Mira. "You're not letting this wise guy talk you into selling the Crown, are you?"

Contempt crackled the glaze of her imperturbable facade. "I'm having dinner."

The man's expression grew lascivious, as if she'd just described her undergarments to him, and he stooped closer, swaying slightly. "I never got to speak to you after the meeting. I admired your grandfather very much. He was real respectable. His son was a piece of work—I knew the guy. But Jack raised a beautiful granddaughter."

She met his eye blandly, unblinking, silent and full of judgment. It seemed to make the man uncomfortable because two heartbeats later he straightened and said, "If you need anything from me, give me a call, sweetheart." He produced a business card from a stack in his pocket. She took it by the edges and laid it on the table, and Fordingham ambled back to his table.

As soon as he was out of earshot, Mira made a sound of disgust. "Grandpa hated him," she muttered. "He thought he could buy everyone's loyalty and bullied anyone who didn't bow down to him. Never did a thing to help this town, either."

The chatter from Fordingham's table dropped, then rose again in earnest. Mira grew quiet and picked at her meal. It wasn't until he peeked over his shoulder that he realized the Fordingham party was staring at them, whispering, laughing.

"I'm not as hungry as I thought." Mira pushed her plate away.

"Then let's go find something that will tickle your appetite." Shane signaled the waiter immediately and got the check. Mira didn't relax until they were back in the car. This was supposed to be a fun night out for the two of them. Instead, it'd become even more awkward and uncomfortable.

"I'm sorry dinner was spoiled," he said once they were on the road. "It's my fault Mr. Fordingham got all up in our business. I shouldn't have antagonized him at the zoning meeting."

"I can handle Bob. I just don't like being stared at and talked about."

"They were staring at you because you were with me."

Her gaze flicked to him. "No, they were staring at me because everyone in town knows about my parents, my past. Some people enjoy rubbing it in my face."

He drove her back to the theater, the gloom of night settling around them. This was not how this evening was supposed to go. He'd meant for her to relax and forget about everything. It was supposed to be just the two of them, learning more about each other.

But business had come between them. Business that wouldn't go away until it was settled once and for all.

He walked her to the door beneath the marquee. After the night they'd had, he was unsure of what to expect. "May I kiss you good-night?" he asked tentatively.

Mira wavered. Shane's guts tied into a knot. If she didn't want him—

She placed a hand on his shoulder, arched up and planted her lips firmly against his. Warmth and relief spread through him. He slipped his arms around her waist, drawing her close. Her softness reminded him of the orchids in her little Eden. They moved deeper into the shadows of the doorway until they were pressed against the boarded-up entrance. Her hands delved through his hair and she softened her jaw, opening to him in invitation.

There was no hesitation in her exploration. He gathered her close, melting into the kiss. He wasn't seducing her—*he* was *being* seduced. And he would gladly climb a rickety ladder to the top of the world to make love to her.

A shaft of protestations and complications briefly cleared the hazy lust fogging his brain, and he broke away, leaning his forehead against hers as he put some space between them.

"Will you come in?" Mira asked breathily.

He throbbed head to toe, and in one region in particular. "I want to. But..." He didn't want to reject her without giving her a really good reason. If she were any other woman, he would be taking Mira hard against a wall right now. But he wanted everything to be perfect.

At one time he might have treated this like part of his grand plan to get what he wanted from her; maybe everything he'd invested in their relationship made this feel like more than a fling. He hated his cynical brain for even thinking it—what was real if this wasn't?

His breathing was ragged as he pried himself away. "I want to, but I have to stop. I know it sounds like a cop-out, but... I don't want anything between us to complicate things. I want to make love to you when we're both clear of all that stands between us. Otherwise you might wonder for the rest of your life whether I only slept with you as part of a business thing."

She stared. "Seriously?" She recoiled. "And you think leaving me like this will make that better somehow?"

He grimaced. "I'm trying to do the right thing here."

"No, I get it." She raised her hands, a cool veil settling over her. "You want to be the good guy.

You want to have it all. You think, 'As soon as Mira sells the Crown, she'll see I was right and we can be together and live happily ever after.'" She shook her head. "You and I both know life doesn't ever work out that way."

"Mira—"

"Go home, Shane. I'm tired and I'm going to bed *alone*."

Before he could stop her, she'd unlocked the front door and slammed it behind her.

"YOU HEAR THE NEWS?"

Arty was doing paperwork in the grocery store's office when Janice's voice startled him out of the mind-numbing task. He nearly knocked over his coffee. "What are you doing here?"

"Pete's out sick, so I thought I'd deliver the shipment myself."

He tried to sound his normal, gruff self. "You didn't have to do that. I would've sent one of my guys if you called."

"Well, I would have if you'd answered the phone. You've been avoiding me."

Arty sipped his coffee, stalling. "I've been busy."

Janice stepped into the office and closed the door behind her. Arty got hot around the collar. Call him old-fashioned, but he didn't think it was appropriate to be in a room with a lady behind closed doors unless they had an understanding.

There was no understanding between him and Jan. None at all. And he had to keep it that way.

"I heard from Stephanie Stephens who heard from her employee, Kira West, who heard from Wyatt Brown that Mira was out with Shane Patel last night at Greenfield's."

Arty perked up. "You don't say?"

"That's not the juicy part. Wyatt saw them kissing outside the theater."

Arty shifted uncomfortably. He didn't want to talk about kissing, and while he was happy for Mira, he also wasn't keen on discussing what she did in her recreational time. "Well, good for them."

"I just hope this lasts, after everything that happened at the town meeting."

"How did that go anyway?" he asked.

Jan blinked. "Wait…you weren't there?"

"Weren't you?"

Her eyes widened. "No, I… I assumed you'd be there and thought…"

"I assumed *you'd* be there."

"Neither of us were there? Oh dear." Janice wrung her hands. "Mira must've been terrified. You know what she's like in crowds."

"She's not a lost child, Jan. I'm sure she did fine." Guilt ate at him now, though. He should've been there. It'd been an important meeting, and even if he wasn't sure saving the Crown was best for Mira, he had to do what he could for Jack's granddaughter to honor his friend's memory. Like he'd been doing by avoiding Jan…

Janice sat forward. "Arty…tell me…what happened the other week? In my shop when you—"

"It was a mistake. I didn't mean to…" He trailed off.

The space between her eyebrows wrinkled. *"Mistake?"*

"I got caught up in the moment, that's all. It'll never happen again."

The florist dropped her gaze. "Why not?"

Why not? Did she have a sadistic streak? He shifted in his chair. "I'm trying to be a decent man, here. I can't dishonor Bill's memory. Or Jack's, for that matter."

She narrowed her eyes. "I can understand your feelings about Bill, but my husband's been dead a long time. And what does Jack have to do with anything?"

Was she yanking his chain? "He told me when he asked you out, you rejected him. He never did get over that heartbreak. A man doesn't—" He cut himself off sharply. What he'd wanted to say was that a man didn't betray his friend by pursuing the woman who'd broken his heart—even if it broke his own in the process.

Janice blinked. "He never asked me out. He flirted, sure—we both know how he was. But I made it clear I wasn't interested in *him*."

Arty stared, his mind swirling with confusion

as he tried to identify what she meant by her emphasized *him*.

"For Pete's sake, Arty, stop gaping. I was interested in *you*." Janice pinkened until she matched the azaleas she sold. "I've waited years for you to ask me out. I'd just about given up. Seemed like the only woman you were interested in was Mira."

He choked on his coffee, started to sputter.

"Not in that way, obviously." Janice huffed out a sharp breath. "God, but you're a blockhead. I don't know how many signals I had to throw your way. It was like trying to flag down a blind bull with a handkerchief."

"But… Jack said…"

"Jack was an idiot, God rest his soul. I told him I wanted *you*." She fidgeted. "That is, he figured it out, eventually."

Arty didn't know what to say. The man he'd called brother had taken this secret to his grave. Jack had known Arty was in love with Janice. He couldn't believe he'd denied him that chance to be with her. All those years they could have had together…

A bleak, black cloud cast his friend's memory in shadow.

"Well? Do you have anything to say?" Janice asked tetchily.

He ran a hand through his hair. "I'm having a hard time wrapping my mind around all this. Jack didn't *really* know, did he? I mean…he didn't actually tell you he'd figured it out?"

"You calling me a liar?"

He shook his head. "I just can't believe Jack would've lied to me about this."

The florist pursed her lips. "Well, he did. To both of us. He told me you had other things to focus on and that you had your eye on someone else. For a while, I thought he might be implying you were…playing for the other team. I got the impression he was protecting you."

Or maybe he had a jealous, vindictive side to him. Arty knew Jack could hold a grudge—it was why he and his son, Mira's father, had been estranged for so long. He just had a hard time imagining his friend would be so duplicitous.

"I… I need time to think about this." Arty got up and left the suddenly stifling office. He should've been overjoyed, should've been kissing the daylights out of Janice Heinlein.

But all he could think about were the long, wasted years, and the man who'd been the cause of them.

CHAPTER SIXTEEN

MIRA SPENT THE week working with Maya and several volunteers to promote the Crown's open house. She was surprised by the enthusiastic support: Maya had enlisted her friends, including the reporter Tiffany Cheung and Stephanie Stephens, who worked at Georgette's Books and Bakery, as well as their partners, Chris Jamieson and Aaron Caruthers, to help clean up the theater.

The open house would take place on the third Friday of July, which seemed too close, considering all the work the theater needed. She only had so many hours in a day, even after she cut back on the number of articles she wrote daily. The volunteers all had day jobs, too, and could only afford a couple of hours in the evening to help out.

And when they got together, Mira had a hard time prioritizing tasks and directing people where to put things. She'd spent years shuffling and reshuffling everything around without actually throwing anything out. Now she found she couldn't bear to lose all those boxes of old flyers and paraphernalia. Everything was infused with the spirit of her grandfather—throwing anything out would chip away at his presence little by little.

Maya and the others were soon exasperated by her need to hoard her grandfather's memories, and that, in turn, made her more anxious. She wasn't used to working in groups. She didn't like being either a captain or a team player—it was easier being alone. Being accountable only to herself allowed her to screw up and act out as much as she wanted to without judgment or consequence. By the end of the week, she was so frustrated she told the volunteers not to come back till she'd figured it all out.

Alone at last, she found she wanted to talk to Shane, but she couldn't face him. She was embarrassed that she'd thrown herself at him and then been rejected. Was she so repellant? She didn't buy his reasoning. What he wanted, first and foremost, was the theater. He probably didn't think he could have her until that happened.

Which pretty much meant they'd never be together.

Being reminded that she was a woman with needs had awakened a restlessness inside her. Her insomnia was worse than ever, but a blessing in disguise: she used those long, dark hours to scrub and clean and fix what she could in the theater. But every job unearthed a bigger one she wasn't ready to handle. And when she tried to start a bigger project, she became distracted by some far less important task. Tasks she could be assigning to those eager volunteers who'd looked ready to give up on her altogether.

She wouldn't blame them if they did.

Part of it was that she simply wasn't mentally prepared to let others into the theater. Putting off the big projects delayed that inevitability. She was baffled by her own behavior—this was what she wanted, what Grandpa would've wanted. And yet, she dreaded the open house almost as much as she'd dreaded going to school when she'd first moved to Everville.

"You'll make tons of friends," Grandpa had assured her. "Who couldn't love a smart girl like you?"

"Mom and Dad don't love me." She remembered how she wouldn't let herself feel pain over the reality of her sad life. The other kids had called her weird because of how little emotion she'd displayed. "They told me so. They said that's just the way it is."

"Well, they don't know any better. *I* love you, Mira. And so will the kids at school. They just need to get to know you."

The memory had her stopping in her tracks. Did she *want* to get to know other people? It was so much easier to be alone, independent, to do as she pleased without anyone being disappointed in her. She got that her parents had screwed her up by treating her like a burden. She'd been more a pet than a daughter, though they'd probably have treated a dog more civilly.

Around eight in the morning, after yet another sleepless night spent cleaning, her phone chimed with a text message. It was Shane. Are you home?

She hesitated. She hadn't answered his phone calls or emails except with the briefest of replies.

A minute passed. Then two. Hands itching, she typed out quickly, Yes. Busy.

I'm outside. Can I come in?

She checked her security feed—sure enough, he was by the back door, but he wasn't alone. Three young men were with him, as well as Sheriff Ralph McKinnon. She hadn't heard her alarm go off. Maybe the battery had died.

She wiped her hands and hurried to the back door, wrestling with both irritation and happiness at seeing Shane. The others she wasn't sure about. Ralph stood eyeing the three young men, hands on his hips. They were in their late teens, tall and scraggly and looking a touch sheepish.

"Morning, Mira," the sheriff greeted. "How're you doing?"

"Fine." Whatever this was about, she wanted it over with quick. "What do you need, Ralph?"

"I think it's more about what *you* need, Mira." He nodded to the boys. "This here's Jacob Massey,

Matthew Smith and Liam Oppenheimer. They're the ones who broke into your theater."

She stiffened, looked the boys over. They shuffled on the spot, hands stuffed in their pockets. They didn't look like hoodlums or ne'er-do-wells. "I see."

"We're sorry, ma'am." The shortest one with the rough voice, Jacob, stepped forward. "What we did was stupid. We didn't mean any harm. Just trying to have some fun."

"You think breaking and entering is fun?" She'd already forgiven them in her heart, but she wanted to make them sweat.

Liam, who had reddish-blond hair, piped up. "We wanted to check the place out. We thought it was abandoned. We thought there might be some interesting stuff in here..." He trailed off at her gimlet glare.

"Stuff you could steal, you mean. Didn't I hear that one of you tried to pick a lock?" Mira slid a look to Shane, who looked amused by her interrogation.

She stuffed down the happiness surging through her and glared at the boys even harder.

"You three were lucky she didn't have a real gun," Ralph said.

"Yes, sir. We know." Jacob grimaced. "But you scared us good. Awesome shot, too. I had some mean bruises from the paintballs."

"I'm sorry if they hurt," she said. "But I thought you were robbing me."

The sheriff hitched his pants up. "Here's the thing. I know these boys and their parents would be grateful if you didn't press charges. But that doesn't exempt them from paying their debt to society. From what Mr. Patel has told me, you could use some help cleaning up before the open house, so I'm proposing they work for you full-time till then, and I'll consider them square with the law. That'll satisfy my obligations without having to do a bunch of paperwork."

Mira's stare bounced from Shane to the boys to Ralph. She didn't want these kids who'd violated her home around.

"If you say no, I'll have to find something a whole lot less pleasant. Probably have to go through juvie to find work for 'em." He cut her a look. "No one wants that."

Matt pleaded, "Please, Ms. Bateman, I can't afford to have a permanent record. Dad says it'll affect my eligibility for college."

Jacob and Liam nodded. "We'll work really hard, seven days a week. Shane's already told us what kind of jobs you need doing. I spent a summer painting houses, and Jacob's dad is an electrician. I bet he'd come in and fix anything you needed."

Mira's jaw worked. She couldn't tell these boys no. Grandpa wouldn't have wanted that. He'd always been about helping the community, giving work to down-on-their-luck folks when he could afford it, handing out free popcorn to hungry-looking kids who could barely afford the matinee ticket. He was the most generous, caring man she'd ever known.

She sighed. "All right, fine."

"Terrific." The sheriff eyed the boys sternly. "Mr. Patel will supervise and make sure you do what you're told. If he's not happy, I'm not happy. Just because I hate paperwork doesn't mean I won't do it, y'hear?"

"Yes, sir." The three youths nodded.

"You start today." Ralph addressed Mira. "If they give you problems, call me."

As the sheriff strode to the exit, Shane grinned at Mira. "So, what do you need done?"

"Can I see you a minute?" Irritation simmered to fury as she strode toward her office, then boiled over as Shane directed the boys without consultation.

"You boys check out that concession stand. Clean out all the cupboards and take stock of any packages of cups, popcorn buckets, anything we can use." The boys jumped to work, and Shane followed Mira into her office.

"What do you think you're doing? Why did you bring them here? Why are *you* here?"

"I heard you needed help. I had coffee with Tiffany Cheung and Chris Jamieson the other day, and they told me you were having trouble getting things done."

Her cheeks flamed as her mind spun out elaborate conspiracies about what they might have said. She couldn't imagine they'd said anything good. People didn't gossip about other people unless it was to say something negative.

"We weren't talking about *you*. They just mentioned they were trying to help out before your open house, but that they didn't have enough time to really be useful. That's when I remembered you were owed a favor or three." He jerked his chin toward the boys. "Sheriff McKinnon agreed."

"This isn't a rehabilitation center. This is my home."

"It's also your grandfather's theater that you want to reopen in less than two weeks." He let out a breath. "It's okay to ask for help now and again, and to accept it. No one is judging you. I just want to help you."

Easy for him to say. "So you can watch me fail and buy the theater from me when all is lost."

"So I can help you realize your dream," he said patiently, softly, as if he were reasoning with a wounded animal. "I understand why you don't want to see me, but this isn't about us. This is about reviving something this town has missed and forgotten about. I want to give the Crown the best chance it has."

Mira shook her head. She could feel her resistance to him melting, wasn't sure if it was his rationale and logic that was chipping away at her stubbornness or the emotion behind it. She kept telling herself he was manipulating her, but she couldn't make herself believe it. "You don't have any reason to want the Crown to reopen."

"If I can be convinced the theater should stay open for the community's greater good, so can Sagmar."

She looked up into his face, saw nothing but sincerity. This was the first time he'd said he'd be willing to consider relocation. He'd refused to budge up until now; maybe he'd gotten permission to consider other options. Hope shone through a pinhole in her defenses.

"Mira, I want this to happen, and not just for the Crown or for the town. I want you to see how much people care."

"They *don't* care." She said it without conviction.

A half smile shone in Shane's eyes. He knew she was near defeat. "Maybe you think they don't, but if you keep pushing them away, you'll never know for sure. If you really want the Crown to reopen, you need to trust people and let them in."

She hated that he was right. She had been pushing people away, not just out of the theater, but out of her life. She might as well have been wearing a Keep Out sign on her forehead, all in the name of protecting herself and what little love she'd known, all of it contained within the Crown. Her grandfather's memory was trapped within these walls, her private sanctuary. As long as she could keep him close by living in the space he'd infused with his passion, that love wouldn't erode. And in this quest, she'd refused to share him, refused to share the theater, making every excuse to keep Jack Bateman's legacy to herself.

Oh, Grandpa. Tears filled her eyes. *I've been so selfish.*

Shane reached out. "I didn't want to upset you—"

"I'm fine." She turned away so he wouldn't see her anguish. Then she decided that she would accept help, whatever it took to make up for lost time. She'd squandered so much erecting a fortress around her—it was time to take those walls down, starting with Shane.

"The boys can help," she said, releasing a breath. "But I'm not good at delegating." The admission made her feel as though she'd let go of a taut rope with a ton weighing it down on the other end, and she flexed her fingers absently. She hadn't realized how tight she'd been clinging to that secret shame—as if owning up to needing help was somehow unforgivable.

"That's why I'm here. If you write out a list of what needs doing, I can prioritize them, and it'll be much easier to get things started. Do you trust me to do this?"

She wasn't sure. She'd never really trusted anyone before. But so far, Shane had fixed her roof, saved her from the stage rigging and put out a small fire. He'd proved himself time and again—so why was she so hesitant?

Then she realized it wasn't that she didn't trust him with the work of reopening the theater: it was that she didn't trust him with her heart. Because if he let her down the way her parents had, she wasn't sure she could trust anyone else ever again.

She thought of that rickety, dangerous stage rigging, thought about how she'd trusted her life to something so unreliable, how willingly she'd thrown herself from it.

Shane was a better bet than that rigging. She had to make a leap of faith.

"Do it," she said before she could take it back.

TWO WEEKS TOILING in the Crown made Shane realize exactly how special the building was—and not in a good way. While a dozen rotating volunteers came in and out to vacuum seats, scrub walls and pick up trash, a plumber and electrician quietly confirmed that the guts of the building were nowhere near up to code, that if the place were to ever be reopened permanently it would need to be gutted and completely redone.

Shane didn't tell Mira that, though. The PI had gone through her financial records and confirmed she wouldn't qualify for a loan big enough to cover the upgrades. He supposed she might get some investors, but who was putting money in old second-run movie theaters these days? The consignment shop owner, Maya Hanes, might be able to fund her for a year. The PI had discovered Ms. Hanes had inherited a sizable sum from her grandmother and had retired to a quiet life in her home town. But even if she did give Mira the money she needed, the theater was a losing business.

Guilt made him quietly pay the electrician and plumber out of his own pocket for the Band-Aid repairs needed. He'd lied to Mira about relocating the condo—it would never happen, even if the whole town came to the open house. He'd run the numbers and knew that with taxes and other bills, Mira would only be able to hang on to the property for another year or so. She'd be forced to sell, or it would be foreclosed by the bank. Either she wasn't aware of her financial situation, or she hadn't accepted that reality.

The bottom line was Mira needed this win. She needed the Crown to have one last hurrah, even if she was in denial that this open house was exactly that. The town needed it, too—a chance to say goodbye to a part of their history. Change wasn't easy, but it was inevitable.

Laura didn't seem to see things his way, though.

"What's this I hear about you working with

the owner of the Crown Theater?" his manager demanded over the phone the Monday before the open house.

"I'm on vacation," he reminded her evenly. "What I do on my personal time is none of your business."

"That's BS and you know it," she bit out.

"Fine. Yes, I'm helping Miriam Bateman, but you haven't seen the place, Laura. It's a demo waiting to happen. A stiff breeze could topple it." It was a lie, but he didn't want Laura thinking he was earnestly trying to save the theater. "Anyhow, the zoning board is withholding their decision until after the theater's open house. I'm 95 percent certain they'll side with us. This is all just a play to give the theater one last blowout. In the meantime, I'm fostering community connections and cultivating relationships with local businesses."

Laura growled her discontent. "'Ninety-five percent certain' isn't good enough. The investors are getting restless. We're supposed to have shovels in the ground before Christmas."

"I know, but Mira's been…difficult." He smiled for some reason. She wasn't difficult, per se. She was just stubborn about her romantic notions and skeptical about her hopes and dreams. She was a paradox, a pragmatic dreamer who lived on canned soup and gardened on top of the world and hung from treacherous stage rigging for fun. And damned if he didn't like it.

"'Mira,' is it?" Laura hummed. "You're not banging her, are you?"

He flinched. "No."

"Would it help our cause if you were?"

He fumed. Laura could be so crass, not to mention too insightful.

"I want to hear from you by week's end whether you think Ms. Bateman will sell. The company's champing at the bit, and I'm hearing rumors that the high-speed rail line might be announced sooner rather than later. You know what happens then, right?"

The price for the property would shoot up, along with investors' tempers and the price for units. "I hear you."

"Good. Then you know you need to seal this deal. Do whatever it takes. We can't afford to wait much longer."

Later that afternoon, while he and the boys were working, Arty Bolton came to the theater. He stared around the place, a pleat between his eyes, as if looking for someone. Shane greeted him. "How's it going, Arty? Haven't seen you around."

"We're having some staffing problems at the store, so I've had to stay in." He looked around surreptitiously. "Where's Mira?"

"In her office. She comes in and out between writing and cleaning."

Arty harrumphed. "Works too hard, that one. Good thing you're here to help her out. Almost too good." He leveled a suspicious look at Shane, and he wondered why the old man was suddenly leery of him. "Heard Ralph has you looking after those hooligans who broke in here."

"Mira needed the help."

"Well…don't get too friendly. You and I both know this place is doomed." He practically growled it out. "Her heart's gonna break one way or another, and I don't think she needs you adding to her misery."

"I would never hurt Mira," he said, put off. Where was this attitude coming from? He thought Arty liked him. He didn't appreciate being accused of duplicity, either, though the guilt that gnawed on his conscience bothered him more.

"We never mean to hurt the ones we love. But we do anyhow." The grocer stuffed his hands in his pockets, glancing about nervously. "Has Janice been around?"

"Not that I've seen."

Arty scratched his nose and shuffled his feet. "All right. Well, I've got a couple of hours in me before I turn into a pumpkin. Put me to work and I'll see what I can do to help straighten this mess out."

Puzzled by the man's mood, Shane directed

him to join the others. He didn't know what was going on with Arty, but whatever it was, he wouldn't let it shake him from his cause.

CHAPTER SEVENTEEN

ARTY STRETCHED, EVERY one of his bones singing, every muscle and joint creaking and popping. Getting old was a literal pain in the neck. He hadn't worked so hard in years. He'd never really paid much attention to the mess in and around the Crown—frankly, he'd never thought it'd open its doors again. But, boy, had Mira let things go. Why hadn't he ever told her to throw out those boxes of old schedules?

Because they were Jack's. The acute headache pinching his scalp intensified. Tossing out all that garbage and scrubbing those walls had been like an exorcism, a cleansing. But it didn't make him feel any better about Jack's lies and secrets.

He'd hoped Janice would be there helping with the cleanup. She'd declared her feelings for him almost two weeks ago, but he hadn't been able to face her since. It didn't seem right to pursue her, even if he'd wanted her practically all his life. She was still beautiful, still vital, and could have any man. He was old and had little to offer…

You're making excuses.

A distant memory of Jack rose in his thoughts.

It'd been decades ago, back when Arty had been contemplating buying the grocery store business from its previous owner. He'd always been conservative about his investments, didn't like big risks, and back then the town's population was starting to dwindle as the local factories and mines closed. He'd been afraid of failure and had made all kinds of excuses about why he shouldn't open his own business. Jack had been the one who'd ultimately convinced him to take a leap of faith.

What's life without a few risks? His friend's jovial voice echoed through his memory.

He shook his head. The theater had a funny way of amplifying the past. It was probably why Jack had loved the Crown. Jack, who'd lied to him, kept him and Jan apart. Jack, whose shadow haunted him.

No. Jack was dead. Arty was just being the coward he'd always been. Janice was waiting for him, and here he was, moping and griping about lost time and friends.

He should've been wooing the pants off her. Maybe not even figuratively. But his doubts still gripped him. Arty had never been a striking figure, especially compared to Jack. Short and compact with dark hair and cheeks like wet dough, he'd been considered "the nice guy" next to Jack's lean form, brilliant smile and long-legged swagger. Now Arty was old and gray, with more wrinkles than a crusty bulldog.

Bone-tired, he drove home to his bungalow on the outskirts of town. A familiar-looking car was parked on the curb. Someone sat on the porch swing, smoking.

He got out apprehensively and approached. The orange tip of the cigarette glowed as the figure inhaled and released a cloud of smoke like a dragon in the dark.

"Thought I'd have to smoke the whole damned pack before you got home." Janice stood slowly and stubbed the cigarette out.

Arty fixed a scowl onto his face, suppressing the relief and joy bubbling up through him. "I thought you quit years ago."

"I only smoke when I'm nervous." She rubbed her fingertips together as if it would clean the nicotine stains from her nails. "Only had two, but I let them burn down, mostly. Wasn't sure when you'd be back and I didn't want to smell like a tavern."

He stuck his hands into his pockets. "What're you doing here?"

Janice pressed her lips together and folded her hands. "Y'know, I'm not sure. I was going to go over to the Crown to help Mira—I hear folks are pitching in to get the place cleaned up. Saw your truck out front and figured you were there. Didn't feel like we should meet face-to-face for the first time in weeks in that setting. So I drove here, decided to wait for you."

"It's awfully late."

"It is. Would you mind inviting me in for a cup of coffee or something?" She was being more blunt than usual, but he couldn't blame her. It was way past both their bedtimes.

He opened the front door and gestured for her to come in. While Jan took a seat at the table, he put a fresh pot of coffee on. The place wasn't particularly messy—he'd been a bachelor all his life and kept his home tidy—but he picked up a few things around the kitchen, keeping himself busy so he wouldn't have to sit down and face Janice.

"Have you talked to Mira?" she asked.

"About the night of the meeting? No, but she hasn't let on that it bothers her. But you know how she hides her feelings."

"Shane's been treating her decent, it seems."

He faltered and cleared his throat. "I told him to back off a bit. I'm not liking where things are going."

Janice's brow furrowed. "I thought it was what we wanted. To get her out of the Crown. To open her mind to dating."

"I don't want her to get hurt. I don't want her throwing herself into something we hope is casual, but turns out to be way deeper. Shane is not going to stick around any longer than necessary. He's only ever been here for one reason, and no matter what else he says, his motives are his own. He'll leave eventually. And when he does, what are we supposed to do? She'll either bury herself even deeper than before or…or…" He trailed off, surprised at how agitated he'd become.

"You're not talking about Mira, are you?" Janice said slowly.

He sighed deeply. "Jan…"

She stood. "You know, I've waited for years for a sign that you were ready to see me as more than a friend. I don't have much more time to wait, and neither do you."

He backed up a step, the small of his back hitting the counter. "I told you. Jack—"

"Jack is dead." The words dropped between them like cement bricks. "What he did or didn't tell you… That's done. This is about you and me. This has only ever been about you and me." She took a step closer. "No one else is in this room with us."

The lightest of floral fragrances wafted from her—not a perfume, but the natural essence of a woman in fullest bloom. She drew closer, her face turning up to his, waiting.

"I…" His voice cracked, and he cleared his throat. "I haven't done this in a long time, Jan."

"Neither have I." A tremulous smile tugged on her lips. "I think we've both waited long enough." Her hands skated over his chest and onto his shoulders.

Her touch undid him. Arty seized her around the waist and dipped his head down, lips meeting, melding. Finally.

She was everything he could ever have hoped for, and so much more. The kiss lay somewhere between sweet and joyous, then things went a different way, and he found himself…

"Well, I guess that answers my next question," Janice purred. Arty gave a soft gasp as she took him in hand, a grip as sure as he was hard.

"What question would that be?" he managed shakily.

She smiled at him seductively. "Whether you'll make me breakfast tomorrow morning."

THE DAY OF the open house, Mira was so nervous, she couldn't stop shivering. With the help of Maya and her friends, Shane and his charges and a handful of other community members, the Crown had been transformed. Every burned-out lightbulb had been replaced, every rug shampooed, every seat vacuumed. She was overwhelmed by the outpouring of support.

Carefully, she placed the sign she'd made onto one seat four rows from the projector room and seven seats from the aisle. She roped it off with a silky gold cord then stood back to admire her work.

"'In memory of Jack Bateman,'" Shane read behind her, and she startled. For a moment she thought Grandpa had been speaking to her, though Shane sounded nothing like him.

"It was his favorite seat in the auditorium. Claimed it was acoustically perfect." She stared at the chair. It was also the seat he'd died in, but she didn't say that out loud.

"He'd be proud of you right now."

She turned away to mask the sudden misting of her eyes. "Are the boys all set up?"

"They're helping Maya with the final touches to her display. Jacob's got first shift in the ticket booth. Liam and Matt are on popcorn and drinks duty." He grinned. "You should think about keeping them on. They've worked really hard."

The corner of her lips tugged up. The boys had worked hard and without complaint under Shane's watch. It'd taken Mira a while to get used to them being around all day—they weren't bad kids. They just needed an outlet for their energy. With Shane directing everyone, it became easier to incorporate herself into the group. And while he was clearly the captain of this ship, she was the admiral, and he always consulted her about where to put things and what to do next, making it look like she knew what she was doing.

"The lineup looks great," Shane said, admiring the flyers that'd been posted all over town. They'd be showing four films, the final being last year's summer blockbuster *Infinite Destinies*. "Maya really came through with those licenses."

Mira nodded. She was still floored by how easily Maya had procured the licenses, though she wouldn't disclose the cost of applying for them. All she'd said was "trade secret" while tapping the side of her nose. "Apparently she has contacts in the film industry. She said all she had to do was whisper 'Save the *blank* theater' and people came out of the woodwork to help."

"Maybe some of those patrons will show up today."

She shrugged. It wasn't that she wasn't excited. It was just that everything had come together so quickly and easily, she wondered how and why she hadn't made it happen sooner. She silently berated herself for not trying harder, for not being the kind of person to ask for help or make a fuss. Then again, she'd lived for so long trying not to draw attention to herself that she wasn't sure she would've known how. If she had been more of a go-getter, more extroverted, she might have reopened the Crown long before this day.

She was getting her wish now, anyway. And it was all because of Shane Patel.

"Shane." He halted. "I never said…thank you. For everything you've done."

"You've said thank you plenty."

"But not for this. You…you keep doing these things for me, and I keep accusing you of ulterior motives when all you've been is a nice guy. I can see it in the way you treat the boys. You care about people."

His eyes darkened. "I care about *you*, Mira."

Under that dark, heavy-lidded gaze, her skin grew hot as she remembered the taste of his lips, his firm muscles pressed against her. Her knees trembled. "I—"

"Mira? Shane?" Matt ran in. "Maya wants you guys to come see the display."

Shane glanced at his watch. "It's almost go time. We'd better make sure everything's ready."

In the lobby, Maya had set up a fabulous display of costumes from the era each film represented. There were dresses from the Roaring Twenties, army uniforms from WWII, sixties-era outfits, and finally, an official Captain Jaxon Killian costume. Maya said she'd borrowed it from a friend of a friend.

Mira stared in wonder, especially at the *Infinite Destinies* costume. It was no cheap Halloween replica: she'd seen this exact costume at the movie premiere in Los Angeles last year. "This is amazing."

Maya beamed. "And you guys did a great job cleaning up. I bet movie studios would flock here to shoot if they knew about it. I never realized what an architectural gem you had under all the cobwebs."

Mira ducked her head, embarrassed. Yeah, the place had been a mess.

“Mira, there’s a lineup forming outside,” Jacob called, peering out the door. “It’s not even time for the first show.”

“That’s ’cause they want to see the Crown in all her glory, remember the good old days.” Shane grinned at her. “Whaddya wanna do, boss?”

This was it. She breathed deep.

“Open the box office,” she declared. “And open the doors.”

CHAPTER EIGHTEEN

THE THEATER FILLED quickly for the matinee showing of *The Jazz Singer*, Hollywood's first "talkie." Most of the audience was older, many from the retirement home. A couple of the patrons claimed to have seen the movie when it had first been released. After the show, Mira was talking to one of them about it when she realized a crowd had gathered to listen to her. She ended up giving an impromptu history lesson on it. At first she was nervous, but she found it easier to talk to a small crowd about her passion than it had been to talk to the zoning board. The group listened intently, then thanked her as they left.

After lunch, they showed *Casablanca*. Mira sat quietly through the whole film with Shane at her side. She noticed several rows down that Arty and Janice were sitting together, heads close. Janice whispered something in Arty's ear and he turned his head and kissed her.

Mira grinned, surprised but pleased. She'd always wondered if something was going on between those two, but everyone in town had known about her grandfather's feelings for Janice, and that knowledge had probably kept their relationship platonic. Arty was a gruff sort, who kept his business to himself, and Janice hadn't ever mentioned a romantic interest. Mira had always treated the two like an aunt and uncle. She hoped they'd be happy together.

While Sam crooned "As Time Goes By" on-screen, Shane slid his hand into hers and squeezed, and bent to whisper in her ear, "No matter what the future brings—"

"Shh." She smiled at him through the dark. His eyes shone and they both turned back to the film.

The midafternoon show was less busy, but there was still a good turnout for *West Side Story*. Apparently the kids at B. H. Everett had done a production of the show earlier that year and they ended up doing an impromptu singalong with the movie's soundtrack. They were practically dancing out of the theater afterward.

The final show of the evening brought almost everyone out. *Infinite Destinies* had made a record-breaking box office gross, and people were still clamoring to see it on the big screen, even if the sound wasn't perfect and there wasn't any 3-D. It was a full house, and after hearing about Mira's matinee lecture on *The Jazz Singer*, Shane suggested she tell her story about going to the Hollywood premiere.

A tremor shook her to the core and her fingers went numb. "Oh, no one wants to hear that..."

Talking to a smallish group of senior citizens who were hard of hearing was different from addressing the whole town after a big movie like *Infinite Destinies*. She didn't need to confirm just how uninteresting she was by watching people walk out of the theater.

"Of course they do." Shane gripped her shoulders. "You're the face of the Crown. You need to say a few words about the Crown, thank everyone for coming out and supporting you, that kind of thing. You stand here in your grandfather's place. He would've wanted you to be acknowledged."

Mira's guts quivered.

"Get Maya to do it."

"Maya's busy talking to some guests," he said hastily, and Mira blinked at him. "It's gotta be you, Mira."

She knew he was right, but it didn't change how much she hated the thought of getting up there in front of everyone. They'd laugh at her. They always laughed at her. She was ridiculous, a nobody trying to be somebody.

No one ever wanted you. You're nothing but a mistake.

Her parents' cruel words echoed through her mind. She ground her teeth.

No. I'm not a mistake. I matter.

You're a selfish nobody who just wants attention, her mother's memory sneered.

Attention is the last thing I want. All I want is to be left alone.

And how alone will you be with all these people marching in and out of the theater? You don't even want them here, do you?

Her argument with herself ceased abruptly, and a chill settled over her skin. Shivering, she retreated into her office during the showing of *Infinite Destinies*.

She sat on her futon as blood pumped into her head until her skull hurt. The past few weeks had brought home an undeniable truth: this whole campaign wasn't about preserving her grandfather's legacy. It was about saving her preferred lifestyle, her special world, the one her grandfather had constructed for her in a house made to hold dreams and fantasies. A life completely removed from the harsh realities of the world and her difficult childhood.

She'd berated herself for being selfish, for hoarding her grandfather's memory, but maybe she'd been right to. She *didn't* want people here, putting gum under the seats, tracking dirt over the carpets, spilling drinks everywhere. She didn't want to play host to a constant stream of people she didn't know. That had been her grandfather's dream, not hers.

The bleak realization was interrupted when Maya popped her head into the office. Her cat-eye glasses and smug smile added to her feline mystique. "Miiiraaaaa," she sang. "I have a surprise for you."

Puzzled, she followed her out. A cluster of people waited in the lobby. Blinding light suddenly flooded the room as several video cameras turned toward her. She shielded her eyes, hissing as she blinked out the spots.

"Guys, maybe not so much with that light," a familiar voice chided with good humor, though Mira couldn't pinpoint or identify who it belonged to. The lights dimmed slightly.

Maya led her toward the group. "This is Mira Bateman. She's the owner of the Crown and the one who's trying to save the last of our old theaters."

"Mira." The broad silhouette striding toward her, hand extended, looked vaguely familiar. His hair was a shade of blond-brown that reminded her of sunshine and sand, and it was with a start that she realized she'd met him once before. He grinned. "Riley Lee Jackson. I heard you needed help saving the Crown. Thought I'd come check it out, see how I could be useful."

She accepted his hand numbly, her tongue lolling as her brain overloaded. "Riley Lee Jackson," she repeated dumbly. "You're Captain Jaxon Killian in *Infinite Destinies*. You're the star of *Infinite Destinies*. We're showing *Infinite Destinies* right now." She pointed stupidly toward the costume Maya had set up. "That's your costume."

"Yes, it is." He chuckled. "I pulled some strings to have it sent over."

She was still pumping Riley's hand. A million questions were going through her head, but only one surfaced. "Why?"

"I have a confession," Maya volunteered. "I'm friends with Riley's wife, Kat. We met in New York years ago while we were both waitressing. I knew we'd have to make a splash to save the Crown, so I reached out to her." She grinned hugely. "I didn't think Riley would be so accommodating."

"Hey, it was in a theater just like this one that I first got the acting bug. I read all about the Crown. Your grandfather saved a piece of performing arts history. If my showing up will help keep the place open, I'm glad to do it."

"I—I—" Mira shook herself, willing her heart to stop slamming against her rib cage. "I don't know what to say." She looked from Maya to Riley to the rest of the crowd standing by. Shane grinned at her from the sidelines. "Did you know about this?"

"Maya told me she was bringing him in, but I thought she was joking." He gave a nervous chuckle. "I'm going to geek out now. Mr. Jackson, I'm a huge fan."

The Hollywood megastar turned his brilliant smile toward Shane. "Thanks. I think we're close to the end of the film. Sam?" He glanced at a petite blonde woman in a black pantsuit with four-inch heels. She pulled the auditorium door open and stuck her head in.

"You've got about eight minutes left," she said a second later.

Riley addressed Mira. "I hope you don't mind the media circus. My agent, Samantha, thought this would be great publicity for the second film. We're actually shooting right now."

"You…you left work for this?"

"For a friend of Kat's and for a cause like this? Sure. I've got some ideas for raising funds for your restoration efforts, too. You into crowdfunding?"

A roar filled her ears. This was all too much. With the support of a Hollywood A-lister like Riley Lee Jackson, she could probably renovate and reopen by next year. Her heart slugged against her rib cage as pressure clamped down on her skull.

"I…" Her vision started to blur. "I…"

"Whoa, easy now." Shane appeared at her side. "Give us a minute, will you?"

He led her back to the office and sat her on the bed. Some of the haze faded as he pulled out a bottle of juice from the fridge and handed it to her. "You okay?"

Mira shook her head. She was panicking enough having to address the audience. Now a celebrity was here with cameras. Her humiliation would be captured for all the world to see. She hid her face as her breath sawed in and out of her lungs. Why, oh, why would Maya put her in this position?

"You want me to tell them to go?" he asked quietly.

She wanted to say yes. She wanted to tell a man who had millions of fans who could throw money at her to go away. She wanted to crawl back under her covers so she wouldn't have to confront the selfishness of her motivations.

She couldn't do any of it, though. She was far too deep into the mess to back out. It would serve no one to be a coward.

She had to go out there and smile and be ever so thankful—even if she was deceiving the whole world.

SHANE HAD THOUGHT a surprise like this might have made Mira smile, but he should've known better. A big celebrity descending on her home with cameras in tow would not have gladdened her. Clearly, she was uncomfortable.

If he felt anger, it was directed at himself. It wasn't Maya's fault that she didn't know about Mira's anxiety issues. He should have mentioned it to the consignment store owner at the start, but he hadn't taken her seriously when she'd said Riley Lee Jackson would be coming.

He also worried what the A-list actor's support

meant for Sagmar. Laura would have a fit when she found out the Hollywood star was throwing his weight behind the Save the Crown campaign. Sagmar rarely faced more than the usual NIMBY objections to their builds. But this kind of attention could turn the Everville condo into a global PR disaster.

He calmed himself. The zoning decision still hadn't been made, and unless people were willing to donate very generously to save the crumbling theater and actually drive down to use it, it wasn't in Everville's best interests to maintain the current zoning, and he was confident Cheyenne Welks and the rest of the board knew it. It was a terrible thing to think when he was supposed to be supporting Mira's cause, but he reminded himself that his ultimate goal would benefit everyone.

So he stayed quiet, politely smiling in the background while Maya gleefully introduced Riley Lee Jackson to the stunned audience. Cheers erupted as the star waved and grinned and took up the mic, espousing the importance of small theaters and the power of movies and storytelling.

Then Mira was invited to say a few words. Shane held his breath—part of him was waiting to hear a rallying battle cry railing against the condo development. Instead, she kept it simple, thanking everyone for coming, then shuffled away, hugging her elbows and looking as though she was about to vomit.

The auditorium emptied in a hurry. Riley Lee Jackson was signing autographs next to his costume in the lobby, and no one would turn down that opportunity. He was probably the most famous person to visit the small town in decades.

It wasn't until the crowd had thinned that Shane spotted Mira making her way down one row of seats, picking up discarded popcorn boxes and empty soda cups. Her brow was deeply furrowed in what he would interpret as a mixture of disgust, dismay and resignation.

"You don't have to do that," Shane said, grabbing a garbage bag. "The boys will clean up."

"They'll want pictures with Riley Lee Jackson. Let them go. They earned it." She cursed as she stepped in a puddle of soda. "Why can't people be more careful?"

He understood her frustration. They'd worked hard to clean the place up, and now, all that work had been undone. A small waterfall of spilled cola and half-melted candies ran down the slope of the stadium seating. One seat was covered in smeared ketchup and gravy from a bag of chip truck fries someone had smuggled in. Apparently, they'd used the seat as a napkin.

He heard Mira swear loudly again. "Some idiot tore the upholstery off this seat!" she shouted across the room. "I knew it was a bit frayed, but who the hell does that?"

"We can get it fixed," Shane assured her.

She shook her head. "They don't make this kind of upholstery anymore. I checked." She sank into the seat next to it, running her hand across the fabric as if it were a dying animal. "It's finished."

"So we'll get some other fabric—"

"That's not the point." Her eyes snapped with fire. "These people know how important the Crown is to me, but they came in here and ruined everything anyhow. They don't care about this place. They don't care about my grandfather or his legacy or the town's history or anything." She slammed the garbage can down. "They don't deserve this place. They don't..." She trailed off, the lines on her face deepening. She looked angry and defeated all at once.

Shane sat next to her. He touched her shoulder, and she flinched away from him. "You must be loving this," she growled.

"Seeing you in pain? How can you say that? Mira..." He took her hand. "I care about you."

She stared at him defiantly, her blue eyes wavering between hatred and longing. She seemed to be daring him to say it again, as if she didn't believe him, as if she *couldn't* believe him, as if he'd made the most absurd statement of all time.

He understood. Why should she trust him? She'd been disappointed and rejected so many times by people, it was inconceivable that he should care for her. Besides, he *was* deceiving her. But that didn't mean he would give up on her.

"I care about you, about what happens to you. You're the most talented, remarkable, infuriatingly belligerent woman I've ever met. And despite all that, I still want to be with you. Get to know you better. Find out what makes you *you*."

"There's nothing special about me," she deadpanned. "I'm not worth anyone's time."

"Hey. Where is this coming from?" Her look of resignation bordered on self-loathing.

She turned her back on him, shoulders hunched. "Forget it. I just want this place cleaned up so I can go to bed."

"Leave it to me and the boys."

"I can't. It makes me crazy knowing this mess is here, soaking into the carpets. And all those people out there in the lobby—they'll be hanging around all night now with Riley Lee Jackson in town." She sounded less than enthusiastic about that.

"I thought you'd be happy about that. You couldn't pay for the kind of publicity Maya got you. Are you mad at her?"

She shook her head. "Of course not. Maya's been great. I couldn't have pulled any of this off without her."

"Well, are you mad at me, then? Is it because I pushed you to speak in public?"

She picked up the trash bin and worked her

way down the row once more. "No." She sighed. It seemed like a great effort for her to admit it.

"It's just… This place was mine and Grandpa's. He always wanted to reopen the theater, but I've never had anything that was my own. And I find myself resenting him now for leaving me with all this and making me share it." She let out a breath. "I'm completely selfish."

"Wanting something doesn't make you selfish."

"Don't you get it? I don't want to reopen the Crown."

Shane's heart stopped. She was saying the words he'd wanted to hear since he'd arrived in Everville. It was the first major step toward giving up the fight for the Crown. And yet, he wasn't happy.

She went on. "This place has been all mine for four years. I like that it's mine and no one else's. I owe it to my grandfather to reopen the Crown—it's what he'd want. But I don't want to have to give up the last bit of him I have left. Worse yet, I know no one will care one way or another."

He stared. "That's not true—"

"I've heard everyone talking. They act like I don't know what they say about the Crown. To them, it's the theatrical equivalent of slumming it at best, and an eyesore at worst. Maybe they don't want a condo, but they don't want a bunch of abandoned buildings around, either. The place could go up in flames and all they'd say is 'aw, too bad' before they start hoping for a shopping mall."

His heart cracked at the bitter despair in her voice. He started to reach out, to tell her that people cared more than that. But she only let out a breath.

"Go home, Shane. It's late." Eyes dim, she turned to leave.

Shane hopped the seats into the next row and stopped her. "Don't give up." He gripped her shoulders, searching her face. "You have to fight for the things that are important to you. The things you…love." He gave her just enough time to push him away, but when she didn't, he kissed her.

It was different from the kiss beneath the theater marquee after their date. Bittersweet, like tears. Shane had no idea how else to help her. Years of parental neglect and abuse had made her believe she was worthless, driving her to withdraw from a world she didn't want to be disappointed by. She desperately wanted to do right by her grandfather, but despite the outpouring of support from the town, she still didn't have faith in herself or others.

A kiss couldn't fix any of that. But he poured himself into it, willed her to accept that people cared—even *loved* her.

I love her.

He broke away, smiling hugely. "C'mon," he

said, taking her hand. "I'll get the boys to finish cleaning up in here. Riley Lee Jackson and his team will be out there a while longer. Once they leave, we'll lock up and you can get some sleep."

"I'm not sure I can sleep after all those people have been here." She rubbed her arms.

"Well..." He swallowed, suddenly nervous. "If it bothers you that much, come stay at my place." Her eyes widened, and he quickly amended, "I mean, there are spare bedrooms. I can make a bed for you with clean sheets and everything." Had he read her wrong?

"Oh." She bit her lip. He hated the uncertainty there, hated that he couldn't seem to hit the right note with her. She was skittish and untrusting, but he'd tasted her desire. Still, he didn't want to push her, or make her feel obligated.

But then she said, "So...you're not inviting me into your bed?"

Shane chuckled, relieved and giddy all at once. He put up his hands. "I wouldn't try to seduce a woman on the brink of exhaustion."

"So I'll have a cup of coffee." She resumed picking up trash.

He raised an eyebrow. He knew he might be getting in too deep, taking this too far. Sex with Mira would complicate things. It would commit him to a path he wasn't sure he could leave. He didn't want to hurt her, to deceive her any more than he already had—she was already conflicted enough right now.

For the sake of their relationship, he had to do the right thing.

CHAPTER NINETEEN

THE BOYS DID a quick cleanup, promising to return the next day to do a more thorough job, while Maya dealt with Riley Lee Jackson's people. It left Mira nothing else to do except pack an overnight bag for her escape to Shane's.

She'd never thought she'd want to leave the Crown, but the place suddenly felt too small, too busy, even after it'd emptied. Strange voices seemed to echo through the auditorium, though no one remained. The tomb-like stillness of the place had been disturbed, chased out with every tread across the lobby's dingy carpet. The town had exorcised her grandfather's phantom presence from the theater. It'd been empty and quiet before, but now, it was simply barren.

Mira brooded about it on the drive to Shane's rented home. Her thoughts were caught in a dozen little eddies, pulling her emotions this way and that. She should have felt elation at the night's success, pride in what she'd accomplished. But all she felt was a sense of desolation, like at Christmas when there was a huge buildup of anticipation followed by a letdown when that magical *something* didn't happen.

Was that why she was going home with Shane? Because she wanted *something* to come out of this endless night?

She'd only half joked about being invited into his bed. On the one hand, all she wanted to do was sleep, and she wasn't sure she'd be able to do that with a second body sharing the space. She'd never even let her college boyfriend, Tom, sleep over. She'd never been comfortable enough with anyone to allow them to share her bed.

On the other hand, she wanted the simple comfort of sex, and she wanted it with Shane. Nothing with Shane was simple, though, and so her thoughts continued their spiral, driving her deeper into her anxiety.

They pulled into a driveway in front of a two-story home with a well-manicured lawn. She could smell the nearby lake, hear the shushing of waves lapping against the pebble beach. Fireflies winked in and out, so brief she thought they might just be fanciful wishes.

"Can I take your bag?" Shane asked almost hesitantly.

"It's not heavy." She'd only packed a change of clothes and her toothbrush.

They walked into the house, and Shane flipped on lights as they went. The home was beautifully furnished with warm beach tones in taupe and sand and pale yellows and blues and whites. Everything was beach-themed, too, with framed shells, pictures of boats and water and nautical knickknacks on every surface.

The place was nothing like her parents' dingy, sparsely furnished apartment, or Grandpa's worn and tired bungalow. It was a home, even if it was a rental. Mira self-consciously plucked at her worn jeans and T-shirt that smelled of sweat and buttered popcorn.

"Can I get you something to drink?" Shane asked. "Midnight snack, maybe?"

Not exactly the seduction she'd envisioned, but she was suddenly so tired, she didn't want to think anymore. "I'm all right. I could use a shower, though."

"Upstairs, first door on the left."

She stood under the steaming hot water a long time, letting the heavy fall wash over her head and back, soothing as a touch. Not like the barely there trickle of her makeshift shower stall in the janitor's closet at the Crown.

Soft, fluffy towels capped off the most luxurious shower she'd had in months. As she completed her evening ablutions the weight of her conscience dropped away. This place might not be her home, but it was comforting in different ways. Maybe she should invest in nicer towels. It'd make her nightly lukewarm dousing a little better. And maybe she could paint her office that nice warm taupe color in the living room…

And maybe she could move out of the theater permanently and into a real house.

When she emerged from the bathroom, she found Shane waiting in the hallway, leaning up against the wall.

"Everything okay?" he asked, scanning her head to toe. She crossed her arms over her chest. Her pajamas consisted of a simple loose-fitting T-shirt and jogging pants, not the sexy lingerie she imagined wearing to seduce a man. Maybe she'd packed these pj's with self-sabotage in mind.

"I was just enjoying the shower." She rubbed the towel over her hair, trying hard to avoid his probing look. Her skin grew hot. "Um…so, bed?"

"This way." He led her to the end of the hall. It was a nice little room with striped gold wallpaper and a queen-size bed with crisp white bedsheets. One thing was clear; this wasn't Shane's room.

"I can set an alarm if you want," he said. "But I think we both deserve to sleep in."

Mira nodded silently. At least the bed looked comfortable. "I think you're right."

He lingered in the doorway. "I'm down the hall if…if you need me."

He turned to go. Mira almost stopped him. Almost. But as much as she wanted to have him in bed with her, she let him leave.

She climbed into the plush linens and burrowed down, inhaling the clean-smelling duvet. Strangely, knowing Shane was only a few doors away didn't make her nervous. She felt safe. Something she hadn't felt in a long, long time.

It was almost enough to let her sleep. Almost.

SHANE SLEPT TERRIBLY.

He'd worried about Mira's safety ever since learning she lived in the old theater. But having her under the same roof tempted him beyond reason. He wouldn't take advantage of her, not when she was tired and vulnerable. He'd made it clear he was waiting for the right time. But while she was in the shower, he'd received an email from Laura.

The company is getting antsy, and the investors are restless. Now I hear rumors you're directly involved with Ms. Bateman's campaign to save the theater. Whose side are you on? Get your head in the game and your ass in gear. I don't need to tell you what it'll cost if you don't close this deal.

Shane didn't like threats. He'd deleted the email, but Laura's words lingered. What would she say if she knew Mira was sleeping down the hall from him?

Every time he was about to drift off, he thought he'd heard footsteps padding down the hall. He'd wait, holding his breath, but no one knocked. No one opened his door and slipped into bed with him. No one snuggled up to him with drifting hands that roamed his chest and lower…

He shot to wakefulness, painfully erect. But he was still alone. He went to the bathroom and splashed cold water on his face. A glance at his watch on the shelf above the sink indicated it was past three. What was it Priti used to say about three in the morning?

"Nothing good happens at three in the morning," he muttered, scrubbing the stubble on his jaw. He snapped the light off and shuffled back to his room.

He lifted the duvet and climbed under the covers of the king-size bed. It wasn't until he turned over that he realized he wasn't alone, and he shouted in surprise.

"Sorry!" Mira scrambled out of the bed, bare legs flashing as she tried to untangle herself from the sandwich of the top sheet and the duvet. "I didn't mean—"

Shane's chest constricted. Moonlight traced Mira's delicate features in silvery-blue light. Her eyes were huge. He caught her trembling hands and drew her closer.

"It's okay. I didn't hear you come in." He didn't want her to doubt he wanted her.

"I didn't mean to scare you."

He chuckled. "Is your bed not comfortable?"

"Oh, no, it's great, but…insomnia." She pushed her hair out of her face. "I'm sorry. Go back to sleep."

"I'm not sure I can now." The heady smell of her skin filled his nostrils, sending his heart into overdrive. His gaze dipped to her bare legs, and he smiled in the dark. "You forget your pants?"

"I was warmer than I thought I'd be. I'm used to being a little chilly in the theater. It's cozy in here."

"It could be cozier." He drew her gently forward, and she didn't resist. He traced his lips lightly up her neck, around the shell of her ear and along her jaw, seeking out her lips in the dark. She softened, allowing him entrance into her sweet mouth, dragging him closer. She slid her arms around him, raking her fingers through his hair. He breathed her in—she was like a drug, sweet, cloying smoke filling his lungs and head until his limbs were heavy.

He sat on the edge of the bed and moaned as Mira climbed onto his lap and twined her legs around his waist. Her nails scraped lightly down his bare back—he didn't wear a shirt to sleep—and she nipped his bottom lip. He flinched in surprise and grinned. He hadn't taken Mira for the feisty sort.

Gathering the hem of her T-shirt, he drew it

up slowly, exposing her belly and chest, then her breasts. When her breathing stuttered, he paused.

"If you want me to stop, tell me."

"Don't you dare stop." She pulled off the shirt, and finally, they were skin to bare skin.

MIRA LOVED SHANE'S BODY, the broad muscles of his shoulders, the crisp-haired expanse of his chest. He lifted her easily, turning them over in bed so she lay on the sheets while he kissed her tenderly, lips moving lower, across her collarbone and shoulder before skimming hot breath over her breast and taking a nipple into his mouth.

She squirmed as heat blossomed in her chest and along her inner thighs. She wasn't a virgin, but she might as well have been. Her college boyfriend, Tom, had been a selfish lover, and not particularly skilled. Shane was something else. A man with experience, who knew himself, knew women's bodies and wasn't afraid to use finesse. The exquisite attention he applied had all thoughts fleeing from her mind.

His teeth grazed the sensitive flesh on the underside of her breast, and she arched into him with a gasp. His tongue trekked down to her navel until he snagged the waistband of her panties, drawing them down past her thighs, her knees, and leaving them somewhere around her ankles. As his mouth traced the vee of her pelvic bones, she panted.

She delved her fingers into his hair and tugged. “I want you so bad—”

“Soon, sweetheart. I just want…this…” And then his kisses descended, and Mira opened for him with a half-gasped cry.

Pleasure spiraled upward, taking her to dizzying, breathtaking heights. And still Shane didn’t stop, his focus singular and riveted on her most intimate heart. Her muscles tensed, stretched taut.

“Come for me,” Shane growled. “I want to feel you come.”

It seemed too indulgent, too selfish for her to let go, to let that happen. But Shane didn’t give her much choice. A strum of nerves, the targeted assault right *there* had her suddenly clamping down hard, as waves of ecstasy slammed up against her like a surging tide pounding the rocks.

He climbed over her, kissing his way up her body. She reached bonelessly for him in the dark, gathering him close as they joined bodies. They sighed together, letting their hearts set the rhythm of their lovemaking.

Mira’s mind emptied of thought, running like the last few inches of a film reel—blank except for the hiccups of imperfect sound and light flashing across a silvery canvas as it spooled and wound tight around the core of her. Heat and friction and Shane’s night-dark eyes became all she could focus on. And as he climaxed, shuddering above her, she could only think of one thing.

La Fin.

The end. Of her, of who she'd been before this encounter. Things would never be the same after this.

CHAPTER TWENTY

THE MORNING AFTER came with alarming speed. Shane had thought there'd be an opportunity to sleep in, to relax with a cup of coffee, to gaze at Mira's soft curves bathed in morning sunlight. He hadn't planned on anything more than that when they'd finally gone to sleep, his arm around her bare waist, her fragrant hair tickling his nose. It felt like the first time he'd allowed himself a slow perusal of any woman he'd ever been with.

Instead, his phone blared a loud, discordant note that had him practically leaping out of bed. He groped for the cell and jabbed blindly at the answer button. "'Lo?"

"Shekhar, you sound terrible. Are you sick?"

"Amma." He shook the cobwebs out of his head and fell back on the edge of the bed. He glanced at the clock—it wasn't quite eight in the morning. Worry furrowed through him—his mother rarely called unless something was wrong. "What's going on? Is everyone all right?"

"We're fine. We're on the road, on our way to see you."

His spine straightened. "What?"

"Your father had a hankering to go fishing, so he left Sanjay in charge of the shop. We left Brooklyn about an hour and a half ago, and we're on the road to Everville. You know he never leaves the shop on weekends, but ever since Priti's party and the way you talked about staying in town, he's been daydreaming." She paused as the garbled sounds of his father's voice came through. "He says he needs you to find out if that guy who took him out on his charter boat years ago is still around. His name's Ben or Bill or something. He can't remember." She made a noise of disbelief and admonished him in Hindi.

All of Shane's good feelings drained out of him, but they were instantly replaced by guilt. "Are you planning on staying long?" He glanced at Mira, whose eyes had cracked open. She watched him warily.

"Well, we don't want to overstay our welcome, but if you'll have us, it'll save us the cost of the motel."

"Of course you will stay here." He bit back a curse. "But I have a lot of work to do, so I'm not sure I'll be a good host."

"You don't have to host us. We know our way around town." He could hear her joy. "I'm just so glad your father's taking some time off. He's been working too hard. It's not good for his heart, not to mention his leg."

"Yeah." Shane rubbed his forehead. "I'm just getting up now."

"It's late for you, isn't it? You don't have a woman over, do you?" she teased.

His cheeks heated, and he glanced at Mira again. She'd pushed up to a sitting position and was reaching for her T-shirt. "I'll see you in a couple of hours."

"Your parents?" Mira asked.

"They decided to surprise me with a visit. My father loves fishing." It sounded like the lamest kind of excuse to get a one-night stand out of his house.

Mira's expression remained neutral as she pushed the duvet off. "I'd better get going."

"You don't have to."

"Not sure how you'd explain me when your parents arrive."

"I'd tell them you're a friend. Someone I'm working closely with."

She looked away. "I'm going to brush my teeth and get dressed. Will you have enough time to drop me off at the theater?"

"Seriously, Mira, it's not a big deal." In fact, he *wanted* her to stay to meet his parents. She was a part of the town and its history, a woman he respected and whom his parents would approve of. Hardworking, dedicated, passionate, intelligent. Shy, maybe, but they'd appreciate that, too.

"I can walk if I have to," she said as if she hadn't heard him. "It's not that far."

"I'll drive you." She wasn't sticking around. She was making that clear. And he knew he shouldn't push her, but last night's magic was fizzling out too fast for his liking.

Maybe she hadn't enjoyed it. Maybe she was regretting it. He thought he'd pleased her—had it been an act? No. Mira was many things, but she wasn't a faker.

"Can we talk?" he asked when she'd returned from the bathroom, fully dressed once more in her uniform of black jeans and black T-shirt.

She held herself still like a deer who sensed she stood in a hunter's crosshairs.

"Last night…was amazing." He took her clammy hands in his. "I want more with you."

Her blue eyes were so pale in the early-morning light they reminded him of turquoise beads, the pupils wide and dark. She glanced away from him as color crept up her neck. "I would like that, too."

He nearly did a double take. She'd been so skittish with him up to now he'd expected her to retreat, to tell him they shouldn't be involved. "But…?" he probed, looking for the caveat.

"But nothing. You should spend time with your family and I really do have to get back to town to clean up, do some work and talk to Maya. I didn't even look at the receipts to see how we did. And all that stuff with Riley Lee Jackson…" She blew out a breath. "I'll have to apologize. I didn't want to freak out like that."

"You didn't freak out. You were caught off guard. It was a perfectly natural reaction."

She lifted her shoulder again, dismissing the excuse. It seemed she'd never believe her feelings were valid.

And how is all your scheming going to help with that? You slept with her, and eventually, you'll be tearing down her grandfather's theater. Her home. She'll never trust anyone again.

"Drive me to town and I'll buy you a coffee," Mira said, interrupting his gloomy thoughts. "You'll probably need to pick up groceries and stuff, too, if your parents are staying with you."

"Good idea." The domesticity of the moment struck him as both odd and comforting. Was it chauvinistic of him to like the thought of Mira as the little woman of the house?

After a quick shower, he drove her into town, where she bought him his promised coffee, then he dropped her off at the Crown. The old building didn't look quite so foreboding in the daylight with the boards off the doors.

"Can I take you to dinner tonight?" he asked before she exited the car.

"What about your parents?"

"My parents will likely want to rest. Dad will get here, gear up and be off in a shot. Mom's not a fisherman by any stretch, but she'll keep him company on the water. They'll make a full day of it, get dinner in town and probably stay overnight."

"I guess that answers my next question," she said shyly. He raised an eyebrow in inquiry. "Should I come over again tonight?"

He grinned broadly. "I've got a better idea. I'll come to you."

MIRA SPENT THE day half floating, half weighted down.

Cleaning up the Crown was easier than she thought—the boys came around as promised and got the auditorium spic and span, or as clean as it was going to get, and all without Shane watching over them. There was no point in doing too thorough a job—who knew if the theater would ever be open again?

It was that singular thought that made her dread her conversation with Maya. Spending the night with Shane hadn't changed her mind about saving the Crown: she still wanted to keep the theater—she just didn't want to reopen to the public.

When she'd gone to bed, she'd been uncertain about selling, but with Shane's parents' early-morning call, she was reminded that the simple bliss of waking up in his arms in his pretty rented house was a temporary thing. He would eventually go back to his life in Brooklyn. They could never have white picket fences—being together meant she'd be reminded daily that she'd given up her grandfather's legacy. And if she let go of the Crown, she'd be giving up the only thing that made her life stable and safe. She might never reopen, but she wasn't going to sell, either.

She bought coffees and croissants and headed to Maya's consignment shop on Main Street. The bell above the door jingled, and the shop owner looked up from her laptop at the desk. "Hey, there you are!" She went and hugged her. "Yesterday was fantastic. Did you see the news this morning?" She gleefully pulled her toward the desk and spun the laptop around. "Riley Lee Jackson's already put something up on his webpage. Look." She scrolled down and hit Play on a video.

Mira stared with a mixture of awe and horror as the handsome A-list actor faced the screen. He was standing outside the Crown under the marquee, talking about the importance of independent theaters, the history of the Crown and why it should be saved. He ended the three-minute video by pointing people to a crowdfunding website for the Save the Crown campaign.

"The video went up this morning. It already has fifty thousand hits, and the campaign has made over twelve thousand dollars."

Mira's jaw dropped. Blood rushed up into her skull. "But...but...why?"

Maya grinned. "I think you underestimate the power of celebrity. People care about stuff like this. At least, they care about some of the incentives Riley's offering. For ten bucks, he's offering ballots for a chance to win a tour of the *Infinite Destinies* sequel set. It adds up quick, and on top of that, people feel like they're donating to a worthy cause."

Mira tasted something sour in her mouth. They didn't care about the Crown—they just wanted to be closer to Riley Lee Jackson.

She knew she should be grateful—twelve thousand dollars was a lot of money. But with her newfound doubts, she couldn't, in good conscience, accept that cash.

"We made just enough last night to break even," Maya went on. "So I'm thinking we should have another movie night, keep the momentum going."

"Maya..." Mira held up a hand. "I don't know about this."

The shop owner tilted her head to one side. "What do you mean? Isn't this what you wanted?"

She sucked in her lip. "It's what my grandfather always wanted. But..." She trailed off at the sight of Maya's disappointment. "I don't know that this is sustainable. People came out because it was supposed to be a one-off thing."

"But it won't be a one-off thing now. If you run regular shows—"

"We broke even, you said. But you were the one who applied for the licenses. Did you get your money back?"

Maya's smile broadened but her eyes slid away. "I just want to see the Crown back in use. And I'd like to see you happy."

Shane had said the same thing. He wanted to see her happy. Why did everyone think she needed their help to be happy? Didn't they think she knew herself, knew what was best for her, knew how to make herself happy?

Maya shifted. "Listen, I'm not going to pressure you or anything. I was happy to help because I believe in you and this theater, but I'll back off if that's what you want. Sit on it for now. Riley's campaign has just begun and will draw more attention. We'll see if we can make the crowdfunding goal and work from there, okay?"

Mira nodded mutely. All she could think about was how much she didn't want this, even if she *should*; even if it was what she'd set out to do in the first place.

She shook her head. Maybe she *didn't* know what she wanted for herself.

"So where did you go last night?" Maya asked with a hint of a smirk. "The boys told me you left with Shane."

"I didn't want to stay here with everyone still hanging around."

"You guys an item?"

She pursed her lips. "No." Skeptical amusement lit Maya's eyes, and Mira blurted, "We just had sex."

"I knew there was something between you two!" Maya grinned hugely and gave her a friendly shoulder punch. "I don't need details, but I have to know—how are you guys getting along? Or are you sleeping together out of hatred?"

"No! I mean, I hated him to start. Well, not really *hated*. We just have different goals." She stopped herself. Except for Janice, she'd never really talked to another woman about her personal life, and even then, she kept her darkest thoughts private. Something about Maya made her want to unburden herself.

"So, it was a one-night stand?"

"I don't know." Mira shifted uncomfortably, embarrassed she was even talking about Shane in those terms. They sounded so…unromantic.

Maya hummed in thought. "So, what does this mean for the Crown?"

"I'm trying not to think about it."

"Is he still encouraging you to sell?"

"No. I mean, he hasn't since…" She couldn't remember. She'd admitted her feelings about reopening, but he hadn't taken advantage of those doubts.

Maybe it was all part of the long game. She hated that she was still looking for deception from him after their night together, but it seemed she'd never shake that need to protect herself, to rationalize every emotion and tender feeling from another person. Even now, she was trying to figure out what Shane's angle was. After all, he'd been the one who'd suggested she get up in front of all those people and cameras and thank everyone for coming. And he'd been in on the surprise celebrity appearance. Perhaps he'd been trying to shock her into a panic attack and drive her into making a hasty decision. He'd achieved one of those things, yet hadn't followed through on that logic. She eyed Maya and asked, "Did he say anything to you about Riley Lee Jackson's visit? Like, suggest it was a good idea?"

"No, I arranged all of that. I didn't tell him until the day before the open house, and I don't think he believed me, either. Frankly, it wasn't a sure thing Riley would make it, considering his filming schedule. We even had a pretaped video ready in case he got stuck on set. Why?"

"No reason. Thank you for everything you've done. Really." She felt bad that she hadn't appreciated all the effort Maya had put into helping her save her grandfather's theater. Had she even acknowledged her in her mumbled thank-you speech? "Even if things don't go our way, I want you to know I'm more than grateful for all you've done."

Sadness tinged Maya's smile. "I know how jarring change can be. Life just keeps rolling on, and if we don't move with it, we get left behind. I'll admit, the condo project could mean a lot for the town, but we have to preserve something of the culture and history of Everville. Besides, it's important to you. That counts for something."

They agreed to meet later that week, after Mira had more time to consider another movie showing, and then she headed to the grocery store. She hadn't seen much of Arty over the past couple of weeks. After catching him kissing Janice during *Casablanca*, she had a good idea why.

She found him stocking apples—an early harvest, as they were small but bright and crisp-looking. He whistled as he carefully piled them on the table, rolling one over his fingers and juggling it so it bounced off his elbow before bumping it into the air and catching it behind his back with his other hand.

"Mira." He tossed the apple at her. She barely caught it. "How are you this beautiful morning?"

"Not as good as you, apparently." She couldn't help laughing. She'd never seen Arty so happy. Lines radiated from his mouth as if smiling had cracked the plaster cast of his frowning visage and wreathed him in newfound joy. "I saw you with Janice at the theater yesterday."

"*Casablanca* was always one of our favorites," he said, grinning. "How did things go last night? Heard there was some excitement with that pirate from that movie in town."

She related everything that'd happened, and gave him a rundown of the receipts. He took it in thoughtfully, reverting to business mode as he set the apples aside. "This internet crowdfunding thing...you think this Riley Jackson fella can drum up the kinds of funds you'd need to get the theater fixed up?"

Mira bit her lip. She pulled out her phone and checked the crowdfunding website. In the time it'd taken her to go from Maya's to Arty's, the campaign had made another five thousand dollars. Her insides flashed hot then cold. "It could..." she said a touch reluctantly. "Though I haven't figured out how much it would cost to fix *everything*."

"No?" Arty tilted his head. "Funny. I thought maybe you had those numbers tucked away in your head, if not on paper."

"I've had to fix a lot of stuff and get quotes for jobs, and things just keep breaking down. But I've no idea what the total cost would be." The electrical alone would be tens of thousands, not to mention restoring the facade *and* the interior.

"Maybe the question you should be asking yourself is what the long-term use for the place would be. Then you could restore it with that in mind. I hear some folks wouldn't mind turning it back into a stage theater."

If that happened, there'd be people at the Crown all the time, rehearsing, building sets, wrecking the place… The thought made her cringe. What was wrong with her? Was she so introverted, so insular, so antisocial that the idea of her building being used for its intended purpose actually made her sick?

She thought about her actual goal. She'd always told herself she would reopen for Grandpa's sake, but what did that mean? Did it mean restoring the Crown to its former glory? Did it mean upgrading everything so it could compete with the theater in Welksville?

Truthfully, she'd always thought of it as an unattainable goal, a "One day, someday, I'll do this" type of promise, like writing the great American novel. Now she was starting to realize that was her excuse for not doing anything significant—why she tended to play on the fly wire rig, set up elaborate traps for trespassers and work in the garden instead of getting any real repairs done.

But that would change now, wouldn't it? If the crowdfunding campaign succeeded, she could get everything fixed. She could keep that promise to Grandpa.

Dread carved a tiny bowl in her gut and it slowly filled.

Arty watched her carefully. "You don't seem too happy about this."

She forced her lips to curl upward. "Everything's happened so fast is all."

"Change does feel that way." He patted her

shoulder. "I know your grandpa Jack would be proud, no matter what you decided to do."

"Yeah..." Her thoughts took a U-turn toward Shane and what would happen if the Save the Crown campaign actually reached its goal. He wouldn't be happy—he might even lose his job.

But that wasn't her problem, was it? They might have had sex, but that didn't make him her boyfriend or anything.

He was temporary. He'd eventually leave Everville, and if he did visit again—well, Mira wouldn't mind seeing him. It was a pretty neat arrangement.

Unless he didn't forgive her and never came back. She swallowed thickly. The thought of losing Shane didn't appeal to her at all.

CHAPTER TWENTY-ONE

"YOU NEED TO move on this."

"Laura—"

"You're running out of time," Shane's manager said. "Why the hell didn't you mention freaking Riley Lee Jackson would be spearheading this campaign to save that shoddy old building?"

"I didn't know," he said. "I only found out the night of the open house."

"Well, that campaign has taken off. A million-dollar goal and they're more than halfway there barely twelve hours in. Do you have any idea how this will affect investors?"

Shane winced. No one wanted to back an unpopular project or take on a world-famous A-list actor. Most of Riley Lee Jackson's fans didn't know or care that the Crown was just an ugly, abandoned building, but they'd back him because of who he was, for a chance to be a part of something he cared about. And slowly, they'd take on his cause, too. People already hated condos; the last thing Shane and Sagmar needed was a reputation for being the company who made the handsome and dashing Riley Lee Jackson lose a fight.

Investors would drop their support like a red-hot cinder if people started associating the Sagmar brand with evil corporate greed, even if that wasn't what they stood for.

"You have to talk to the mayor again, see what she and the others on the board are thinking. All the money in the world won't help Ms. Bateman if the rezoning goes through."

"Mayor Welks has been pretty adamant that we not be seen talking with each other," Shane said. And he knew now that Cheyenne was right. This was a close-knit community, and any canoodling with interested parties could be misinterpreted.

He wondered how many people had noticed him and Mira canoodling and whether that gossip would get back to Laura.

"Well, figure something else out to convince them to rezone. Have you learned anything else about Ms. Bateman?"

He'd learned a lot. She preferred old classic movies over summer blockbusters. She was a hard-core film critic, a bona fide expert. She liked gardening and swinging from dangerous stage riggings. She knew her own mind and didn't like the public eye on her. She was quiet and thoughtful, which some mistook for unfriendly and closed off—she simply preferred her own company and that of a select and honored few.

And she tasted like popcorn butter and maraschino cherries. And her skin felt like warm water over white velvet. And when she gasped in pleasure, it made every muscle in his body tighten.

"She's a woman of her own convictions," he replied casually.

"I mean do you have something we can use against her." Laura huffed in exasperation. "I'm disappointed, Shane. You were always a closer. Considering the personal investment you've made in this project, I'm surprised you haven't worked harder to seal the deal."

He ground his jaw, rubbing the knot forming at the base of his skull. "This is a much more delicate situation than I anticipated. The community has banded together to help Mira—Ms. Bateman out."

"The community doesn't always know what's best," Laura said plainly. "C'mon, this isn't your first rodeo. Everyone bitches about condos lowering property values, but that's never been the case. When that high-speed rail deal is announced, people will be begging us to get shovels in the ground. You think a decrepit theater is going to stop change from happening? Even Riley Lee Jackson can't stop this project. But you need to put your ass in gear and get the town council to do something."

"And what, exactly, do you propose?"

"Eminent domain."

Shane flinched. Getting the Everville town council to seize Mira's private property for the purposes of bettering the community was so against his values, and what the town stood for, it made him ill to think about it. "They wouldn't go for that."

"They would if they knew about the high-speed rail project."

"We can't divulge that information. Besides being highly questionable as a business ethics issue, these folks are already clinging to what they have. We start telling them about the train lines, they'll circle the wagons around the whole damn town."

"I think you overestimate the community's interest. Everywhere I've ever been, people learn to accept change, or at least resign themselves to it. Your email about the zoning meeting said it was mostly older folks who were there to hear themselves talk."

He grimaced. He had said that. He hadn't been impressed by anyone's deputation, except maybe Mira's, and he got the sense that the zoning board had their minds made up. The delay had been Cheyenne's way to give the theater the goodbye it deserved—that'd been his reading of the situation, anyhow. "That doesn't mean they won't fight."

"They can fight all they want, but Cheyenne Welks is smart. If Everville really is 'the town that endures'—" she quoted the town's motto "—then she knows that the condo project must go ahead. And the town will accept it once the deal is done."

"You don't think the mayor will change her mind if the project becomes unpopular? It could lose her the next election."

"I think people have short memories. I think humans are only ever looking for the next shiny new thing. I think old folks eventually die and the newer generation values nostalgia without wanting to bear the burden of reality." The most cynical side of Laura was always difficult to listen to, but it was what had earned her a management position. "Eminent domain, Shane. We do it now while the price of the Crown property is low."

Shane drummed his fingers against his thigh. He knew she was right. If the price for the Crown shot up to its estimated projected value, the cost of the condo would skyrocket and he'd never be able to afford that unit he wanted more than ever. His time in Everville and his parents' visit had solidified that deepest wish. They looked so relaxed and happy here. He couldn't deny them a place in town upon retirement.

But getting town council to declare eminent domain would force Mira out of her home. She'd be well compensated, but where would it leave the two of them? He'd worked so hard to gain her trust, to open her up to him emotionally.

"I'm not sure I'm comfortable using that tactic," he said honestly.

"Well, if you're not, we can send someone else to do the job. You can enjoy the rest of your vacation and then…we'll see where things go from there."

Her crisp tone made her words an unmistakable threat, and one Shane did not appreciate. "You don't need to do that."

"Are you sure? Because if I recall, you were the one who said Everville deserved this kind of investment. We could've moved the project to Welksville, but you insisted, and the senior partners listened."

Shane rubbed the back of his neck. When he'd first joined Sagmar, he'd talked over her to keep the project in the small town despite her objections. She was still sore about it, and he didn't really blame her—she was his manager, and he'd undermined her. She went on, "If the welfare of the town means anything to you, you know what the right thing to do is."

Yeah, he knew. A dark cloud hung over him as he considered his options.

SHANE WAS QUIET. Pensive. Mira supposed she understood—she was still feeling a little stunned and shy about the night they'd spent together, but she was happy in his company, too. Content in a way she'd never experienced.

Well, not *entirely* content. She allowed herself a private smile as a thrill pulsed through her.

She'd changed the sheets on her futon and cleaned her room in case they came back to the theater for dessert, as she would suggest. She'd even found her one cute matching set of lingerie to wear tonight. Just thinking about it made her squirm, though simply holding Shane's hand had an effect on her lady bits, too. At a different point in her life, she would have been disgusted by how pathetically needy and starved for sex she was, but it didn't matter just then—she felt as though she could fly.

"Where are we going for dinner?" she asked a touch nervously.

"Actually, after our first date, I thought it'd be nice if it was just you and me and a picnic basket down by Silver Lake."

She blinked, feeling warm and fuzzy inside. "You packed a picnic?"

"To be fair, Arty did. He seemed to know what you'd like. All your favorites are in there, apparently. I haven't sneaked a peek, so it'll be interesting to see what you like."

"I'm not *that* hard to please."

He raised an eyebrow, and she sighed. "Okay, so I gave you a hard time with all those platters and chocolates and things. Not without good reason."

He lapsed into silence once more as they drove past the beach by the lake. Families and groups of teens lingered by the water, playing in the cool surf and enjoying the sun and sweet summer breeze.

Mira grew tense at the sight of the crowds, but Shane kept driving. "Don't worry, we're not stopping there. I bumped into Chris Jamieson at the grocery, and he told me about a secret little place by the lake that would be much more private."

The way he said it sent shivers down her spine. They parked, and instead of taking the trail that would lead them to the edge of the beach, they went down a barely there path through the trees. Mira wasn't much of an outdoorsperson, and the hike seemed to take forever. Ten minutes later, though, as the view opened into a sheltered cove, she realized it was totally worth it. No one was around. The place was pristine. Shane laid a blanket beneath a big willow tree and set the basket down.

"I feel like I'm about to open Pandora's box," he said as he eyed the basket. "What if you like pineapples on your pizza?"

Mira made a face. "Pineapple? Gross."

Shane laughed. "Whew. Okay, at least we made it past that deal breaker."

He took out containers of ready-made items from the grocery's take-out counter, and Mira grinned. Arty really did know all her favorites, but of course, he'd been delivering them to her for years. Bean salads, chicken and pasta, breads and dips and her favorite herbed cheese spread.

She couldn't afford them regularly, but when she could, Arty always treated her to an extra helping.

"Cheetos?" He pulled out the big bag of bright orange cheese snacks.

"Only on my birthday," she clarified. "But you've seen my fridge. Frankly, I can't be bothered to cook most days."

"I guess you don't have the facilities to make anything elaborate, either."

"No," she laughingly agreed. "Grandpa taught me to cook a few things, though. And I actually made myself a lot of food when I was still living with my parents. Following instructions on mac and cheese boxes was crucial to survival."

When Shane next spoke, there was a catch in his voice. "What'd your grandfather cook?"

"A lot of pasta. Spaghetti, mostly, but now and again he'd make lasagna. Arty and Janice would come over sometimes, too, and we'd do a potluck. I'd make grilled cheese sandwiches and they'd bring fancier stuff." She blinked, thinking back on those memories. "Weird. I haven't thought about that in a long time."

"You and your grandfather didn't both live in the theater, did you?"

"Oh, no, though you wouldn't know it considering how much time we spent at the Crown. Grandpa had a place, but after he died..." She cleared her throat. "I had to make a choice. There were bills to pay. But I couldn't sell the theater."

"So…that's why you live there?"

She wasn't sure about the hesitancy in his voice. "You know why I live there."

His smile was tentative. "I thought maybe you had an apartment in town and chose to sleep over."

She wasn't sure why he was asking these questions…or maybe she did. "How are your parents?"

"Good. They'll probably be out for dinner, though. I thought they'd need me to play host, but they're really at home in Everville. Mom can find her way around any kitchen, and Dad is so focused on fishing he won't care what he eats as long as he catches a few fish." He regarded her. "You should meet them. My mother worked in film production in India. I bet she could tell you all kinds of stories about Bollywood."

She paused. "That'd actually be nice."

"Really?" He blinked. "I thought you'd flat out say no."

She understood his reaction—she wasn't exactly a social butterfly. "India has a rich and thriving movie industry. I'd love to talk to your mom. Maybe she'd be willing to do an interview for one of the online publications I write for."

"I'll ask. We can have lunch together tomorrow and you can meet them."

Already they'd planned a third date. And she was meeting his parents. Though she didn't feel too uncomfortable about it, it struck her as perhaps a little too intimate. "I don't want to impose." She pursed her lips. Shane had said his parents were only there for the weekend. It wasn't as if they'd want to spend time with some stranger who was making their son's job harder.

"I wouldn't have asked if I thought for a second it was a bad idea. Mom loves talking about the old days. She'd love you."

But do you *love me?* She'd had no designs on Shane, no thoughts toward anything more serious than a fling. But her heart clung to hope like a fist around a handful of sand.

They ate quietly, enjoying the breeze that stirred the curtain of willow fronds around them. Shane checked his watch and said, "I actually thought we could go to the theater in Welksville. There's an evening show of a movie I've wanted to see…"

Mira wanted to say no. She liked spending time with Shane alone, out of the public eye. Besides, she'd never been to the theater in Welksville—going there would feel like she was betraying her grandfather.

But she saw the hopeful look in Shane's eyes and found herself saying, "Sounds great."

They were back on the road within the hour and got to the theater in Welksville with more than half an hour to spare. Mira stared up at the colossal building plunked down in the center of an enormous parking lot. Posters advertising coming attractions that spanned two stories hung from the lip of the roof. Shane parked, and she stared up at the marquee. There were fifteen big-screen digital auditoriums, nine of which were showing films in 3-D. There was even an IMAX auditorium.

"There." He pointed at a title for a critically acclaimed movie that had been released earlier in the year. "Let's go."

As they walked in, Mira was assaulted by noise and lights and the vastness of the space. Giant prop spaceships hovered above the enormous concession stand in the center of the main lobby. A café, bar and arcade resided in the wide-open space. Escalators led to a second unseen level where Mira imagined most of the auditorium entrances were.

The place was mostly empty just then—a lot of the more recent popular films had started an hour ago—but the cacophony of constantly playing previews on screens placed everywhere, the flashing digital movie poster displays, the arcade's chaos and the music blaring from the bar made the whole place frenetic with activity.

Shane got the tickets and ordered a ridiculously large bucket of popcorn, along with two gallon-size drinks and a bag of candy as big as her face. Her eyes grew huge at the cashier's total.

"Thirty bucks for popcorn and candy?" Grandpa had never charged more than five.

"They're refillable," Shane said with a smirk.

She shook her head as they headed for their auditorium.

It was supposedly one of the smaller theaters in the building, but it was more than double the size of the Crown's auditorium. She fell back in the plush, roomy seat. There was enough space for her to stretch out her legs, even. No bruised knees to be had here. Then Shane pulled up the armrest dividing their two seats and pressed closer to her. "Love seats," he said, and she laughed.

"I didn't realize this was something people wanted in their moviegoing experience."

"You didn't expect me to keep my hands off you while we sat in the dark, did you?"

"Sorry to disappoint you, but I go to the theater to enjoy the movies," she teased.

She devoured nearly half the bucket of popcorn while watching the preshow slides and commercials playing on the screen. They had nearly the same picture quality as the high-end projector Shane had brought her, though the surround sound of the theater was much better. And this wasn't even the real show. When the curtains around the screen drew back to accommodate the wide-screen picture, Mira slowly felt her heart sinking.

No hissing or popping or lines or unfocused pictures. No banging a projector to make the color balance straighten out. The picture was crisp and clear, the sound immaculate. The latest in digital projection, she reminded herself. She spent the whole hour and forty minutes spiraling down into depression.

The Crown could never compete with this. Not even if she got twice the crowdfunding goal.

It was time to face the facts: her grandfather's legacy would never survive.

CHAPTER TWENTY-TWO

THE MOVIE HADN'T held Shane's attention as he thought it would, but that was mostly because of the woman next to him. He'd held her hand throughout, but nothing more—she hadn't made any move to be intimate with him in the nearly empty theater. He might have initiated, but they weren't horny teenagers. He had manners and control.

Besides, she seemed to be enjoying the film. Or at least she'd watched it more closely than he had.

They didn't say much as they left the theater. He'd started the night on the pensive side—he was still mulling over Laura's demand that he get town council to expropriate the Crown. It meant they were skipping on offering Mira an even better deal for the property. He wasn't sure that was the best idea—using eminent domain to seize the Crown could end up costing Sagmar even more than a buyout would, especially if anyone on the town council learned about the high-speed rail line. But he didn't want to contradict Laura again. Going over her head in the first place to get the project approved had been bad office politics. And spending all this time in town and involving himself with Mira was putting his job in jeopardy, regardless of the fact that he was technically on vacation.

He was on rocky ground with Laura and Sagmar. But he was finally on smoother roads with Mira. He glanced at her as they drove back to town. She was staring out the window into the dark. The roads between Welksville and Everville were well lit, though not much thrived here now. That would change soon. The high-speed rail line would bring a lot of new developments to this part of the county. It could save the small towns in the area from extinction.

"How'd you like the movie?" he asked.

"It wasn't bad, though a bit derivative. It takes after an Italian film done about fifteen years ago."

"I had no idea."

"This wasn't as bad as some remakes. I can find the original for you, if you like."

"Thanks." He wasn't sure he'd watch it, but sometimes the originals were better.

He pulled up outside the Crown. The marquee was lit and the lights in the lobby had been left on, giving the theater a warm, cheerful glow. Lighting made such a huge difference when it came to big buildings like this, but it didn't hide the fact that it was the lone holdout on a deserted block. The empty department stores flanking the theater remained as forlorn as ever. They'd be torn down soon for the first stage of construction.

"Would you like to come in for coffee?" she asked. "I know your parents might be waiting up for you. I don't want to presume..."

He grinned. "I'm a big boy, but you're sweet for thinking of them. Let me give my folks a call to let them know I'll be out past curfew." It wouldn't keep *Amma* from sticking her nose in his business, or *Baba* from interrogating him about his whereabouts, but he didn't want them to worry.

Mira went in ahead of him while he made the call. His mother picked up. "We were starting to worry. Your father and I are back at the house. Where are you?"

"Out with a friend."

"A lady friend?"

"Yes, in fact," he said, beaming. "Her name's Mira. Miriam. She's the owner of the theater I'm trying to buy."

Silence. "Shekhar...you're not trying to bamboozle this girl, are you?"

Bamboozle? "No. How can you say that?" He felt as if she'd slipped a cold damp cloth over him while he burned with a fever, and he shuddered. He was affronted and uncomfortable and a little sick all at once. He cleared his throat. "In fact, she wants to meet you. I told her about how you used to work in Bollywood. She's a film critic for a bunch of websites. I thought we could do lunch together. I'll make spaghetti."

Another hesitation. It was uncharacteristic of his mother to be so reticent. After all, he was telling her he wanted to bring a woman to meet her. She should have been jumping for joy.

"You cooking something more than peanut butter sandwiches? This girl must be pretty special," his mother teased. And yet, a note of doubt hung in her tone.

"She is," he said without thinking. He really did want his parents to meet Mira.

"All right. I'll tell your father. We were going to leave early but delaying our trip home by a couple of hours won't make much difference."

Shane hung up and hurried into the theater, grinning. He found Mira making coffee in her office/bedroom. The futon had been pulled out into its bed form, and he arched an eyebrow saucily.

She looked up, cheeks pinkening. "All's well?"

"I told them where I am like a good son would. And they said they'd love to meet you for lunch tomorrow."

She nodded and glanced back at the brewing pot. Shane slid in behind her and wrapped his arms around her waist. She was trembling.

You're not trying to bamboozle this girl, are you? His mother's words echoed. The way Mira made him feel, the way he felt for her… It wasn't an act. It wasn't him manipulating her. He wanted what was best for her and for everyone. That was all.

He buried his nose in her hair and breathed deep, kissing the tip of her ear. She shivered, turned her head slightly and leaned into him.

"You okay?" he asked.

She chuckled nervously. "I've never had a man here before. It's not the nicest place to stay overnight. I mean, if you do stay." She bit her lip. "My futon is lumpy and old and probably smells funny. The shower's in the janitor's closet—I attached a showerhead to the old spigot that's used for the mop bucket. And this place is really drafty—"

"I can manage."

"It's also… It was the space my grandfather inhabited, you know? He lived and died here. I've always felt as though he's watched over me here. It just feels kind of weird, you being here with me."

"We don't have to do anything. If you'd rather just watch a movie or go to bed…"

"I only want to go to bed if you're in it," she said, turning in his arms and snagging the front of his shirt. A mix of doubt and wickedness flickered across her face. "I mean, if you can stand being here."

Shane grinned slowly. All doubts vanished as their mouths came together.

They made noisy love on the creaky futon,

driving the hollow groaning of the old, empty theater and all of Shane's misgivings away with their pleasure.

But later, as they lay in that cramped double futon, his worries returned. He had to make a choice eventually, and to him, there was only one way he and Mira could have everything. She had to give up the Crown. It wasn't safe or healthy for her to keep living here. She would earn a hefty sum on the sale of the theater and could have a nice, quiet life elsewhere, maybe even with him. And he had so much he wanted to show her and share with her...

They were good together. He'd convince her of that, no matter what it took.

SHANE'S PARENTS, NISHA and Ranjeet, were delightful. Mira had never used that word for anyone, but it was the only one she could think of to describe them as they sat with her in Shane's living room, drinking tea and eating biscuits while Shane made lunch.

Mira usually did interviews for her articles over the phone or via email, so talking to Nisha in person was a completely different experience. The woman was animated and lively and had all kinds of stories to tell about her formative years working as a manager on the set of several big Indian film productions. She showed her photos from parties she'd been to that she'd saved on her phone, pictures of her with some of India's biggest movie stars and directors. She still went back now and again to visit family and reconnect with old friends and folks in the industry.

It was her stories about meeting Ranjeet and giving it all up to come to America that fascinated Mira the most.

"He was a businessman's son, and a big technology nerd," she said. "While I was one of the first and only women working in my industry in my position. Back then, it was practically impossible for someone like me to get that kind of job so young. I'd spent years clawing my way to that position. Then Ran proposed and I left it all behind to become his wife and a mother."

"Don't sound so disappointed," Ranjeet said, slurping his tea. "I brought you to New York after all."

"Where we lived in a tiny little apartment that had rats and roaches—"

"While I built an empire—"

"While you built a small business that took *decades* to establish itself." She pinned him with a look. "Just think of the wasted four years in film school and another six fighting my way to the top, only to end up running a cash register..." There wasn't any real bitterness in Nisha's voice. Just a good-natured ribbing tone.

"Admit it, you loved every minute of it," Ran teased.

"I suppose I can't argue with steady hours and a comfy stool to let my butt get big on." She beamed at her husband. "Especially when Shane came along. That boy never stopped moving."

Mira's mind was boggled by the woman's choice. She couldn't imagine giving up her career, especially if she'd worked so hard to establish herself. She waited until Ranjeet had gotten up to go to the bathroom to ask, "Why'd you leave your job? It sounded like a dream."

"I got a new dream," she replied simply. "Ran was the love of my life. I knew being with him meant things would be very different. And I knew it would be hard to adjust to life in the States. Yes, I gave up everything that had been important to me at the time, and Ran knew it. But it was worth it. Change isn't ever easy. I couldn't imagine being without him, though."

That stuck with Mira for the rest of the afternoon, even after she and Shane said goodbye to his parents. They were heading back to Brooklyn, but before they went, Nisha told her, "It was very nice to meet you, Miriam. I hope you'll come and visit me."

She agreed. Normally, she was uncomfortable around people she'd just met, but Shane's mother was friendly without being overbearing, and she didn't seem to want anything from Mira. She didn't study her as if she was some freak at a sideshow, either.

"They really like you," Shane said as she helped him with the dishes. "That went really well."

"I thought it did, too." She regarded him thoughtfully. "Have you brought other women to meet them before?"

"No one who stuck."

Mira didn't ask, though she wondered what these other women had been like, how Shane's parents might have received them.

They finished cleaning. Mira was tired. Last night's exertions had made her a bit sore, but it'd been sharing her cramped bed with Shane that had kept her from getting a full night's sleep. She'd had the same problem the first night they'd slept together: despite his king-size bed, she wasn't used to sharing, to feeling the other person's slightest twitches. She was accustomed to being alone.

"I should probably get home," she said. "I've got a ton of work to do and I haven't watered my tomatoes in a couple of days. Poor things might've shriveled by now."

"I can help." His lips had peeled back in a rictus of a grin. She had to give him points for volunteering despite his phobia. Maybe it was an empty offer, but she knew from the look in his eyes that if she accepted, he'd do it.

"It's all right. It won't take long, and I'm sure you have other things you need to do."

He looked relieved. Something else lingered

in his eyes, though. She wasn't quite sure what it was—maybe her paranoia about overly helpful Shane was making her see things that weren't there. She needed to accept that he liked her, that his parents liked her, that maybe, just maybe, she was worthy of his love.

Not that she expected it from him. If it were love, it wasn't the kind of romantic love she saw in the movies. Not head-over-heels, happy-ever-after love. The English language wasn't adequate in describing the complexity or nuances of her feelings for Shane, or his feelings for her, she imagined.

When he dropped her off, he lingered under the marquee. "Is something wrong?"

He tapped his fists together rhythmically. "I've been meaning to talk to you about something, but I don't want you to think anything between us had anything to do with it."

A leaden weight suddenly dropped into the center of her chest. "What is it?"

He took a deep breath. "Sagmar wants to get town council to declare eminent domain on the Crown."

She sifted through his words for meaning. "I don't understand."

"It means they want to convince council to expropriate your property. They'll pay you market value for it—"

Mira stumbled back a step, as if she'd been punched. "No. No, they can't do that..."

"You said it yourself—you don't want to reopen the theater."

"That doesn't mean I'm willing to sell!" Her lungs shrank to half their size as she tried to suck in air. "When were you going to tell me this?"

"I only got the call yesterday—"

"And you thought it was okay to not tell me and sleep with me?" She forked her fingers through her hair. "How could you? Was this your plan all along? Soften me up? Make me think you actually care about me?"

"Calm down. I told you, this has nothing to do with what's between us." He said it so quietly, it hurt. She glared at him, eyes hot.

"Maybe you've convinced yourself of that, but you're only lying to yourself. God, why did I even—" She cut herself off ruthlessly. She'd been the stupid one. She should never have trusted him. "Who's coming to town to talk to council? Or have you already done that behind my back?"

"That's not fair."

"*Fair?* You think this has anything to do with what's *fair*? All this time, I bet this was in your back pocket. Of course it was—you wanted my property from the get-go. Eminent domain had to be your last resort. It's going to cost your precious company, but not as much as it would if..." She thought hard. She wasn't stupid—she'd watched enough movies to know there was always some other motivating factor to drive a man to desperate measures. But she was missing a puzzle piece—some nugget of information Shane had withheld, something that meant eminent domain would cost Sagmar less than trying to convince her to sell with a last-ditch effort.

That there were secrets like this between them bothered her, but not as much as his betrayal did.

"I swear, Mira, I didn't think Sagmar would go this route. If they'd planned to do this all along, Cheyenne and the town council wouldn't have wasted their time with a zoning hearing. I turned my world upside down trying to convince you to sell while keeping everything transparent and aboveboard. I'm sorry if I fell for you, or made you feel something for me, but those feelings had nothing to do with Sagmar or this project. I'm only doing my job."

"And doing me was just a bonus?"

His eyes flashed with pain. "That's not fair to either of us."

She hugged herself, shaking as her skin alternated between hot and cold. "So what's supposed to happen now? You going to go to the next council meeting to make some kind of case against the Crown?"

"If I don't do it, Sagmar will send someone who will. And I'll lose my job."

"So that's it. All this…fixing the roof, the

projector...your parents!" She glared. "Were they in on this?"

"Of course not. Look, I know you're upset—"

"*Upset* doesn't begin to cover it. You lied to me, manipulated me. You made me believe you cared."

Shane clenched his fists. "I *do* care. Everyone in this town cares, but you're too stubborn to see that. You think everyone's out to hurt you when all they're trying to do is help you. This building—this place is just a pile of bricks with a leaky roof over top. You're sleeping on a lumpy futon and taking showers in a janitor's closet, for God's sake. The place is falling down all around you, and costing more in taxes than rent would."

"My grandfather—"

"Your grandfather wouldn't have wanted this for you, and you know it. You're unhappy here but you won't admit it because you don't know how to be happy anywhere else. You're afraid of the world. You're afraid everyone's going to let you down and take advantage the way your parents did. You don't have any self-esteem because if you did, you would've realized you're better than this place. I'm sorry your grandfather died, but things change. You can't bury yourself in his so-called legacy just so you can be with him!"

His chest rose and fell rapidly. Mira stared at him, the fury she'd felt moments ago limp and ragged as a weathered flag after a storm. She'd been cut to ribbons by his razor-sharp remarks.

His image fractured as tears dropped from her eyes.

"Get out." She uttered it on a hot exhale past the lump in her throat. When he didn't move, she clenched her teeth. "I said go. Get out of my sight."

"Mira—"

"Just go!" She flung open the door and pulled it shut tight behind her, locking it before Shane could get to it. With the boards gone, though, she could see his anguish plain through the glass. He took two steps back, and for a frightening moment, she thought he might kick the glass in.

He didn't. She stood in the theater's vestibule between the sets of glass doors, like a fish in an aquarium, and watched as his expression settled into a cool mask. He backed away, turned on his heel and headed for his car.

Only after he was out of sight did she make her way deeper into the Crown. Into safety. Into her sanctuary. She thought about going to the roof to water her tomatoes, but she suddenly didn't have the energy to climb the ladder, much less stay on her feet. She sat in front of her laptop and stared blankly.

"Grandpa..." The theater remained silent. He wasn't here. He hadn't been here in over four years.

She was alone.

She curled into her chair, put her hands over her face and wept.

CHAPTER TWENTY-THREE

"MR. PATEL. PLEASE, sit down." Cheyenne Welks looked up from a thick file on her desk as he walked into her office at city hall. It'd been three days since his blow-up with Mira, and he'd finally convinced himself that approaching town council about claiming eminent domain on the Crown was the best course of action for everyone.

Apparently, the mayor was not impressed by this move. Her weighted gaze rested somewhere between indifference and contempt. The chair across from her was piled with folders, leaving him only a narrow ledge to perch on. He moved the folders onto the floor, but the tower toppled, creating an avalanche of paper. Cheyenne waved him off as he tried to gather the files together, just barely suppressing a sigh.

"A representative from Sagmar called me yesterday—a woman named Laura Kessler," she said. A knot of frustration tightened in his chest as his suspicions were confirmed. Laura had sent him a terse email this morning saying things were being "handled." Apparently, she didn't trust him to deal with the situation in Everville anymore. Cheyenne went on. "She told me there was a high-speed rail project in the works for Upstate New York, and that the nearest proposed stop was so close to Everville, it would, and I quote, 'Jack real estate prices sky-high.'"

Her next words were crisper than fallen leaves in November. "You never mentioned this in your presentations, Mr. Patel."

He silently cursed Laura—she was clearly too eager to get the Crown property squared away, probably so she could get a nice fat Christmas bonus, regardless of the cost of divulging that secret. Giving away highly sensitive information like that was a bad business practice all around. Then again, he'd seen Laura talk her way out of bigger trouble, especially if it meant the bottom line remained intact. She wouldn't be above blaming Shane for the leak, either. After all, he had an established relationship with the townsfolk, and an inappropriate relationship with the Crown's owner. She could rightfully say his judgment had been affected.

He rubbed his temples. Laura may have screwed him, but this was his mess. "It was in everyone's best interests that we keep those details under wraps. Sagmar has always—"

The mayor snapped a hand up as if she were swatting a fly, silencing him. Her features pulled tight as she pushed out of her chair and paced the cramped office space.

"I campaigned very hard against Fordingham and his cronies," she said. "My platform was based on transparency and fighting corruption at the municipal level. Those men made hundreds of thousands of dollars in back room deals because of investment tips like this. Do you have any idea what kind of position you and your company have put *me* in?"

Shane pressed his palms together. He had no excuses. He'd wanted to help Everville and see it thrive, but he'd known from the beginning that withholding this vital piece of information would change everything. "Please understand, I couldn't disclose this information. My intention was never to hurt anyone," he said.

"The rumor mill suggests you're too late for that." She glared down her nose at him with the scorn of a displeased mother-in-law. He squirmed.

She turned to look out the window, arms crossed over her chest. "As mayor, I have a decision to make. I could deny the rezoning of the block, save the Crown and watch the town stagnate. I could go against my ethics, not tell Miriam Bateman about the high-speed rail line and convince her to take your money and run, though I doubt that would work. Or—" she turned to face him, her red hair lit from behind like a ring of fire "—I could expropriate the theater, spend a boatload of cash the city doesn't appear to have and make myself even more unpopular with Riley Lee Jackson fans and Fordingham supporters, losing me the next election and undoing all the good I've striven to accomplish."

He hated his part in the trouble he'd caused her, but said nothing. He'd done enough damage as it was.

"Tell me something honestly." Cheyenne gripped the back of her chair and bent toward him. "Do you love her?"

"Love who?" He said it almost automatically. Again, that flickering look of contempt and utter disappointment. He'd let Cheyenne down. Let everyone down. But he had to do his job and he had to win. It didn't matter if no one else realized he was trying to help. They would understand later.

She turned her back to him, picking up a file and speaking without looking at him. "Town council will have a special meeting next Thursday to decide this matter, Mr. Patel. I expect to see you there and not beforehand."

Shane couldn't let the meeting end like this. He had come here to finalize things, and he couldn't have the sale of the Crown further delayed. He'd already screwed everything else up—it was time to win back his reputation as a closer.

He'd come to Everville to help the town. To get the Crown. To win.

He cleared his throat and sat forward. "Before

you make your decision, there's something else you need to know about the Crown…and about Miriam Bateman."

THE GYMNASIUM AT B. H. Everett was only half-full, though that shouldn't have surprised Mira. The notice of the special town council meeting had only gone out last week, and it was the first week of a sweltering August. Many townsfolk were on vacation and not particularly interested in spending an afternoon in the high school's stuffy gym. Not even Bob Fordingham was present, despite his proclaimed interest in the matter.

Her stomach churned as she took a seat. She didn't want anyone talking to her right now—she was far too nervous. She doubted she'd be given the opportunity to make one last plea for the Crown, but even if she had that chance, she wasn't sure she could get up there and beg town council to reconsider.

She kept her eyes glued to the front, refusing to look around for Shane. The tables for the council members were arranged around the lectern, which looked for all the world like a guillotine platform.

"Mira." Janice slid into the seat directly behind her and squeezed her shoulder. "Honey, are you doing all right?"

"I'm fine." She wished she had something to

fidget with. She might start tearing strips of skin off her arm otherwise.

"Arty'll be here any minute. He had to finish up some things at the store."

She nodded absently. Janice's presence wasn't irritating, exactly, but she wasn't in the mood to talk or be comforted. She just wanted this meeting to start.

It did, five agonizing minutes later. The town council members walked in together, looking slightly flustered and perhaps a little irritated to have their summer holidays interrupted. They weren't even meeting at their usual space, the Everville Tavern, so they couldn't get drinks or snacks. From what Mira knew, council had always been fairly relaxed about proceedings, which made this gathering all the more nerve-racking.

Cheyenne took the lectern, presiding over the meeting. She ran through the usual reading of minutes. The crowd grew bored very quickly, fanning themselves with greater fervor as the heat in the gym slowly suffocated them.

"I want to thank everyone for coming today. This special meeting has been called for the purposes of determining whether the Crown Theater on Main Street should be expropriated by the town for the purposes of redevelopment and rejuvenation." She didn't look up from her notes. "While the decision to rezone is a separate issue from today's venture, I was forced to call this meeting due to some new information that was passed to me regarding the future of Everville. As mayor, I had a decision to make, and in the interests of full disclosure and transparency, I decided it was my duty to share this information as soon as possible."

It took nearly ten minutes for Mayor Welks to explain the high-speed rail project that'd been proposed for the area. A station had been proposed near Welksville, making it and Everville perfect sites for commuter towns. It meant that people who couldn't afford to live in Manhattan could buy a home out here and travel to work in under two hours via an express train.

It meant Everville would be changing. It meant there'd be more people moving in. It meant there'd be new construction and more jobs. It meant the land the Crown sat on was worth more than the building itself or the memories it housed.

A buzz filled Mira's ears. It wasn't in her head, though—people were excited, nervous, apprehensive. A few were angry. The voices rose and rose, and it took the mayor an extended banging of the gavel to get everyone to settle down.

"None of these plans have been finalized," Cheyenne clarified. "But I have it on good authority that the proposal is in its final stages, and that we should be hearing about it within the next month or two. Ground won't be broken for another year or so, and the project itself may not be completed for another three to five years, if not longer. If the high-speed rail project does happen, our town is going to get a huge boost. Getting started on new housing will ensure we're capturing the first wave of new residents. And the Sagmar condo project is the perfect place to start."

"We can't allow this to happen!" Mira recognized Mrs. Abbot's shrill protest immediately. "We don't need all those people here! No one wants things to change."

"Change happens, whether we want it or not," Cheyenne snapped, and the crowd went still. "As mayor, it's my job to make sure we can roll with the changes and make the most of what comes our way. If you don't cozy to that, Kelly, then you can speak with your ballot at the next election."

At some point during the talk, Arty had come in and sat next to Janice. Mira felt his strong hand give her shoulder a little shake. "You need to speak up now if you're going to save the Crown," he said quietly.

But she didn't. Even when the floor was opened to questions, she didn't say anything. Even when Cheyenne looked her way expectantly, she said nothing. Her tongue had crawled down her throat and her whole body was shrinking into itself.

"Madame Mayor." Mira glanced up to see Maya standing amidst the audience. "Perhaps this is the least of your concerns, but what about the Save the Crown campaign? There's been significant national interest paid to the theater since the open house. Surely we'd be better off keeping the theater open for these supposed new residents to patronize? It would be a tourist attraction."

"I'm aware of the campaign and the celebrity endorsement, Ms. Hanes. Unfortunately, it has come to my attention that in order for the Crown to be brought up to code, the entirety of the electrical and plumbing systems would have to be restored. As it was, it was against regulations to have the open house and we cannot, in good conscience, allow for another event there until such upgrades are made. I've also been informed that there have been…residents living illegally within the building."

Mira felt the stares on the back of her head, and her body burned beneath the scrutiny. The mayor went on, her tone devoid of emotion. "Regardless of its historic or nostalgic value, a theater house cannot be used as a place of residency for the health and safety of the inhabitants and their neighbors. According to the bylaws, the Crown must be condemned."

Gasps and whispers echoed through the gym. It wasn't a secret that the reclusive Miriam Bateman, Jack's granddaughter, the weird girl with the dead and jailed drug addict parents, lived in the Crown. That it was being used against her now could only mean one thing—Shane had brought an official complaint to council.

Yes, it was illegal. Yes, it was unconventional and, in some people's eyes, dangerous. But it'd been her property, her choice. She'd been happy there. And she'd invited Shane, a man she had no reason to trust, into her inner sanctum.

And he'd betrayed her.

She worked on autopilot for the rest of the meeting. She barely heard Cheyenne as she read the list of building code violations the Crown had infringed upon. Then she said something about the fines being waived in favor of expropriating the Crown. Mira's vision blurred as the votes were counted. The motion passed, and she went numb. One by one, her senses shut down; her emotions drained out of her. She could no longer comprehend the world around her. She had no home. The one place she'd always felt safe was being taken from her. The one place where she could cling to her grandfather's memory was being condemned, knocked down and sold to the man who'd betrayed her.

It was a long time before she realized her hands were bleeding. Her nails had torn bloody crescents into her palms. Janice was exclaiming something as she pushed tissues into her hands. Arty was rubbing her back and cooing some words of sympathy.

The banging of the gavel brought her back sharply.

"I'll have order." Cheyenne's voice sounded rusty, but was no less forceful. The audience quieted down. "The motion has carried. Miriam Bateman, the current owner of the Crown Theater, will be allotted the market rate for her property. Ms. Bateman—" finally, Cheyenne looked her way "—I do personally regret that it has come to this. I understand how important it was for you to keep this part of Everville's history alive, but for the town to endure, we must adapt." She pushed her glasses up her nose and referred to her notes. "After numerous consultations, the council committee agreed on the price, and so it is with a heavy heart that we will be awarding you the sum of $2.5 million for your property."

The gasp that resounded through the gym sucked all the air from Mira's lungs. She hadn't heard that correctly, had she?

Arty's hand nearly crushed hers. "Oh, my God."

"Mira..." Janice's hand touched her shoulder.

But Mira couldn't say anything. Couldn't do anything.

This wasn't winning the lottery. It was losing everything.

SHANE PACED THE empty school hallway, his cell phone pressed against his ear. When Laura finally picked up, he nearly shouted, "I hope you're happy with your Christmas bonus, because it might be the last either of us get."

"You got it?" The smile in her voice made him want to punch a wall.

"Town council expropriated the Crown," he said through clenched teeth. "For two and a half million dollars."

Laura was quiet a moment. "Oh."

"'Oh'? That's all you have to say? This was what we were trying to avoid! Why did you tell the mayor about the rail project?"

"Because I had to play hardball. This is the big leagues, Shane. If I hadn't—"

"You jeopardized the whole project with your selfishness. When the investors find out what it cost to get the property—"

"Will you relax? The unit prices will all be padded accordingly. No one's going to lose money and we nipped that silly Save the Crown campaign before it reached its goal. That high-speed rail project is as good as gold." But she sounded a little less sure of herself now. Shane made a fist and banged it against a locker.

"Dammit, Laura, when I get back—"

"Don't threaten me, Shane. You nearly ruined the deal by getting personally involved with the seller. Who's to say you weren't the one who leaked the information? It'll be your word against mine." She paused, and then gave a nervous chuckle. "Just relax. The deal's done. That Podunk town won't have that kind of liquid cash to fork over to Ms. Bateman, so they'll have to sell to us. It's the only way the whole thing could've gone down. Anyhow, your girlfriend's rich now. Isn't that great? We should all be happy."

Laura didn't get it at all. Money didn't matter to Mira.

"You did a good job tonight. Go and celebrate or something. I'll be in touch to finalize the property sale." She hung up.

He stared at his cell phone. He wanted to whip it at the wall, dash it to 2.5 million little pieces. The problem was that he knew Laura was right. The unit prices wouldn't go up so much that potential buyers would shy away. There might be some tweaking to the designs to balance the books, but it wouldn't be dramatic. No, the condo would be built. People would still buy the units. Everville would change and grow. And he'd be the guy who'd helped make that happen.

A figure in black slinked out the side door, just as he'd predicted she would. He followed her as she drifted out at speed, a wraith on a mission.

"Mira," he called. But she kept walking. He called her name again as she exited, her strides lengthening until she was practically running across the hot asphalt. "Mira!"

"Leave me alone." She didn't even turn around.

Shane caught up to her and grabbed her arm, swinging her to face him. Her blotchy cheeks were wet, and she glared at him through puffy eyes.

"I did the best I could for you," he said by way of apology. But no, he had nothing to apologize for. He had 2.5 million nothings to apologize for. He straightened. "You have to understand, I couldn't say anything about the high-speed rail line. It wasn't even a sure thing. I could've gone to jail for disclosing that information to anyone who might have profited, and that means everyone in this whole town. It's not personal."

"'Not personal'?" She clutched her hands in front of her. "What does that even mean to you? You came here and...made me *feel* something for you. And like an idiot, I let myself believe—" She cut herself off sharply and turned away.

"Don't run from this. We have to talk. I did what I had to. This is my job."

"And that's all you care about. Your job, your career, the condo... It was never about *me*."

Shane stared. "How can you believe that? After everything I did—"

"You may have convinced yourself it was because you liked me, but we both know those motives were never pure. I *never* should have trusted you."

Heat suffused Shane's chest. "You've *never* trusted me! You don't trust *anyone*. You don't even try making connections with others. I was the one to reach out to you nine out of ten times."

"Keeping score. Yeah, that's real attractive." The contempt in her critical look had him squirming. "You betrayed me. You let me down. Just admit that it's always been a game for you. I was something else for you to win. Another prize on top of the Crown." She shook her head. "You know what? I don't care. You win, okay? You got everything you wanted. Now leave me alone."

"Mira—"

Something snagged his arm then, and he whirled around to find Arty Bolton and the florist, Janice Heinlein, glowering at him. "Leave her alone," Arty said. "She needs space right now."

"I have to explain things to her. She doesn't understand what I've done for her."

"Is that how you see it?" Arty shook his head in disgust. "I told you not to hurt her. I don't know why I bothered. I knew you were nothing but trouble."

Shane was fed up with the old man's judgments. "You were never keen on her living there, Arty. I just did what you couldn't and finally got her out."

"You broke her goddamned heart."

"That's the cost of doing business sometimes." He wrenched himself away, but Mira had already disappeared, melting back into the shadows.

It wasn't too hard to figure out where she'd gone.

"Mr. Patel," Janice called, huffing as she caught up to him before he got in his car. "I'm sorry about Arty. He's always been very protective of Mira. You did what you came to do—I respect that. Please, let me go talk to her first. She'll be quite upset, and I don't know that you confronting her right now is the best thing."

He ground his jaw, but saw the reason in her argument. "All right. But please, tell her it was never my plan to suggest eminent domain. It's all very complicated."

"I'm not sure any of that will do you or her any good at this point." Janice's parting look straddled the line between pity and contempt. She walked sedately back to a fuming, glowering Arty.

As Shane got into his rental, he caught a few more dirty looks from people leaving the meeting. Someone shouted, "Get out of our town!" and he flinched—he'd never been met with such hostility before.

All he'd ever wanted was to help make Everville a better place.

He'd never expected they wouldn't want his help.

CHAPTER TWENTY-FOUR

MIRA RIPPED THE stubborn ivy vines clinging to the trellises and stuffed them into garbage bags. *No sense in holding on,* she thought angrily. *This'll all be gone soon.* Maybe it would've been better to set the whole thing ablaze, give the Crown a proper funeral pyre. But the last thing she needed was to be charged with arson or fraud or whatever. She was already a vagrant. A millionaire vagrant, but a homeless unloved orphan nonetheless.

She gave a bitter laugh, wiping the tears from her face with the back of her dirt-covered wrist. It was getting dark—she could barely see, except by her lantern and the solar-powered lawn lights jutting from the garden boxes like tombstones, each casting a dim, ghostly glow.

"Mira?" Janice's voice floated toward her.

"Go away."

"Honey, where are you? It's dark up here, and I can barely see."

"Then go back down the ladder."

A pause. "You shouldn't be alone right now."

"Why? Do you think I'm stupid enough to

fling myself off the roof?" The thought had occurred to her. She was angry and hurt and betrayed. Taking her own life felt like the only way she could have control over the situation. Killing herself would make people sorry they ever—

A sudden gust of wind groaned through the garden, sending the pinwheels whirling, the wind chime she'd made for Grandpa clattering like old bones. She exhaled sharply as tears burned in her throat. Of course she wasn't going to kill herself. She wouldn't give anyone the satisfaction of confirming their worst thoughts about her.

"There you are." Janice's shadow edged into the lamplight. "What are you doing?" She squinted into the dark and gasped.

"If anyone is tearing up all this, it's gonna be me." She gestured around at the carnage she'd wreaked so far. "It's not like any of it was going to be harvested."

"The council didn't condemn the building yet—Cheyenne did that to make sure you had time to pack and say goodbye, otherwise the sheriff would be here putting bolts on the doors. No one's forcing you out tonight. Mira, stop!" The florist grabbed her wrist as she yanked a potted flower out of its terra-cotta hearth and shook its roots violently.

"It doesn't matter. I can't take any of this with me." Fury boiled through her as she glared around the half-ruined garden she'd worked so hard to keep up. Plants won't do me any good where I'm headed."

"Where are you going?"

"I don't know." Her mind hadn't been clear enough to formulate any kind of plan. The truth was, she'd never been able to bring herself to think about what would come next if she was forced to leave. She'd assumed she'd always live in the Crown. She gave another bitter laugh to hide her despair. "Maybe I'll drive to LA, live on Sunset Boulevard like Norma Desmond. I could get a house for a cool two mil there, right?"

"Mira..."

"Or maybe I should give my money away. Do something useful with it, like build a church. I could live in the bell tower. Sanctuary, sanctuary!" She mimed a hunch and hobbled around as she grabbed a tomato plant. One of the small, green fruits exploded in her fierce grip as she tore the whole thing out of the box, scattering clods of dirt all around her. Janice cried out.

"Mira, stop!"

"Why? What does it matter? Nothing here is going to live. Not even if we tried to transplant it. At least this way, I can make sure they don't die slowly." She grabbed another tomato plant. She could feel the delicate roots tearing as she ripped the plant up easily, their grasp on the life-giving earth tenuous. Several little green tomatoes rolled and bounced off the plant. What a waste. It would've been a good crop this year if she'd taken better care of them.

"You want to save something, take the succulents." She pointed at the greenhouse. "Otherwise, I'm pitching them." Over the roof, most likely. She'd always wondered what it would sound like, all that pottery crashing to the ground below.

Janice almost seemed afraid Mira would do just that if she didn't hurry. She opened the greenhouse and gathered an armful of plants, hastily stacking them into a wooden tray. Mira suddenly felt bad for making the older woman work so hard in the dark, and in fear. Mira had never acted out like this—she was admittedly half-crazed, but could anyone blame her? She'd lost everything that meant anything to her because of Shane. She was allowed to freak out. But she didn't want to inflict her pain on Janice.

Give her the succulents. Get her out of here. Continue with your rampage. That was the coolheaded thing to do. She strode over, and Janice recoiled. "I'll help," she said tersely.

Together they emptied the greenhouse. Some of the succulents had been put in there by her grandfather—Janice deserved to keep those. Most of them were Mira's, though. But she knew she couldn't keep them. In her mind, she was packing her car, filling it with her movie collection—there wouldn't be room for much more.

Mira's chest squeezed as she took out the potted orchids Shane had given to her. They'd flourished under her care. There were even a few new buds dripping from the stems. She touched their delicate shape. One of them snapped off readily, and she moaned.

"Don't worry, dear, that happens. Those were the ones I—" Janice paused, snapped her mouth shut and went back to straightening the plants in the trays.

"These were the ones you what?"

"Nothing."

No, not nothing. Mira could see the lie burning in her eyes even in the half-light with all those shadows around her. She felt as though in the dark she could see everything much more clearly, like a film projected on a screen. "Tell me about the orchids, Janice."

"They were gifts from Shane, weren't they? I remember them now. I picked them out myself."

Mira sifted through her words, plucking the lies out like weeds. "They weren't from Shane at all, were they?"

The florist's eyes widened. Slowly, she shook her head.

Mira's hands were already raw, her arms aching, but she didn't care. She grabbed the first orchid and lobbed it as far as she could over the edge of the roof. It sailed through the darkness and landed somewhere over on the next building's roof with a tinkling crash.

That building belonged to Shane, to Sagmar and their ilk. She was just sending them a housewarming gift.

She picked up the next orchid, the white egret Shane had brought her from New York. She hesitated only briefly before sending it to its oblivion.

"Orchids are just parasites, anyway." She kicked the door of the greenhouse.

"You're going to hurt yourself."

"No one cares," she snapped. "Everyone *knows* I live here. Everyone. And no one said a word to help me save my home."

"This ain't a home." Arty's voice emerged from the darkness, gruff and unpleasant. He climbed over the edge of the roof, scrambling away from the edge and pushing to his feet. "It's a tomb you've been haunting since Jack's death."

She rolled her burning eyes. "Great, now it's a rooftop party."

"Don't use that sarcastic tone with your elders, young lady. Jack would be mortified with the way you're treating us."

"The way *I'm* treating you? I didn't ask you two to treat me like a child."

"Well, you're certainly acting like one. You're throwing a tantrum when you should be celebrating."

"Celebrating what? You think money means

anything to me? They're taking the only thing I have left of Grandpa." *The only good thing in my whole miserable life.*

Arty's mouth firmed. "Your grandpa's dead, Mira. He was a good man who lived a good, long life. He was flawed, too, but he did what he could for others. And he never would've wanted you worshipping his ghost. He wanted you to live a rich and meaningful life."

"I *was* living a rich and meaningful life!" Why didn't anyone accept that? Tears of pure frustration edged into the corners of her eyes. All she wanted to do was stomp her feet and scream.

"Come inside," Janice coaxed. "It's late, it's dark and you need to get some sleep. Things will look better in the morning."

"You two go. I have things to do here."

"Mira—"

"I don't need you two interfering with my life. Not anymore. I'm not a lost little girl who needs protecting. And by the way, that thing you pulled with Shane and the flowers? Pretty shitty of both of you."

Arty stiffened. "We did that for you."

"No, I think I get it now. You did that for yourself. You wanted to foist me off. You thought Shane would sweep me off my feet and take me away from Grandpa's theater. 'Let's get Mira a man, then maybe she'll be more normal and we won't have to look after her anymore.'"

"It was never like that," Janice said.

"I never needed either of you. No one's ever wanted me, so I've had to learn to be on my own, and I'm doing fine."

"How dare you say that. Your grandpa Jack wanted you. Show him some respect."

"Respect? Is that what you're showing him?" She sneered at Arty through the darkness. "You two carrying on while he's cold and dead in the ground, even though he loved Janice all his life."

"What happens between us is of no concern to you," Arty growled.

"Right, but you think it's fine to meddle with my life." She scoffed, trying desperately to keep herself from crumbling. She hated that she was being so nasty and cruel, but she needed everyone to leave her alone. "Get off my roof. For as long as it's still mine, I don't want to see either of you around here." She spun and tromped back into the darkness.

This was why she didn't let people into her life. They were constantly trying to manipulate her, to find ways to use her. Ultimately, everyone let her down.

The decision was simple then. When they took the theater, she'd leave Everville for good.

"THAT WAS AWFUL."

Arty said nothing as he passed Jan her coffee and sat heavily next to her on the couch in her home. He'd always liked her house—a place that'd been made for a small, tight family. Of course, her sons were grown and gone, and he and Janice wouldn't be having kids. Though Arty had always wanted a dog…

He gripped that dream hard, then let it go on a tired exhale.

"What do we do, Arty? We can't just leave Mira on her own."

"She needs space," he said pensively.

"But where will she live? What will she do when the town evicts her?"

"I talked to Cheyenne. She's not so cruel-hearted that the council would turn the poor girl out onto the street without advance warning. But the law is what it is. She'll eventually be given a notice to vacate. Sheriff McKinnon will have to come in to oversee the whole thing, make sure she gets out safe."

Janice ran a hand through her hair. "Oh, what a disaster. This is all my fault."

"Don't blame yourself. Nothing we did amounted to more than harmless matchmaking." Though the words were bitter now. It had been anything but harmless. Mira was heartbroken, and the financial compensation was cold comfort to her. Even Arty recognized that.

"She should stay here with me," Jan said decisively. "Just until she can find a place of her own."

"No. She can stay at my place. I'll move into the motel down near the lake."

"Don't be ridiculous. If you're giving up your space, then you can move in here with me." She gave him a small smile. That tiny upturn of her lips made Arty swallow thickly. He'd only just kissed those lips, and now it felt like poison was taking hold, wending its insidious way through his system.

"Jan..." He sighed. "There's no easy way to say this. But I think Mira's right. We shouldn't be together."

She was quiet a moment, her thoughts flickering in her eyes. "We've been through this before. What's changed your mind?"

"Don't you see? We failed Jack. We were supposed to help Mira, but instead we got caught up in each other, and all we've done is hurt her. Jack would be mad as Hades to know what we did."

"So you're punishing us both for something you yourself admit wasn't wrong?"

"It was wrong in different ways." He didn't know how to articulate it. He'd never been a man of many words; all he knew was that some things came too little, too late. It wasn't just about what Jack thought, either. "Jan, we're both too old to be messing around with...with this." He looked down at his liver-spotted hands, feeling the arthritis singing in his bones. He wasn't a young man anymore. Was it fair to make her a grieving widow twice? "We shouldn't be together. If it wasn't meant to be then, it isn't meant to be now."

Janice's mouth crimped into a steep frown. Her eyebrows knitted and her hands clenched over her knees. "I thought you loved me."

He didn't respond. He didn't want this melodrama dragged out any longer than it had to be. "We each have our own lives, things we need to take care of. You've got your boys. I've got Mira. I have to do something for her."

"So you're choosing her over me?" She glared.

Arty decided not to take the bait. She was angry at him—he got that. He was being a class-A jackass. Jan was no more jealous of Mira than he was of their dead friend Jack. "I'd better get going."

He left icy silence and everything he'd always wanted behind him.

It didn't matter what he wanted now—he'd given up on that a long time ago. There was no point in chasing what didn't belong to him. What would never belong to him.

CHAPTER TWENTY-FIVE

SHANE SPENT THE next month finalizing the sale of the Crown with Everville town council. Things moved much more expediently now. The suddenness with which the town had taken the Crown from Mira had galvanized the condo's greatest opponents, though not enough to actually do anything more drastic than criticize Mayor Welks in the local papers.

The online campaign run by Riley Lee Jackson got play in global media, as well. They'd nearly made their goal before the theater had been expropriated. The story showed up in a few entertainment blogs and online magazines, but people noticed, and Sagmar's name was portrayed in a less than positive light.

"Any publicity is good publicity," Laura had insisted. "And no one actually remembers company names. For now, though, it puts us on the map."

"Is that what the senior managers and investors are saying?" Shane asked skeptically.

"Relax. I promise you won't get any flack." Of course, he knew that if he did get called in, it would be because she'd blamed the situation on him, and he, in turn, would tell them what she'd done. It would be mutually assured destruction.

When the paperwork had been filed and there was nothing left for Shane to do regarding the Crown, he decided it was time to end his so-called vacation. With a heavy heart, he packed his bags, locked up the house and got in his car. Nothing about his time there had been terribly relaxing. Except for those stolen moments with Mira.

But she wasn't answering his calls or emails or texts anymore. She probably wouldn't ever again.

He made one more last-ditch effort and went to the Crown. As with all the other times, she didn't answer his knocks, didn't even come when he stood directly in front of the hidden cameras and yelled. He tried the back door, hoping the lock was still broken, but by some miracle it was working, so there was no way in.

He circled the building and noticed one of the ladders from the fire escape had been pulled down. Had Mira done that? Or someone from the city? He stared up, trying to fathom who might have left such a blatant security risk.

And then he realized there was only one way to find out.

It took him the better part of an hour to climb the riserless fire escape steps to the balcony entrance and then scale the scorching hot ladder to the roof. Four stories wasn't nothing, even to someone who *wasn't* deathly afraid of heights. Only the thought that Mira might be up there pushed him upward. He had to talk to her.

By the time he crawled over the lip of the roof he was drenched in sweat and shaking, his hands raw and cramping. What he saw made his heart sink. The rooftop paradise had been completely uprooted. Dirt was scattered everywhere. The greenhouses lay open and vacant. A pile of broken pinwheels and patio umbrellas had been discarded in one corner like old bones in an open-air mausoleum. The only plants that had nominally survived were a handful of stubborn dandelions, their partially crushed heads peeking from the soil.

Had vandals torn up the garden? Why would they wreak such devastation on such a beautiful place?

He called Sheriff McKinnon to report the crime, but Ralph only grunted.

"Wasn't vandals. It was Mira."

"What?"

"Had herself a bit of a party after the meeting. I got called by some concerned neighbors, but Arty told me what was what, so I let her be. Long as she wasn't hurting anyone or herself, I figured it was best she let off some steam. I should probably ticket the girl for littering but I'm not inclined to add insult to injury." He harrumphed. "You wanna tell me what you're doing trespassing up there?"

Shane stiffened. "I was looking for Mira."

"Seems she doesn't want to be found," he deadpanned. "You better run along before I'm asked to press charges. As you've pointed out, that place isn't safe to be around." The iron in his voice was all the warning and admonishment Shane needed.

He hung up and began the terrifying climb back down the ladder. A mixture of anger, hurt, worry and fear for Mira distracted him from the ground below. His jumbled feelings for her were stronger than any phobia he had, it seemed.

Or was that love? He shook his head as he got into his car, taking a deep, calming breath before starting the engine. He would have to live with the bitter stench of fear, sweat and failure on his drive home.

He knew he should just walk away. Mira was too scared, too stubborn, too paranoid, too challenging. He needed to find someone who didn't suspect his motives at every turn. He'd met plenty of women who hadn't given him anywhere near as much trouble as Mira had.

But he didn't want any other woman.

Surely his attachment to her was related to how hard he'd worked to win her over. Nothing worth having ever came easy, after all. But he suspected he had a serious white knight complex when it came to Mira. That was reason enough to leave this place and forget about her. A relationship wasn't supposed to be about how he felt when he gave. Love was supposed to be about mutual respect and attraction.

He firmed his jaw. He didn't love her. He'd been fooling himself, the same way Mira had tried to fool herself into believing she would one day reopen the Crown when deep down she didn't want to. He'd tricked himself into believing he cared for her more than he cared for the rest of the town, his family, his own future. He'd come to Everville for one reason, and now that that job was done, he could continue on with the rest of his life. It would take time for people to forget his role in building the condo here, but things would change in Everville soon. Then he could get himself the condo unit he'd dreamed of owning. Dad could go fishing on Silver Lake anytime he wanted, maybe even retire here…

And Shane would, what? Be reminded of what he'd done to first earn then break Mira's trust every time he had to deal with the property? Be forced to relive all the memories they'd created together?

He gripped the steering wheel, wanting to pull over so he could rub at the headache drilling into his temples. He'd barely left town, and he was already too tired to drive. Maybe he was coming down with something after that climb to the Crown's rooftop.

He decided a quick pit stop at Georgette's Books and Bakery was in order. At least bringing some of Georgette's cookies and croissants back to Brooklyn would make him feel as if he'd accomplished some good in town. A muffin and a coffee would take some of the bitter taste from his mouth, too.

He parked and entered. The warm space filled him with a sense of nostalgia at once, though it had changed since he was a child. The dining room had been converted into a bookstore run by Georgette's grandson, Aaron. The old baker wasn't there herself—instead, a pretty blonde and a teen were running the counter. As they packed his order and prepped his coffee, Shane perused the books.

"Shane?"

He looked up in surprise. It was Maya. She plucked the cat-eye glasses from the bridge of her nose, putting down a book she'd been browsing through. "I haven't seen you around since…" She trailed off.

"I've been busy getting things squared away with the property sale." He cleared his throat, unsure of how this woman saw him now that he'd destroyed their plans to resurrect a piece of Everville's history. "I'm on my way back to Brooklyn now."

"Oh." Surprise and concern rang in her exhalation. "I thought… You and Mira…"

He gave only the slightest shake of his head. "I've got to get back."

The muscles in her jaw worked, as if she were chewing over his words. "You haven't talked to Mira since the town council meeting?"

"No." He decided not to mention the number she'd done on the rooftop garden. He remembered how Mira hated people talking about her, and he didn't want to feed any rumor mills. "She won't answer my calls. I even went to the theater."

"She's not at the theater." Maya's brow wrinkled. "She's staying with me."

"What?"

"She left the theater days ago. Said she couldn't stay there. She spent the past few weeks clearing everything out, putting it into storage. I didn't think she should be alone so I invited her to stay in my guest room." Her lips pursed. "She really needed a friend."

Shane balled his fists. It was on the tip of his tongue to demand to see Mira. He had no right wishing she'd turned to him first. He had to remind himself that her welfare wasn't his responsibility. She'd made that very clear, and besides, his meddling had only made things worse. So instead, he said, "Thank you for taking care of her."

If Maya thought he'd take some other course of action, she was sorely disappointed. "Did you hear about her fallout with Arty and Janice?"

He hadn't expected that. "No. What happened?"

She explained the deception the two had played on her. Shane listened, the tension in his shoulders telegraphing to his stomach as she concluded the sordid tale. At first he felt a little put off by Arty and Janice's matchmaking. It made him feel as though he'd been manipulated. But then, he'd taken credit for that first potted orchid, and had thus made himself complicit in the scheme. No wonder Mira wasn't talking to him. There was no way she couldn't see his involvement as a long-term scam taking advantage of her.

"I could apologize to her to the end of days, but something tells me it'll never be enough," he said, aching.

"I'm sorry, I don't know how else to be helpful." Maya's shoulders slumped.

"I think the best course for me would be to leave town."

"But you'll come back, right? I mean, the condo still has to be built."

"At this stage, my involvement is almost nonexistent. It's all paperwork and then contractors and building permits. I don't handle any of that." And even then, after all the shenanigans he and Laura had been through, he wasn't sure he'd still have a job with Sagmar, much less the Everville account. "The only reason I'd come back was if I had to sell something else to the town." Or if someone asked him to come back. A very specific someone. "I doubt Everville's ready for a second build just yet."

Maya smiled. "I don't know. People get over change pretty quick around here."

"You're not mad at me?"

"Not for doing your job. Frankly, I knew the chances of the Crown surviving were pretty slim."

He blinked. "But…you were so passionate about the whole thing."

A secret smile tugged at her lips. "I'm passionate about a lot of things, but mostly, I want to help people in town be the best they can be." Her gaze grew distant. "A long time ago, I was told I'd never amount to anything. Suddenly, I was gifted with opportunity and means to accomplish whatever I wanted. I knew the people of my hometown needed that same kind of opportunity. That's why I came home."

He remembered her inheritance, but decided not to mention it. "So you're the town's fairy godmother?"

She gave a small shrug. "I try not to draw attention to myself." She peered up at him. "You, though… You want to be this town's savior, don't you? And Mira's?"

Heat crawled up his throat. Was he that transparent?

"That's not a criticism," she added gently. "Times change. After all the factories closed the community isn't what it what it was. But some people don't realize that. And they take umbrage that anyone thinks they need a hand up, a chance to flourish again, no matter what form it takes. Change is a threat to the way things were always done, to people's perception of themselves as self-sufficient and successful."

"You've given this a lot of thought."

"It's why I do what I do. No one wants to be looked down upon."

Was that what he'd been doing all this time? Looking down on Everville? On Mira? Had he been that condescending? "I never meant to hurt anyone."

"I know. And eventually, Mira will get that, too."

The ladies at the bakery counter called his name, indicating his order was ready.

"I guess this is goodbye," Shane said, holding out a hand. "No hard feelings?"

"None from me," she replied wryly. "And if living here has taught me anything, it's never goodbye. Just...see you later."

Shane picked up his pastries and got back in the car. The fresh-baked croissants and coffee filled the interior with a sense of hominess and hope he hadn't felt before. Or perhaps it was Maya's words that had bolstered his spirits.

The feeling followed him back to Brooklyn. Despite the fact he was going home, his mission accomplished, he knew he wasn't yet done with Everville or Mira.

"LOS ANGELES OR VANCOUVER," Mira declared as Maya walked in. "Or possibly Toronto. It's going to be one of those three, though I'm not sure about the West Coast. Nice weather, but earthquakes..." She shivered. "Toronto, then. Or maybe Montreal?" She scrolled across Google Maps and considered the metropolitan areas of Canada, a country she'd never been to but knew plenty about from all the film festivals she covered remotely.

It would be so different to get a job somewhere else, live in an apartment and work in the city. Maybe she'd even have a desk in an office. How weird would that be? She laughed drily at herself. She never would've contemplated such a mundane existence before, but since moving out of the theater, she felt...rootless. Drifting, like a bit of dandelion fluff on the wind. Not having the Crown like a millstone around her neck to watch over and worry about was completely freeing.

Maya set a box of croissants on the coffee table and sat in the wingback armchair across from where Mira was curled up on the red velvet settee. The place was as stylish as the consignment shop owner's outfits—vintage chic with all the flair, but none of the gaudiness. Somehow, she made it all work together.

"I'll admit a partiality to Toronto," Mira said. "More media jobs, plus I won't have to learn French." She reached for the box of baked goods.

Maya toed it just out of her reach, and she looked up into her serious face. "What?"

"You really want to leave town?"

"Of course I do." She cleared a frog from her suddenly sticky throat. "I can't stay. There's nothing left for me here."

Maya was silent. She plucked a croissant from the box and set it on a plate, but didn't slide it over to Mira. "I wouldn't try to stop you. But saying there's nothing here for you… I thought you loved Everville."

She did. But it would be too painful to stay. She'd probably lose her mind watching the Crown get knocked down. After that, people would forever be whispering about her, pitying her, the orphan recluse in the old theater who'd been evicted. At least in another city, another country, she could reclaim her anonymity. She couldn't stay in Everville. She would never again be someone's emotional charity case.

"Have you thought about moving to New York? I mean, that's where all the action is moviewise, right? And there are tons of media and publishing jobs there."

She bit the inside of her cheek. "Thought about it. Doesn't appeal."

"Because Shane lives there?"

"Don't be ridiculous. It's a city of, like, eight million people." Which wasn't enough to put between her and the man who'd taken her home from her. She needed real, physical distance. "It's too…expensive."

"You don't have to live in Manhattan, you know. Even if you wanted to, two and a half million can get you pretty far."

Mira didn't say anything. For the first time in her life, she didn't have to worry about feeding herself, paying the taxes, keeping the lights on or fixing some busted plumbing. Sure, she'd have to find a place, pay rent, get some new furniture, but that would hardly make a dent in $2.5 million.

She swallowed. God, that was a lot of money.

Speaking of money… "What's Riley Lee Jackson going to do about the crowdfunding thing?"

"Don't worry, it wasn't for nothing. They were really close to the target, and he did a lot to help raise awareness for endangered independent second-run theaters. He doesn't hold it against us."

Mira nodded. Maya had called the actor after the town council meeting and handled everything while Mira had licked her wounds, packed and moved her things out of the theater. Arty and Janice had tried to convince her to stay with one of them, but she couldn't even look at them right now. Maya had come to her rescue and given her a place to stay. She'd never really had a girlfriend like her. Mira would miss her when she left.

"Tell me something," Maya said as she pushed

the plate with the croissant toward her. "If your grandfather were still alive, what would he have done with 2.5 million dollars?"

Mira's more cynical side had wondered at first if the shop owner had only invited her to stay with her to get access to her money, but the check from the city wouldn't be ready for a week or two. And judging by Maya's decorating tastes, she was doing better than all right with her shop.

Mira thought about it. "Buy back the farm, maybe. He loved growing things." She thought about the rooftop garden and how she'd demolished it in her fury. She'd regretted it the next day, but the violent act of ripping it all out—it'd been cathartic in a weird, messed-up way. All that careful weeding and planting and work—and she'd trashed it all.

What was wrong with her?

"What else?"

Mira blew out a breath. "I dunno...he always said he wanted to take me to see the world. Travel to all the places great movies are set. London, Rome, Paris..."

We'll always have Paris...

She banished the image of Shane's glittering eyes from her mind with a frown.

"Maybe *you* should do that now. I know the Crown meant a lot to you, but it wasn't the building, right? It was all about your grandfather's memory."

"The Crown was his legacy," Mira parroted, and Maya gave a sad chuckle.

"*You* were his legacy. He may have loved films and going to the theater, but he would never have taken you in if he thought the Crown was more important."

"That's just it. I'm the reason he closed the Crown." She slumped forward, the truth cork-screwing through her. "He mortgaged the theater to send me to college. I came back after less than a year and the theater was barely earning enough to stay open. He needed to keep that money to repay the bank, but instead he shut down operations and put the money into a trust fund for me. I told him I wasn't going back to school. I wanted to stay with him. He was the only person who'd ever cared about me…" Tears pooled in her eyes as the floodgates of her pain burst. She hid her face in her hands.

"Oh, Mira…hon." Maya sat next to her and wrapped an arm around her, squeezing. "You know that's not true."

"I have to get out of this town." She wiped her eyes hastily. She hated crying in front of people. She'd done plenty of it as a child, back in school when it was so easy to tip her over the edge. It was a game to the other kids, to see what it would take to make the weird girl cry. And people were still playing that game, only now it was all about seeing what she could endure, see what it would take to drive her out of town for good.

Well, they'd won.

"Okay." Maya stood. "If you're going...then I'm coming, too."

Mira stared up at her blankly. "What?"

"I'll come with you. To Toronto, Montreal, Vancouver, LA...wherever you wanna go. Hell, if you want to hit London, Rome and Paris on the way, I'll come with. I haven't been out there in years."

Mira squinted at her. "What're you talking about?"

"You can't be alone right now. You're making hasty decisions about your future. But," she added with a smile, "you're also doing it with a nice little nest egg to back it up, meaning you can afford to take a few chances, make a few mistakes. Still, I'd like to be there to make sure you don't make too big a mistake."

"I don't think I'll be a very good traveling companion."

"I think you'll make a great traveling companion. I can show you all the best places to eat and stay. And you don't need to worry. I can pay my own way." She took Mira's laptop and went to a discount travel website. "What do you think? One month? Two? Personally, I can spend a whole year in Paris and never get bored, but I think we should do a whirlwind tour now, and then go back to your favorite places another year."

Mira gave a low chuckle, but Maya's expression didn't change. "Wait...you're serious?"

"Of course I am. You have a fortune to spend and you're looking for a fresh start, and I've had the itch to travel for a while. Feels like I haven't been on vacation for years." She tapped away on the keyboard. "Oh, the Ritz Paris has a great deal."

"Just like that?"

"Just like that." Maya grinned.

Mira stared. "How can you afford it?"

Maya cleared her throat. "My grandmother, the one who gave me those dresses... Well, she left me pretty much everything when she died. And she was kinda loaded." She rubbed the back of her neck. "It's not really a thing I talk about."

"But...you run a consignment shop." As if that somehow made her wealth impossible. Why was she even in Everville?

"I like old stuff. I like to catalog what's past, understand why people give up the things they do." Compassion shone in her eyes. "The thing I've discovered is that people don't just unload things they don't need, they give up things they cherish and believe have value in exchange for something they want more."

A slow, hot burn grew in Mira's gut. "Are you

telling me *you* could've saved the Crown single-handedly?"

"Is that what you would've wanted?"

She opened her mouth to say yes, to shout it to the rooftops. But her voice snagged. It was a lie. Maya had helped her reopen—she'd made her grandfather's dream come true, even if it was only for a day. And Mira had found it was not at all what she'd wanted. Even if she'd been given all the money in the world to fix up the theater, she wouldn't have enjoyed running it full-time the way Grandpa had. She loved the movies, yes, and there was a certain satisfaction to be had in sharing that experience and enjoyment with others. But the day-to-day of business would've slowly killed her.

"I think," Maya began lightly, "that we should look into a backpacking trip. So much more fun to stay in hostels and meet the people there than it is to stay in stuffy hotels. Although that can be fun, too." She turned the laptop around. "How about we start in Paris?"

CHAPTER TWENTY-SIX

"A EUROPEAN TOUR?"

Janice nodded eagerly. Arty had been surprised by her visit to the grocery store after the way they'd parted three days ago. "She's taking a mental break."

"Having one, you mean. Why on earth would she leave town? Everything she knows is here." Arty wrung his hands. "The girl's barely been out of the state, much less the country. Where would she go? And why?"

"She won't be alone. Maya Hanes is going with her. Those two are thick as thieves these days."

Yeah, he knew that. Mira had rejected his offer for a place to stay. He'd never felt so stung in his life. Janice watched him pace his tiny office. "I thought you'd be happy. This is what we both wanted for her, isn't it?"

"What *we* wanted?" He shook his head, running both hands over the thin pate of gray hair. "I don't think what we wanted ever played into anything that girl did. She's too much like Jack that way. If she leaves..." He trailed off.

If Mira left, Jack left with her. He didn't want

to admit it, but his memories of his friend lived in the man's granddaughter. Arty was so used to thinking of his life in Jack's shadow, then as Mira's caretaker, he wasn't sure what he'd do with himself without their presence.

And wasn't that the crux of it? He'd been struggling since his breakup with Janice, asking himself why he continued to deny himself happiness and the pleasure of Jan's attentions. Maybe it was just easier being miserable and alone.

Wait. Hadn't he lectured Mira about this exact thing? Miring herself in misery because she was too afraid to explore, take risks and find joy? Was *he* such an old curmudgeon that he didn't know how to be happy?

Your problem is that you're willing to wait and wait for things to happen, Jack's voice floated to him from a distant memory. *Carpe diem, Arty!*

He never had been one to seize the day. He'd been afraid of rejection, of getting hurt. And he couldn't blame Jack for that. His friend hadn't told Janice about Arty's feelings because it wasn't his place. Arty had to do it himself. For years, he'd made excuses by telling himself that handsome Jack Bateman had a far better chance. He'd let his friend flirt and woo while he'd stayed on the sidelines, convinced Jan wouldn't want him.

Now he was rejecting her for those same reasons, making excuses when he should've been seizing the day.

Janice glanced down as if checking the time. "Well… I thought I'd let you know, in any case. She can go anytime, soon as she cashes that check. You might want to bury the hatchet with her." She got up to leave.

"Jan, wait." He rounded the desk. Every nerve in his body strained toward her. "Things ended badly between us the other night… I'm sorry about that."

She let out a breath. "But you're not willing to give us another try?"

He kept his lips firmly shut for fear he'd burst out saying what he really wanted to say—that he would do anything for them to be together. But he didn't want to sound like a romantic idiot.

Janice laughed bitterly. "I suppose I shouldn't have expected more." And when he didn't do anything because he was still a coward, she sighed. "Goodbye, Arty."

The light in his life drained out of him as he watched her go. She made him feel something other than tired and old. She made him feel as though life had more meaning than just the day's take and getting groceries delivered to his customers on time.

Dammit, what the hell was wrong with him?

His feet carried him forward. Suddenly, he was running out of his office and down the dairy aisle. He nearly crashed into Mrs. Abbot, who gave him a dirty look as he hurried out. One of the stock boys called his name.

"Not now." He'd always made everything else a priority—his business, the town, Mira. It was time he stopped denying himself. Mira no longer needed him. Jack had never needed him to be loyal to his memory. And Arty didn't need to keep being a martyr.

The only thing he did need was Janice.

"Jan!" Her step faltered as she glanced over her shoulder. He caught up to her, out of breath, his heart hammering. "Janice. You're right. I'm being ridiculous."

She challenged him with a look. "About what?"

"About everything. I'm letting Jack get between us as much now as he did back then, but that's on me. I've been using his memory as an excuse because… I've always been intimidated by you. You're beautiful and smart and funny. I never thought of myself as worthy. I've loved you since you were a girl in Mary Janes and a ponytail."

The doubt in her eyes made his heart strain. "Really?"

"What'll it take to prove it?"

When she didn't respond, he hastened over to a bench and stepped up onto it. "Listen up, everyone!" He shouted. There weren't many people on the street, but those who were coming out of the grocery store, lingering in the parking lot or sitting in the shade turned to stare. "My name is Arty Bolton and I'm in love with Janice Heinlein!"

"Arty, get down! You're going to hurt yourself," Jan whispered harshly.

But courage and maybe a little insanity had taken hold, inflating his chest and suffusing his limbs with vital heat. He'd always been afraid of looking like a fool for love—it was time to face that fear. He raised his voice further. "Under the witness of God and everyone who can hear me, I love Janice Heinlein and I'll do anything to make her believe it!"

Someone across the street whistled and whooped. He heard a child start to cry. A few people turned and walked away quickly. And then, Arty heard the blare of a siren.

A county sheriff's car pulled to a stop right in front of the bench. Ralph McKinnon slowly got out, hitching both thumbs in his belt loops, grimacing. "Arty," he greeted casually, then nodded to Janice. "Everything all right here?"

Janice waved her hand hastily. "He's fine, Ralph. Arty, get down from there."

"Only if you tell me you'll believe me," he said, desperate to make her understand. To make her *believe.* In that insane moment, as all his pent-up feelings coalesced, he realized he didn't want to be without her for another minute. He would go to jail if that was what it took to convince her.

"Tell me you know I love you. If you don't love me back—"

"Oh, will you shut up. Of course I love you."

He nearly toppled over with relief. He climbed off the bench stiffly as Janice wrapped her arms around his shoulders and kissed him.

Ralph coughed discreetly. "I'll be on my way then," he said. "Unless you need a ride home? Or possibly to the loony bin?"

"We can walk from here," Arty insisted, gathering Janice closer. Their audience laughed and hooted their approval. He found he didn't care.

"Crazy kids." Ralph shook his head as he got back in his patrol car.

Arty was grinning so hard tears squeezed from his eyes. Janice held him, head pressed against his chest. "You didn't need to do that. All I wanted to hear was that you cared enough to try."

"Life's too short to just try. I'm going to do my damnedest to show you how much I love you. I can't spend what time I have left moping and stalling."

She smiled and kissed him once more on the lips. "Then there's no point wasting time." She opened his palm and placed a key there. "Move in with me, Arty."

"I'll do you one better." He got down on one knee. "Let's get married."

Janice grinned in delight and sealed their agreement with a kiss.

"ARE YOU WATCHING that movie *again*?" Priti plopped onto the couch next to Shane and snagged the bowl of popcorn next to him.

"*Casablanca*'s a classic." He kept his eyes focused on Rick, brooding as Sam played "As Time Goes By." He'd felt a weird kinship with the gin joint owner since leaving Mira behind in Everville. Though he supposed in that analogy, he was more like Ilsa in Paris. Or something. He didn't care. He just wanted to watch the movie over and over, and remind himself that at the end, Rick did the right thing in making Ilsa leave Casablanca with Victor Laszlo.

If that condo doesn't get built, you'll regret it. Maybe not today. Maybe not tomorrow, but soon and for the rest of your life. He laughed at himself bitterly. Priti peered at him curiously.

"Did I miss something funny?"

"No. Is dinner ready?"

"Not quite. *Amma* sent me in here because she was afraid you were still moping over your breakup."

Shane groaned. "Is that what she thinks happened?"

"I dunno, you tell me. *Amma* told me all about this girlfriend of yours. She's the theater owner, right? The one you were trying to bully into selling?"

"She wasn't my girlfriend." Not really. Not in the way he'd wanted. There'd been too much deception, too many underlying motivations to make it a real relationship. "And I didn't bully her. It was complicated."

"They really liked her. Wish I got to meet her, too."

He lifted a shoulder nonchalantly. He probably shouldn't have introduced Mira to his parents, given them hope for their bachelor son's happiness. And he *had* been happy, despite everything. It all felt so faraway now, like a dream that had ended with a rude awakening.

We'll always have Paris.

Priti studied him. "So what happened between you two?"

"Nothing. I did my job like I was supposed to. It was what was best for her. For everyone." His sister's silence made him itch and he felt the need to explain himself further. "The theater would've been condemned eventually anyhow. The place was falling apart and she was living there illegally. She's lucky she didn't get in any serious accidents. Did I tell you how I found her dangling from a stage wire once? She could've been hurt or killed and no one would've known." He clenched his fists just thinking about it.

Priti tilted her chin. "So you did her a favor?"

He ignored her patronizing tone. "It made no sense for her to hold on to that property. It was costing her thousands a year in taxes, and she wasn't getting anything out of it. Now she's a multimillionaire. She's way better off."

"You sound like you're trying to convince yourself of that."

He glared at his sister. She smirked and shoved a handful of popcorn in her mouth. "Can't admit that maybe winning isn't everything, huh?"

"What're you talking about?"

She gave a put-upon sigh. "C'mon. You were never good at compromise. You went full Shekhar on her and drove her into the ground in the name of winning. You had to be *right*. You thought everything would work out for you once you got her property, that she'd thank you. But she didn't."

"I had her best interests at heart," he argued.

"Right. Because that's what every woman wants to hear from a man—that he thinks he knows what's best for her." She rolled her eyes. Shane froze, realizing his sister had him pegged. "Just admit that what you did was wrong. You've never accepted failure as an option. You would've arm wrestled her for that property if that's what it took. Whether or not you meant to, you led her on. You should have stepped away the moment you realized you had feelings for her, but you didn't. You had your eye on the prize. You thought you could have it all. But you can't. And now you're moping about it instead of actually feeling bad about what you did to her."

It galled him to admit she was right, except for

that last part. He *did* feel bad. He felt guilty, not self-righteous.

His cell phone rang. He answered. "Hello?"

"Shane? It's Arty Bolton."

His heart leaped into his throat, and he sat up. "What is it? Is Mira all right?"

"She's fine. I mean, as fine as she can be. I haven't talked to her much… She's a bit cross with us right now."

Shane caught the smug look on his sister's face and got up to get away from the noise of the TV and her inquisitive ears. "Listen, Arty, I hope we're still good."

"I've made my peace with it. It's Mira I'm concerned about right now. She's got it in her head to travel around Europe with Maya."

"Oh." He sat back, a mixture of jealousy and regret filling him slowly. "Well. That's…that's great."

"Great?" Arty harrumphed. "Didn't you hear me? She's leaving Everville. Her home."

"Maybe that's what she needs to do," Shane said, even though every cell in his body screamed that he should be the one with her, guiding her, protecting her. "Anyhow, she won't be alone. She'll be with Maya." Someone who cared. Someone who didn't have an agenda. His throat tightened.

Arty grumbled a curse. "I thought you'd care enough to do something about it."

"Mira's her own woman. I've never been able to convince her of anything." He bit his lip. "Sometimes you gotta let go of the things you… love." His throat tightened.

Arty snorted. "That's a stupid thing we tell ourselves when we're too afraid to confront our feelings. A bunch of meaningless words someone cobbled together 'cause they were a coward."

"What are you saying, Arty?"

"Don't be reading me wrong. I like you, despite everything that's happened. You have a good heart…when you listen to it, that is. I just thought maybe you'd be more of a man when it came to Mira. This trip would be good for her, but I don't cotton to women traveling alone. What if someone takes advantage of her?"

The way I did? Shane swallowed thickly. Mira was too cautious and wary of people to ever be conned. She wasn't naive. Still, Mira could meet someone on her travels, someone who'd see what a gem she was and sweep her off her feet…

The thought left a sour taste in his mouth.

"We don't get to decide what's best for her." He said it reluctantly, but knew it was the truth. "Whatever she wants to do, we should show our support." Even if it was from afar. He could pretend that he didn't care, but he always would. His greatest regret would be that he was not the one to share those new experiences and triumphs with her. To see Paris with her. "Besides, I'm not sure there's much I could do. Our relationship will always be tainted by what I did."

"Dunno about that. Memory's a funny thing." He paused. "Mira's a lot like her grandpa Jack. But she's different, too. She only ever wanted to please him. To have someone love her unconditionally."

I love her unconditionally. The thought tore a strip from Shane's heart.

Arty went on. "I remember his falling-out with Rick, Mira's father. Back when Jack had the farm, he was a real ballbuster. Rick could never please his old man. It drove him toward a life of crime and debauchery. Damn near broke Jack's heart. That's why he let Mira hide herself away when things got tough. He didn't want to make her do anything that might stress her out. Didn't want her to walk away from him the way her father had. 'Cause of that, he didn't give her the push out of the nest she needed, especially after she came running home from college."

Shane hesitated. "Why are you telling me this, Arty?"

"Because I want you to understand Mira better. See, she only ever remembers Jack as being this godlike figure who saved her from her terrible home life, a man whose love she felt she had to earn. She doesn't remember a lot of the other things about him, like how he let her skip school if she wanted to, or how he let her have the run of the theater during business hours. She doesn't remember him telling her it was best for her not to see her father in jail. She just went along with what he wanted because she thought the world of him." Arty sighed. "Jack always had good reasons for what he did. But he could be a son of a bitch sometimes."

Shane had never even considered that Mira might have missing pieces in her life, like an incarcerated father who wanted to see her. "I don't understand how I'm supposed to help."

"Truthfully, you can't. It's like you say—Mira's her own woman. She's got to find her own way, and whether or not you like it, you were the one to put her on that path. You'll need to accept that at some point. But—" Arty cleared his throat "—if you *were* still feeling guilty, I might have an idea about how you could make amends."

Shane would do almost anything to stop the gnawing in the pit of his stomach. More than that, though, he wanted Mira to look him in the eye again. Even if she didn't feel the same way, all he wanted was for her to be happy. "I'm listening."

CHAPTER TWENTY-SEVEN

Three months later

MIRA STARED OUT at the snow-covered landscape, flat and white and quiet. It was a palate cleanse for the senses. Three months of touring Europe with Maya had inundated her with a never-ending smorgasbord of sights, sounds and smells. Now, driving back to Everville for the holidays, a strange mixture of dread and longing permeated her. Why was she even going back? She could have stayed in Europe indefinitely, though she hadn't wanted Maya to miss Christmas with her family and friends.

"Be it ever so humble, there's no place like home," her friend said with a sigh. "I thought I'd hate the idea of another winter in New York State, but coming home to this?" She gestured at the pine boughs dusted in white, the houses along the roadside festooned with lights and giant inflatable snowmen on the lawns, and she sighed. "Christmas isn't the same without all this."

"Are you sure you're okay with me staying with you?" Mira asked.

"Hey, if I didn't like spending time with you, you would've known by now. Of course you'll stay with me. Where else would you go?"

Where indeed? Since she'd left town, Arty and Janice had moved in together, and she didn't want to be a third wheel in their relationship. She'd eventually forgiven them—she'd called to apologize for her abominable behavior, and they'd made amends. They still worried about her, but she'd assured them she was doing fine. Time and distance and long talks with Maya had given her a chance to get some perspective on her new life.

It'd taken a couple of weeks to deal with her anger and sadness over losing the Crown. It'd been like grieving her grandfather's death all over again. Maya had helped distract her by dragging her from one end of Europe to the other. There were too many things to see and experience, and Maya wouldn't let her stay still long enough to wallow.

At some point after the first three weeks, she'd realized she didn't miss living in the Crown. She'd slept in some of the world's most luxurious hotels, taken long, hot, languorous showers, eaten exquisite meals and sampled the best of everything life had to offer. She'd met fascinating people, explored world-famous attractions—Grandpa would've been blown away by the gardens in Versailles—and not once did she worry about broken locks, trespassers or what she had to fix next.

It was while visiting Notre Dame Cathedral in Paris that she'd found peace. Walking into the magnificent church with its polished floors and vaulted ceilings had made her turn her thoughts inward. She wasn't particularly religious, but in that space, the setting for one of her favorite stories, *The Hunchback of Notre Dame*, she'd felt closer to Grandpa than ever. She'd sat in a pew and stared up at the stained-glass windows. She could almost feel the warmth of her grandfather's smile, refracted through the rainbow of colors raining down on her, like a benediction that allowed her to let go of fear and anger and the burden of the Crown.

The money she'd gotten from the expropriation had made it all possible. And as much as she'd resented it at first, she now understood that what she'd been holding on to was not her grandfather's legacy, but her own. She'd mired herself in her past, in the idea that she was useless and unworthy and ultimately better off alone, cloistered, protected from the world, just like Quasimodo in the bell tower. She'd been her own jailor, convinced that dreams and living vicariously through the silver screen were enough.

In a roundabout way, Shane had freed her. He'd forced her to face the fact that trying to take care of the Crown on her own was a nearly impossible task—she never would've been able to fix the roof on her own, or reopen the Crown had he not been there. In her quest to protect the theater from him, she'd made friends, opened up to the rest of the world and seen what life had to offer.

The car crested the hill overlooking the town. Mira studied Everville from that vista and her heart sighed. Everything looked smaller. Different, somehow, too. The water main projects had been completed on most of the main roads, and the traffic cones and detour signs had been cleared away to show perfectly straight, blacktop roads clear of debris and mud.

They pulled into town and slowly crawled along Main Street to admire the Christmas decorations. The business improvement association had stepped up their game—every storefront had a Christmas display in its window. The streets were bustling with shoppers, too.

"Is that a new store?" Mira pointed to an unfamiliar-looking sign in a building she'd previously given little thought to—it'd been closed for the longest time, and now it was some kind of Christmas shop. "Look how busy it is."

They kept driving. It wasn't until farther up that she realized she didn't recognize where they were. "Hang on—where's the Crown…?"

Maya parked by the curb. Mira popped her seat belt and got out, heart in her throat. She stared around at the unfamiliar landscape, the bruise-purple sky too big above her. She felt shadows where there were none, thought she saw ghostly silhouettes hanging above her. But all that was left of the block where the Crown Theater once stood was a pile of rubble ringed by temporary fencing.

"Oh, my God." She looked around for the landmarks, any sign of the old department stores, the chain-link fence, the empty lots and floating garbage that'd once danced there.

It was all gone. And in its place, a huge sign: Coming Soon! Crown Condos By Sagmar, Starting in the mid $200,000s!

Maya got out of the car. "Oh… Mira."

Her face felt numb. "They didn't waste any time." She supposed she should've been glad she hadn't been in town to witness the wrecking crew tear down the place she'd called home. But she hadn't thought she'd feel so empty coming back to that gaping hole in the sky.

Through one of the viewing windows, piles of red brick, twisted rebar and broken concrete lay like tombstones dusted with snow. She couldn't tell if it was all from the Crown, or if it was mixed in with the other buildings' detritus. Did it matter? In the end, this was all the theater amounted to. Rubble and dust and some fond memories.

She felt a hand on her shoulder.

"I'm okay," Mira said, throat tight. "I just

thought that…somehow, even once it came down… This is going to sound crazy."

"What?"

"I thought I'd see my grandfather come out of all this." As if he'd be standing there, a phoenix from the ashes. "I think part of me believed Grandpa still lived there. That I was protecting him, keeping him alive."

Maya wrapped an arm around her shoulders and hugged her. "He lives on in you."

Mira lingered a moment longer. There was nothing left now of her grandfather's legacy. Nothing for her to fight for or save. It was over.

But life would go on. The condo would be built. The town would change.

She probably wouldn't be here to witness any of that, though she hadn't entirely decided on what she was going to do next.

Back at Maya's house, they opened the windows to the frigid cold December temps to get the stale air out and ordered Chinese from the Good Fortune Diner. Mira called Arty and Janice to let them know she and Maya had arrived home safe. Arty sounded relieved.

"You'll join us for Christmas dinner, won't you?" he asked.

"Of course."

"We missed you, Mira. We're glad you're home."

She didn't reply. She wasn't sure what the word

home meant anymore. The only place she'd ever called home was gone.

Jet lag kept Mira from sleeping; she went online and caught up on her emails and internet news. Maya had zonked right out. She was a light sleeper and Mira didn't want to bother her friend.

When the phone rang, she picked up quickly, wondering who would call so late.

"Mira? It's Shane."

The air in her lungs stopped. "Shane Patel," he clarified unnecessarily when she didn't respond. "I heard you were back."

"I just got in today." She was confused by her emotions—elation with a heavy dose of longing and wariness. The last time they'd faced each other was after the town council meeting. They hadn't even said goodbye—she'd done everything in her power to avoid seeing him. The truth was, she'd been afraid of what she might say or do. She hadn't wanted to subject Shane to her wrath. She'd realized during her trip that part of her had still cared enough about him to preserve him from her backlash.

"I know. I asked Arty to call me as soon as you returned. Did you have fun?"

"It was...amazing." She didn't have the vocabulary to talk about the trip in detail. Shane had stolen it all from her with one phone call. Her heart pattered softly.

A pause. "I've missed you," he said.

Her stomach tumbled. In Europe, she'd met interesting and interested men, but the only person she'd been able to think about was Shane. She'd even turned down a chance to slip into a hot tub with a Swedish professional skier named Sven. Maya had teased her mercilessly about that. "I missed you, too. But you didn't have to call."

"Actually, I did. Can I see you?"

"When?"

"Now. I'm outside Maya's house."

She went to the window. Sure enough, Shane's car was parked outside, and he was sitting in the driver's seat, cell phone pressed to his ear. He waved tentatively through the darkness.

"Have you been here all this time?"

"No. I got the call from Arty around four-thirty. I drove from Brooklyn as quick as I could. I didn't think traffic would've been so bad on the roads, but there was a snowstorm and…" He trailed off. "Well, I'm here now. Can we talk?"

He'd driven more than three hours from Brooklyn through a snowstorm just to see her. The least she could do was say hello. "Hang on." She slipped on her shoes and hurried through the biting cold to Shane's car. She didn't feel right inviting him into Maya's home, and she didn't want to wake her friend.

She opened the door and slid into the passenger seat, and was immediately enveloped by Shane's spicy, clean scent. "Hey."

He smiled briefly. He looked a little haggard, probably as bad as she did after her long flight. And yet, she'd never felt more alive and refreshed seeing him here. "Hey."

He glanced away, grim lines etching his face. "Guess you must've seen the site on your way into town."

The site. As in the condo, not the theater. It was no longer the Crown, except in name. Strangely, the fact that they'd adopted the theater's name for the project didn't bother her as much as she thought it should.

"It was bound to happen sooner or later," she said finally. "I'm sure the project has been stalled long enough."

"It may have to be stalled a bit longer. There are some new plans. But before they go ahead, I needed to show them to you." He flicked on the car's overhead light and pulled out a folder. Perplexed, Mira glanced at him. It wasn't as if she had any say in construction.

He opened the folder filled with blueprints. "Originally, the condo was going to have a swimming pool," he said. "But it turns out people don't really like paying the maintenance fees for an amenity most residents don't use. Frankly, the lake is way better for swimming anyhow. So I thought we could do something else. Something better." He handed her a piece of concept art—

one of those computer generated images with smiling people placed in it to make it look real.

She did a double take. Red velvet curtains with gold fringe, plush red upholstered seats, aisle lights…

"It's a movie theater," Shane explained unnecessarily. "A mini version of the Crown to replace what we took down."

Mira looked up at him, astonished as he pointed out the features in the concept drawings.

"The demo crew saved a bunch of the old seats to get reused, though they'll all be reupholstered. And the equipment will all be brand-new and state-of-the-art. It'll be open to the public for special occasions, but it'll also be available for private parties, and as a facility for the condo residents. But we need your permission."

"My…permission?"

"We want to name it the Jack Bateman Memorial Theater." He fidgeted. "I didn't want to go ahead with this until I had your okay. I insisted on it, really."

Her chest hurt. "You held up construction just to talk to me about this?"

He nodded. "It took some convincing, but the board at Sagmar agreed we needed to reestablish a rapport with everyone in town. And I didn't want to just email you. I had to see you…show you and ask you myself. I didn't want to go behind your back on this. I won't ever lie to you or trick you into anything ever again. Arty thought it would be a nice surprise if we just went ahead, but I couldn't, especially if you're not okay with this—"

"I'm okay with this," she said quickly. "In fact, I'm…stunned. And honored." She touched his arm as happy tears threatened. "Grandpa would've loved this."

"It was Arty's idea to save something of the old Crown to keep for you. I just ran with the idea and talked to the designers and engineers. The whole company loves it. On top of that, I got them to add a rooftop garden. It'll add to the building's LEED score and give the place a beautiful green space."

Mira's vision blurred, and she wiped her tears away, smiling.

Shane set the folder aside. "I'll have some paperwork for you to sign. Nothing major, just a letter that says you'll let us put his name on a plaque. I promise, nothing hinky."

"That's fine. I trust you."

"Do you?" His lips pinched and he released a breath. "I haven't been able to sleep wondering what you must think of me, of the way I've handled things. You have to know I didn't set out to deceive you…not consciously. But my manager went over my head and told the mayor about the high-speed rail line even when she wasn't supposed to—"

"It's okay, Shane. I understand." She folded her

hands to keep from fidgeting. "You were doing your job. And you meant well. You're trying to make things better for the whole community. My grandfather tried to do the same when he bought the theater in the first place. He gave up all he had to save the Crown. But there's a season for everything and now…well, that season is over." She glanced out the windshield. Large flakes of snow drifted down, settling on the ground.

Shane sighed. "I never wanted to hurt you, even in the end. I convinced myself I was helping you by forcing you to move out, but it wasn't my place to make that decision for you. And I shouldn't have ratted you out the way I did." He wiped a hand over his mouth. "I wouldn't blame you if you were still mad."

"I guess I should still be mad, but I'm not. I worked so hard to keep the theater. I convinced myself it was what I really wanted." She shook her head. "I thought I could only honor my grandpa and keep his memory alive through the business he loved. But I see now there's so much more I can do."

"Like what?"

"Like doing all the things he dreamed of doing. I watched the sun set from the Eiffel Tower. I went on a tour of Buckingham Palace. I ate gelato on the Spanish Steps." She smiled. "And I met all kinds of people. People who didn't judge me, who were interested in who I was, what I did, what I had to say. People who wanted to be my friend, who I wanted to be friends with, who didn't have any agendas and weren't looking to screw with me." She chuckled drily. "I never realized how cynical I was. It took getting away from Everville to gain perspective."

"I understand. And you have every right to be cynical. I wouldn't want you any other way." At that, she blushed. Shane cleared his throat. "Anyhow, it sounds like you had quite an adventure."

"I did." She lifted her eyes. "But something else I've discovered is that I don't want to travel alone. After three months away from the shop, Maya won't be able to go on more trips for a while." She bit her lip. "I was hoping… If you have any vacation time coming up, maybe you'd like to go with me?"

Shane blinked. "You want me to travel with you?"

"Not far," she said. "I was thinking something more local. I haven't seen a lot of New York City. I don't suppose you know somewhere I could crash?"

His lips slowly spread into a smile. "When do you want to go?"

"I'd say now, but I just got back, and I feel like I need to spend a few days here. Have Christmas dinner with Arty."

"How about Boxing Day?" Shane suggested.

She laughed, unable to contain her happiness.

She reached across the console at the same time he reached for her. Their lips met over and over again, reacquainting, overjoyed by the reunion. She grasped him tightly. "I'm sorry for making life difficult for you. I've been stubborn. About everything."

"You were never difficult. Challenging, but not difficult. You held your ground and you didn't budge on your principles. It's what I love about you." He pressed his forehead against hers and kissed the tip of her nose. "I'm sorry I made *your* life difficult. I was a real pain."

"But if you hadn't been as persistent as you were, we would never have gotten to this point. It's what I love about *you*."

"So...we're in agreement for once? We love each other?" He grinned impishly.

"That depends." She cut him her naughtiest look. "Where are you staying tonight?"

He exhaled a shuddery breath. "I've got a room at the Sunshine B and B."

"Well, I think we have notes to compare. How about we head back to your place and we'll see just how much we agree on?"

Eyes alight, Shane put the car into gear. Mira quickly buckled herself in and turned to him.

"I think this," she said, pecking him on the cheek, "is the beginning of a beautiful friendship."

* * * * *